Country Scene Digest

Editorial Director, James Kuse

Managing Editor, Ralph Luedtke

Production Editor/Manager, Richard Lawson

Photographic Editor, Gerald Koser

compiled and designed by

Marty Zens

David Schansberg

Country Scene Digest

Ideals welcomes you to *Country Scene Digest*, a compendium of the best of *Country Scene* and with a broad collection of related topics for your enjoyment.

Country Scene Digest will enlighten and entertain you with wisdom from some of America's greatest poets, naturalists, and artists. It is also filled with sound advice from the practical and hardy country dwellers whose sturdy lives are reflected in their art and daily living.

Rural simplicity, strongly unique in its way, is evident in each of the sections in this book. We hope a greater appreciation of nature and those who love it may be found by the reader as each article presents a fascinating element of country living.

Country Scene Digest

Country Gardening

With the approach of spring and the thawing of the soil, many people long for the fragrant odors of the earth to fill the senses with new life. A most convenient way to experience this rejuvenation is by preparing the soil for a garden. With proper cultivation methods, the earth will reap an abundance of wholesome and healthy vegetables and plants to preserve or just enjoy during summer and later months. A plot of land, well-tended, is itself a simple and rewarding activity, and will draw all persons to the pleasures of the countryside with its promise of a good harvest.

THE
SEED CATALOGUE

Midwinter's traditional harbinger of spring—
still well read and still priced right

Ken and Pat Kraft

THE SEED CATALOGUE, so it is often claimed, was one of three books found in every home in nineteenth-century America, the other two being the Bible and an almanac. The reading habits of most Americans have changed considerably since then, but an estimated twenty-five million American gardeners still receive seed catalogues by mail each year. The reasons for the continuing popularity of seed catalogues are not difficult to understand. Not only are most catalogues free, but they also offer the customer the convenience of ordering by mail and the choice of an immense number of varieties—twenty-one different kinds of beans, to give some examples, sixty-two different petunias, forty-four cucumbers, and so on. But the most important reason of all is that seed catalogues contain the ingredients that armchair gardeners' dreams are made of.

January, a month in which most gardeners can do very little else but dream about spring planting, is when most seed catalogues are distributed by mail. Some of the smaller specialty houses issue only simple price lists, but the larger seed companies usually print magazine-sized booklets replete with splendid, shimmering, four-color photographs of the glorious vegetables and flowers that will sprout from their seeds. The exact costs of producing each catalogue are a closely guarded secret, but thirty-five cents a copy—exclusive of postage and mailing-list costs—seems to be an average figure. The returns on this investment, however, can be substantial. At the turn of the century, orders usually ran between fifty cents and a dollar; today an average order amounts to about ten dollars. Experience has demonstrated that a time of economic uncertainty is a good time to sell seeds.

© 1973 American Heritage Publishing Co., Inc. Reprinted by permission from AMERICANA (November 1973).

BURPEE'S PERFECTION WAX BEAN.

Introduced by us last year, when the supply being very limited, the seed was sold only in sealed packets, Burpee's Perfection Wax Bean has given splendid satisfaction. It was perfected by eight years' careful selection, and named in our honor by our friend, A. H. Ansley, of Yates County, N. Y., well known as an experienced grower of beans for more than a quarter of a century. In visiting Mr. Ansley the past summer, we were much struck by the exceeding beauty and purity of a ten-acre field of these beans which he was growing for us. It was a grand sight—the plants all uniform and vigorous in growth, free from runners, and so crowded with the magnificent golden-yellow pods (with not a sign of rust), that the whole appeared as might a field of gold. We quite agreed with Mr. Ansley, that "it was the finest field of beans in all New York." The illustration herewith represents two mature pods, natural size, and also a plant showing habit of growth. For *vigor of growth* and *immense productiveness*, it is *unequaled* by any other dwarf Wax Bean, the plants being loaded with the long, rich pods. One of our customers in Massachusetts, (Mr. Saml. Seagrave, of Uxbridge) has sent us a single dwarf plant of BURPEE'S PERFECTION WAX BEAN, on which we counted *fifty-seven matured pods*. In comparison with the Golden Wax, they are as early, or *earlier*; they are of more vigorous habit of growth, and have larger pods on a stronger bush, by which they are held well up from the ground; they have never blighted. Several other new varieties of dwarf wax beans were introduced last year, all of which we *carefully tested*, but found none to equal Burpee's Perfection Wax in productiveness or size of pods. The magnificent, large, golden-yellow pods are of the most handsome appearance and finest quality, being stringless, tender and of very rich flavor.

Per packet 15 cts.; per pint 40 cts.; per quart 80 cts., postpaid, by mail. By express or freight, per quart 50 cts.; 4 qts. $1.75; per peck, $3.00; per bushel $10.00.

The Burpee Farm annual of 1888 contained 128 pages and the added bonus of two pages of color. Compare this with today's catalogs, which are often in full color—cover to cover.

Probably the first seed catalogue issued by a seed company still in business was published by the Geo. W. Park Seed Company, of Greenwood, South Carolina, in 1868. (Two other major producers of seeds today include the W. Atlee Burpee Company, which was founded in 1876, and the Joseph Harris Company, whose first catalogue, printed in 1879, numbered thirty thousand copies.) Since then seed catalogues have changed greatly in appearance—due to the introduction of four-color photography—but in conception they have remained much the same. Basically they are descriptive listings with flowers and vegetables presented separately in alphabetical order. Some fifty years ago one innovative seedsman tried to vary the formula by listing his vegetables according to which part was edible—seed, root, fruit, or foliage. Two years later he was alphabetizing them again and licking his wounds.

Modern seed catalogues, however, are bland and businesslike compared with earlier ones. Nineteenth-century catalogues could be quaintly helpful: Spanish peanuts were, one wrote, "splendid to fatten hogs and children." Or disarmingly honest: "I was completely carried away with this new celery last fall, but I have lost much of this enthusiasm." Or just plain jocular: "Plant the six-foot-long snake cucumber and scare the girls out of the garden." And seed-catalogue customers responded in kind to this personal touch. In the 1880 Harris catalogue, the section headed "Testimonials" included a letter from Alson Rogers, of Warren, Pennsylvania, stating that he was able to raise heads of Early Fottler's cabbage weighing ten pounds and that "some of them sold as high as twenty cents apiece." H. M. Grisham, of Readsville, Missouri, wrote that from one Harris seed he grew a beet measuring nineteen inches in circumference.

Years ago a business tycoon chided a seedsman for hopelessly underpricing his product; no one in the seed industry would ever get rich, he predicted. At the time most packets of seeds cost five or ten cents; today the average is about forty cents a packet—a modest rate of increase in these inflationary times. The newest developments can cost a good deal more—but then they always have. In 1883 seeds of a fancy new geranium fetched fifty cents the packet, and in 1890 seedsman W. Atlee Burpee coolly priced his brand-new Burpee bush lima beans at seventy-five cents for a mere four seeds. Those

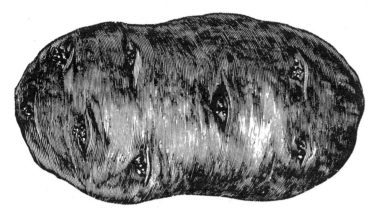

WHIPPLE'S SEEDLING POTATO.

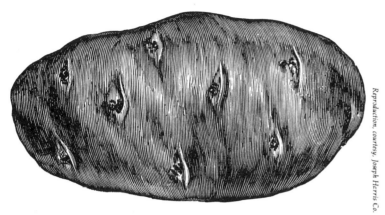

CENTENNIAL POTATO.

A word of warning from Joseph Harris in his catalogue of 1882: "Please remember this, and do not order potatoes to be sent as freight unless you can wait from the middle of April to the first of May for them. If sent by Express, they can go much earlier, but express charges, to distant points, often cost more than the potatoes."

Park's Floral Magazine boasted a circulation of 362,000 in 1898. In addition to information about flowering plants, it contained poetry as well as advertising for health aids, bicycles—even corsets.

beans are still highly popular, by the way, and it is comforting to note that Burpee's now sells them at sixty-five cents for about fifty seeds.

While the smaller seed companies usually specialize in certain types of seeds, the larger companies offer a vast selection of practically every kind of popular flower and vegetable. But even these giants excel in special areas within the business. The Geo. W. Park Seed Company, for example, is especially noted for its wide selection of flowers; Stokes Seeds, Inc., carries a tremendous number of tomatoes; the W. Atlee Burpee Company and the Joseph Harris Company are strong in independent research leading to the development of new varieties; and the De Giorgi Company carries a number of Italian vegetables. Among the smaller specialty houses, Le Jardin du Gourmet features European seeds; the Kitazawa Seed Company supplies Oriental vegetable seeds; Johnny's Selected Seeds and Metro Myster Farms offer the gardener grains usually associated with farming; and F. W. Schumacher Company and Mellinger's sell seeds of trees and shrubs.

As always, gardeners with an experimental bent eagerly await each new catalogue for announcements of new varieties. Among the "New Creations in Vegetables" heralded for the year 1900 in the Burpee catalogue were a "Willow-Leaf" bush lima ("A Most Unique Novelty—Uniformly of Perfect Bush Growth"), Burpee's "Quarter-Century" tomato, Webb's "Wonderful" lettuce, and the Boston "Unrivaled" ("An Improved 'Telephone' Pea"). New developments in that era were accidents of nature discovered by observant gardeners and refined by seedsmen through a process of trial and selection over several growing seasons. Modern new varieties, on the other hand, are products of planned scientific manipulation, which makes the seed industry a fast-changing, competitive and exciting business. Recent innovations include Lady Godiva pumpkins, developed by the U.S. Department of Agriculture, which produce "naked" or hull-less seeds for eating raw or toasted, and a yellow watermelon, reputedly crisper, sweeter and with fewer seeds than standard varieties. This year will see the introduction of a zinnia as wide as a saucer that will bloom continually until frost and of a corn called Candystick that will grow ears up to two feet long with narrow cobs the size of pencils.

Cantaloupes are ripe when the melon will slip from the stem with a slight touch of the thumb.

To help the gardener who might be overwhelmed or confused by the enormous number of choices their catalogues offer, the seed companies usually indicate the varieties they consider superior with common printer's symbols or boldface type. If such varieties meet your needs, they are usually good choices. Seed catalogues are also helpful aids in planning next spring's garden. The catalogues all specify, for example, how much space different crops require. You can grow a nice crop of radishes on a plot the size of a pillowcase, but corn and watermelons need a lot of room and might not be practical for the gardener with just a small plot. Other helpful information found in seed-catalogue descriptions includes:

Maturity time. The number of days for a plant to mature from the time the seed is planted to the first harvest is given in the catalogue description of each kind of seed. Radishes, for example, mature quickly in about twenty-five days; cabbages, depending on the variety, take from sixty to a hundred and ten days. To make best use of this information, you should know the length of your growing season. Your local weather bureau, agricultural extension service, or newspaper will tell you when to expect the last frost in the spring and the first one in the fall. Some plants, such as tomatoes and peppers, are usually transplanted to the garden as seedlings. In such cases the maturity time is figured from when the plants are set out. To grow seedlings yourself, seed the plants indoors eight weeks beforehand.

Plant size and spacing. Knowing how tall plants grow and how far apart they should be planted is an invaluable aid to planning the garden. Seed catalogues usually include such information. Tall plants should be placed so that they don't shade smaller ones, with the tallest plants—tomatoes perhaps—grown on the north or west side of the garden. The catalogues will also tell you how much space to allow between plants so that they won't be too crowded when they attain full size.

Special purposes. Seed catalogues usually specify which vegetables are best eaten fresh and which ones can be frozen, canned, or dried exceptionally well. The Joseph Harris Company offers a variety of pickling cucumber called Greenpak for gardeners who want to get their pickling done all at one time. The catalogue reads: "It sets fruits extra-early in a concentrated set, and just a couple of picks will practically clean off the vines." Since even a small vegetable garden will produce more than one family can consume at one time, it makes economic sense to plant some varieties with preserving in mind.

Disease resistance. Catalogues stress this factor when present because it makes for happier gardeners. Last year's Burpee catalogue advertised a hybrid cucumber with "built-in resistance to mosaic and mildew" that allows it "to produce heavy crops where these diseases are a problem," while the Tendercrop bush bean is said to resist "common bean and N. Y. 15 bean mosaic and pod mottle virus." Hybrid plants, by the way, are bred for vigor and usually are more resistant to common diseases.

The larger catalogues are loaded with information on growing the seeds they sell. You can learn a lot here. Some examples: Keep the spikes of snapdragons picked for continuous bloom. When growing Brussels sprouts, pinch out the growing points in the top of each plant about the middle of September. Cantaloupes are ripe when the melon will slip from the stem with a slight touch of the thumb. Such helpful advice has been a longstanding feature of seed catalogues. Listen to a seedsman of 1896 instructing customers on the virtues of kale:

"This is more hardy than cabbage, and makes excellent greens for winter and spring use. The leaves are curly, bright green, very tender and delicate in flavor. Sow seed in May or June, transplant in July and cultivate same as cabbage. For early spring use, sow in September; protect over winter with a covering of straw or litter." The passage of eighty years has not altered the advice a whit; it is as sound as ever. Follow it this summer, and next winter you'll be glad you did. ⑤

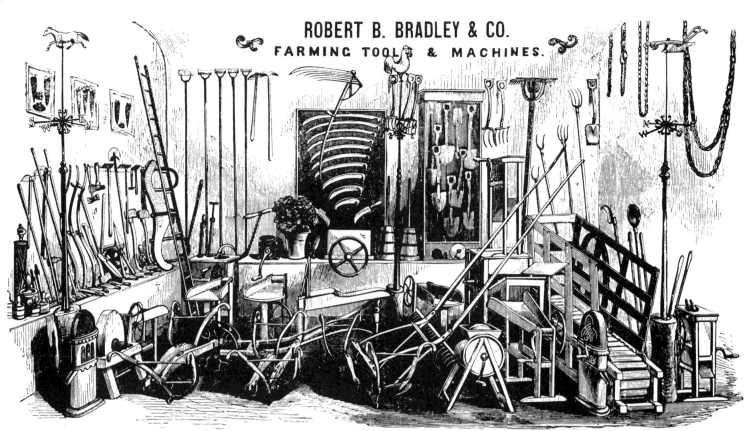
SOURCES OF SEED

Arthur Eames Allgrove
North Wilmington, MA 01887

Burgess Seed and Plant Co.
67 East Battle Creek St.
Galesburg, MI 49053

W. Atlee Burpee Co.
Warminster, PA 18974

De Giorgi Co.
Council Bluffs, IA 51501

Farmer Seed & Nursery Co.
Faribault, MN 55021

Henry Field Seed & Nursery Co.
Yankton, SD 57078

Joseph Harris Co., Inc.
3670 Buffalo Road
Rochester, NY 14624

L.L. Olds Seed Company
P. O. Box 1069
Madison, WI 53701

George W. Park Seed Co., Inc.
Box 31
Greenwood, SC 29646

Pearce Seed Co.
Moorestown, NH 08057

R.H. Shumway Seedsman
P.O. Box 777
Rockford, IL 61101

Stoke's Seeds, Inc.
86 Exchange Street
Buffalo, NY 14205

How Does Your Garden Grow

Vegetable Gardening

Richard L. Hawk

You really can't beat vegetables that come right from plot to pot or salad dish. But to make sure they really are good, the gardener should know the simplest, quickest, best and most convenient ways to make his garden grow.

One of these ways is to establish a permanent mulch garden.

Start with a layer of loose hay about 8 inches thick, which may be spoiled. Maintain the mulch as it rots down by adding any and all vegetable matter that will rot quickly. Materials you can use include straw, leaves, pine needles, sawdust and wood chips, weeds, garbage (no, it doesn't smell bad), grass clippings, marsh or salt hay, corn cobs, cornstalks, peat moss, buckwheat hulls or other cereal chaff, sugar cane, manure, cranberry tops and spent hops. If any of the vegetable matter, such as sawdust or oak leaves, seems to make the soil too acid, wood ashes or lime may be applied.

To sow seeds or set plants, pull the mulch back a little so that your furrows or holes may be made. With small seeds, pull the mulch around the plants after they appear; but with larger seeds, or plants, you may replace it immediately after sowing or setting. The thick mulch will prevent the growth of most weeds.

Whatever gardening method you use, be sure that your garden plot is located in a place with plenty of sunshine and good drainage. If it is on a slope or hillside, plant crosswise rather than up and down to prevent the rows from washing out in the rain.

Vegetables are classified as very hardy, hardy, tender, very tender. Read the package or ask your seed dealer to determine hardiness of the vegetables you plan to plant.

Hardy vegetables should be planted as early in the spring as the garden can be worked, tender crops only after danger from frost is past.

There is no need to buy plants of cabbage, tomatoes, peppers or other early starting vegetables. You can grow them inside in small containers of soil. For later crops, you can even sow seeds right in the garden, then thin out the plants and transfer some to new locations.

When you sow your garden seeds, don't put them too deep or too thick. Cover them with soil to a depth of about four times their diameter or follow the directions on the seed package. Firm the soil either by walking on it or by tamping it down with a hoe. If you sow seeds during a dry period, keep the soil moist. In a large garden, allow plenty of room between rows for easy harvesting.

For a steady supply of vegetables such as sweet corn and baby beets, either plant successionally (small amounts planted periodically), or plant several varieties of the same vegetable, that will produce early, midseason and late.

When transplanting young plants, allow as much earth as possible to cling to their roots. After you set the plants in the holes and pack earth around the roots, give them a good watering. Best times to set out plants are in the evening or on a cloudy day.

Maintain a regular schedule of fertilizing and watering during dry weather. A good soaking once every week is preferable to many light sprinklings which will result in roots staying close to the surface of the soil.

Happy gardening!

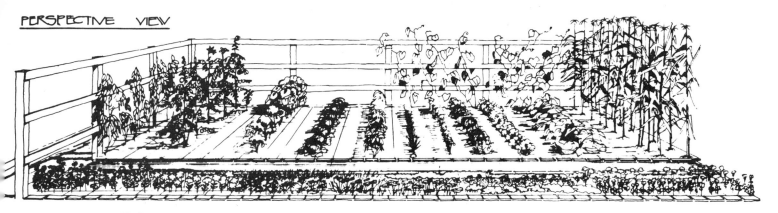

COMBINATION VEGETABLE-FLOWER GARDEN

Vegetables

1	Pole Beans
2	Tomato
3	Sweet Peppers
4	Eggplant
5	Cabbage
6	Bush Beans
7	Beets
8	Carrots
9	Lettuce
10	Broccoli
11	Squash
12	Sweet Corn
13	Cucumber

Herbs

14	Basil
15	Chives
16	Dill
17	Thyme

Flowers

18	Marigold
19	Ageratum
20	Petunia
21	Alyssum
22	Periwinkle
23	Dianthus
24	Celosia
25	Zinnia

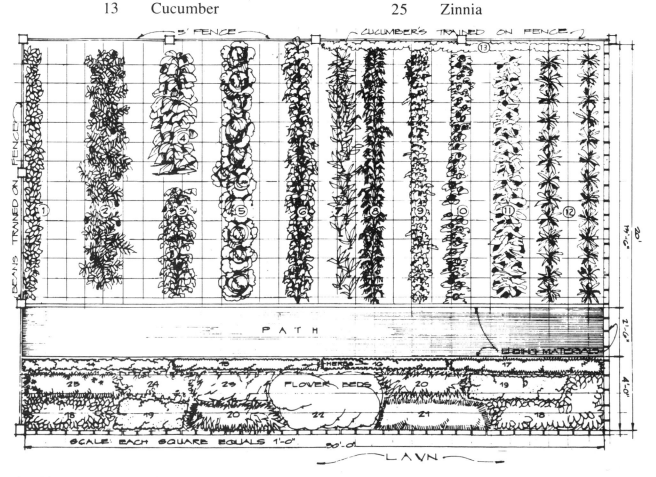

*Special thanks to the George W. Park Seed Company
for supplying us with the garden plan shown here.*

Tomatoes: Misunderstood Beauties

Article and photos by Peggy Flynn

Ever have a friend you loved so much that you assumed the rest of world did, too? I count tomatoes as one of the great loves in my life. What a shock it was to find that tomatoes have a history of bringing fear and dread into the hearts—not the stomachs—of the human race.

Our modern dictionaries and encyclopedias give straightforward definitions of tomatoes. But it wasn't always so. Philip Miller's 1731 Gardener's Dictionary had this to say: "The Italians and Spaniards eat these Apples as we do cucumbers—with Pepper, Oil, and Salt—and Some eat them stewed in Sauces, etc., but, considering their great moisture and coldness, the Nourishment they afford must be bad."

Tomatoes! My friends! Those scarlet, smooth, globular, vine-ripened Greater Baltimores, Matchless, Oxhearts, Pritchards and Bonny Bests that every gardener loves to plant and that we all know are loaded with Vitamins A and C.

"Bad"?

Besides, it's the moisture, the slightly sticky, sweet juices rolling down my chin that makes me love tomatoes. Apples? No, Miller's reference really is to tomatoes, although they were once called "love apples." And Miller, unfortunately, was by no means the lone catsup hater of the century. Sad to say, but eating my favorite *Lycopersicon* is not exactly an old tradition in this country.

But let's back up a bit. The tomato is a native of the coastal regions of South America. Agricultural records show, however, that the large, smooth, round beauties we eat today (and that are so delicious with a sprinkling of pepper or celery salt) are seeds and slices and years of hybridization away from the small, rough-skinned originals.

And the Spanish must have eaten tomatoes because the credit for nicknaming them "love apples" goes to them. This nickname supposedly came about because the tomatoes were valued as aphrodisiacs. I can see it now. The shades of night are falling, the Pyrenees tower behind, a few couples lounge in the grass; then they gorge on my favorite salad ingredient and turn into Latin lovers of renowned fame.

But what about the rest of the world?

Well, the British may be responsible for starting the non-gourmet custom of growing tomatoes as garden ornamentals. One section of *The Early Horticulturists*, by Ronald Webber, reports that tomatoes were identified in England as early as 1544, "But these tomatoes were ribbed, rather ugly fruit, which were grown more as a curiosity and regarded in Britain as unfit for eating, though known to be enjoyed by Spaniards and other foreigners."

Able to turn even the shyest young swain into a latin lover?

Ah, so the secret was out.

But who were these other foreigners?

Historian Philippa Pullar sheds some light on the mystery. In *Consuming Passion,* the author notes that it wasn't until after the Napoleonic Wars and the development of trading companies that ground was broken for the British and tomato eating made acceptable.

Were the French the "other foreigners"? Perhaps, they might have been in need of a new aspic ingredient.

Across the Atlantic, in that unknown and mysterious land of Virginia, America's first public relations expert, John Smith, was unable to find any tomatoes to write home about. His diaries tell of "Salvages" and their cornfields. But yes, they grew no tomatoes in America.

How and when did tomatoes first immigrate to our shores? In 1899 the Department of Agriculture reported that tomatoes were first introduced into the New World in 1798. Their port of entry appears to have been Philadelphia and it's a nice fantasy to think of the Third U.S. Congress taking a tomato break while they were debating the eleventh amendment. Alas, that's rather doubtful. For, in the great tradition of their English forebearers, the inhabitants of our first capitol brought with them the custom of *not* eating the jewel of the nightshade family.

If it won't play in Philly, why not head back to the state of the Pilgrim's first landing? That's exactly what Michael Corne, an Italian painter did. He's credited with taking time out from his palette to try and stir things up in Salem, Massachusetts, by unveiling an eatable tomato, circa 1802. Another bomb. The New Englanders refused to indulge their palates. Perhaps they'd had enough of toads and turtles and dared not tempt the devil (again) by biting into the love apple.

And diplomatic foreign relationships had an impact on our diets—even back then. In *The Rise of Urban America,* Richard Arno Cummings notes that "Following the French Alliance of 1778 French cuisine was taken up by the fashionable . . . they (French) introduced bonbons and encouraged use of soups, sweet oil, tomatoes and fricassees."

So! The French *were* in on it!

But who in our country took that first bite? We may never know; another unsung hero of our land. Thank goodness someone finally did; eating tomatoes is simply too good a treat to bypass.

And times do change. Harsh attitudes soften. So the tomato grew and grew and turned into a Burpee Big Boy. Well, not quite. The development of greenhouses had a great influence on the commercial development of tomatoes. Sure, if you can grow them all year, why *not* eat them?

The development of canning and refrigeration also helped to spread the bounty throughout the country, as did scientific breeding and cross-pollination experiments. Sixty-seven years after the Philadelphia debut, over a thousand acres of Pennsylvania farmland were devoted to tomato growing. Not bad for a relative newcomer. Today, California leads the nation as the number one tomato state, where last year alone tomatoes were grown on over 300,000 acres.

Of all the scientific studies and experiments, the most novel was undertaken by the great plant developer, Luther Burbank. He titled his 1877 work, "The Tomato—And an Interesting Experiment"; subtitled, "A Plant Which Bore Potatoes Below and Tomatoes Above." Burbank knew that tomatoes and potatoes are of the same genus. He grafted a tomato to the stalk of a potato, and then reversed the procedure. The results, he said, were "the fruit that appeared in due season was a tomato differing in no very obvious respect from other tomatoes of the same variety. They, however, were not of as good quality."

Burbank had better success with tomato seeds he brought with him to California from his home in Massachusetts. He saved the seeds for nineteen years before planting them to see if they could retain the "power of germination." They did, but only two plants fruited.

Even Burbank, with his great mind and curiosity, didn't make a federal case out of his tomatoes. That job was left to Mr. Nix.

Mr. Nix was an importer who started another tomato controversy stewing. He was unhappy when told he had to pay duty on tomatoes he imported from the West Indies. Tomatoes, he assumed, were duty free under the 1883 Tariff Act because they were "Fruits, green, ripe or dried . . . " A witness for the plaintiff argued that Webster listed only cauliflower, cabbage, turnips, potatoes, peas, beans and the like under the heading "vegetable." The case went to the Supreme Court. The decision, written by Horace Gray, said that neither "fruits nor vegetables had any specific meaning in trade or commerce different from that given in the dictionary and that they had the same meaning in trade today that they had in March of 1883." Justice was done. Down went the gavel. The historic May 10, 1893, decision: The tomato is a vegetable, not a fruit. Thanks to Mr. Nix we know to look for our red beauties next to cabbages and turnips in the market, and not alongside the apples and peaches.

Of course, we home gardeners, pizza lovers and tomato juice addicts know the legal issue doesn't tell the entire story. Tomatoes, botanically speaking, really are still fruits, as are beans and any number of seed pods.

If you've given up caffeine, cigarettes and smog, eat assured that tomatoes really are good for you. The Department of Agriculture made it official in 1911: "It is perhaps needless to say that attributing cancer to the use of tomatoes, as was formerly done, is like most such ideas, regarded as without foundation."

No, my love, the tomato, is not a carcinogenic, and I'm glad that, today, the rest of the world loves them as much as I do. ⑤

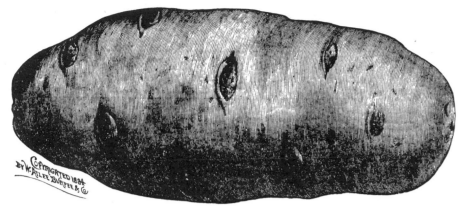

BURPEE'S EMPIRE STATE POTATO.

GOLD FLESH POTATO.

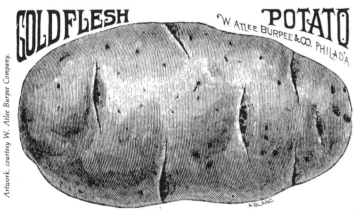

Artwork, courtesy W. Atlee Burpee Company.

The Various Virtues of a Valued Vegetable

Devon Reay

"Oh, how I love that lowly tuber, rotund, prolific, earthy, springing from Mother Earth to the delight of both famished worker and bon vivant! A few potatoes a day can be heaven," observed gourmet Iles Brody. He amended the maxim, "The best thoughts come from the stomach" to "The worst thoughts can also come from the stomach. But it is vegetables that can keep those thoughts away, and it's potatoes in particular that can ensure tranquillity within."

During one lean period in his life, Mr. Brody ate pratically nothing but potatoes for several months. "Steaming, boiled potatoes, enormous, snow-white and flaky—I ate with all my being, with every particle of my body. Believe me, I never revolted, never wished for a better or different fare."

Actually, the potato, *Solanum tuberosum*, is not a true root vegetable; it is classed among the green vegetables that grow above ground. It probably originated in

or near Chile. When Sir Francis Drake landed in southern Chile in 1577, the vegetable was a staple of the inhabitants. Soon after, the potato was among the foods stocked on Spanish ships, and during the 1580s it was grown in Italian gardens.

Although potatoes from Bermuda were introduced in Virginia in 1621, potato growing in this country began in Londonderry, New Hampshire, in 1719 from seed potatoes brought over by Irish immigrants.

Considering the quality of machine-harvested market potatoes, the person who appreciates a good potato, whether Idaho, Russet, or Green Mountain, should grow his own if he has a sunny yard. "Potatoes were long a crop that could be grown successfully only in cool regions; now, if adequately mulched, they can be grown where the summers are fairly hot," according to a gardener who advises acid soil and moisture for potato growing. To keep the soil from becoming dry and render the bed weed-free, the potatoes are grown under a six-inch mulch of leaves or freshly cut and dried grass clippings. This mulch, which settles to three inches, assures a forty to eighty-nine percent higher yield than that of an unmulched bed.

Knaggs believes the potato to be the most effective of all food remedies. "Indeed, it may seem revolutionary that an exclusive potato regimen can cure disease, but such is actually the case. The potato diet has been found to possess remarkable powers in clearing up colds and fevers, bronchial and digestive troubles which for the most part are due to an excess of acid poison in the system. And obstinate skin disease and chronic nettle rash have yielded to this diet after all other remedies have failed."

He adds that potato treatment stops influenza in four days, rheumatic fever in eight. Raw potato, grated or shredded makes an effective poultice for bruises, rheumatic pains, and even certain skin conditions.

Polish cooks appreciate the potato; they prepare potato pancakes and patties, potato biscuits and cakes, stuffed potatoes and potato noodles, potato soup and a variety of excellent potato salads. What is more memorable than a perfect potato pancake?

Then there is cold vichyssoise and real country fries. Best of all, perhaps, is a crisp-skinned, baked Russet or Idaho which bears little resemblance to the "baked potato" served in restaurants. Of their foil-wrapped potatoes, a diner observed, "Just a plain old soggy steamed potato; whoever initiated the foil wrap probably concocted the fake cream you often get with coffee. And the potato is always too big—if it was baked right, you could make a meal of it."

To ensure a crisp-skinned baked Idaho, Russet, or Green Mountain, the potato can be put in a saucepan of cold water, covered, brought to a boil and simmered six minutes or so before being removed from the water and placed in a hot oven for half an hour or longer. When it is cooked within and crisp outside, it is quickly taken out and immediately split open to let the steam escape and keep the skin crunchy. At this time it can be buttered and peppered (or served with sour cream). At least one Eastern family eats the crisp skins only; they refrigerate the insides for tomorrow's home fries, potato salad, or stew.

An Englishman of the eighteenth century, Sidney Smith, was canon of St. Paul's Cathedral and a gourmet. Especially fond of salads, he wrote his salad recipe in verse and recited it from the pulpit. It begins:

Two large potatoes passed kitchen sieve
Smoothness and softness to the salad give—

A recent study conducted in Pennsylvania compared three ninety-square-foot plots, all harvested in early August. The one mulched with grass clippings produced forty-seven pounds of potatoes, the leaf-mulched plot, forty-four pounds, while a control plot, unmulched and weeded, produced just under twenty-eight pounds.

The potato, one of the most alkaline of all foods, contains calcium, potassium, iron, and more than sixteen other minerals and essential trace elements. Besides vitamin C and several B vitamins, it provides twelve amino acids and protein comparable to the complete protein in eggs. In a series of studies of men performing hard work, the subjects, for three to six years, maintained excellent health with potatoes as their only source of protein. In the everyday German diet, ten percent of the protein comes from potatoes.

For balance and good nutrition, potatoes, cooked by baking or boiling, should be included in the diet. Dr. Derek Miller, dietician and nutritionist advises, "A well-balanced diet is essential for keeping weight down, and including potatoes can help people stay slim."

"Irish peasants and the crofters of western Scotland, when they lived chiefly on potatoes, did not become fat; they were just healthy and well-proportioned," says researcher Dr. Valentine Knaggs. "There is every reason to believe that potatoes were used freely as an article of diet in prehistoric times. The vegetable was first heard of among the Incas and other South American tribes who are the direct descendants of the ancient races of those times." Ⓢ

THE CHARLES DOWNING POTATO.

An Easy-to-Build Greenhouse

Albert S. Jetter

Build your own greenhouse with redwood framing and plastic sheet materials. It's easy—and in every sense a permanent-looking structure to be proud of. We did ours for $350 in three weekends.

The location of the greenhouse is very important. It should get as much sun as possible, be protected from strong or persistent winds, and the land on which it sits should have good drainage. All things considered, a spot near a deciduous tree is ideal, the shade shielding the greenhouse from direct heat in summer and allowing direct sunlight in the leafless winter.

It would be a help, too, to have a convenient source of water and electricity—not necessarily a permanent hookup when a hose and an extension from the house would do as well.

And to keep the tax man at bay, examine local building codes carefully to determine what con-stitutes a permanent, assessable building. Our greenhouse is classified as a movable or temporary structure (thus, not assessable in our area) because of the mortarless brick foundation we used. This method is shown in the basic construction sketch.

We also show in a detail sketch an alternate foundation which uses concrete blocks at the four corners—a permanent anchor to be sure and, as surely, a feature that puts the greenhouse in the assessable category.

Preparations begin with levelling the ground and setting up the course of loose bricks all around. This done, treat and cut the plates: 4x4 cedar soaked in Woodlife (in the shade, please, to slow evaporation of the stuff) and half-lapped at the ends for good, strong corners. Use diagonal braces to keep the corners square.

In order to provide some kind of toe-hold on

Reprinted from MECHANIX ILLUSTRATED Magazine.
Copyright 1975 by Fawcett Publications, Inc.

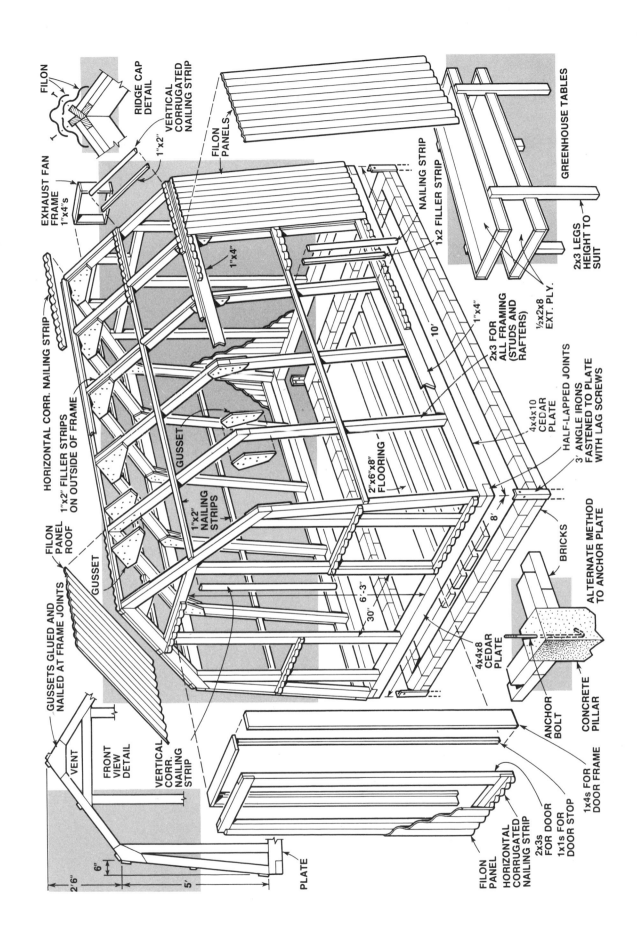

FILON

RIDGE CAP DETAIL

VERTICAL CORRUGATED NAILING STRIP

1"x2"

FILON PANELS

NAILING STRIP

GREENHOUSE TABLES

EXHAUST FAN FRAME 1"x4's

1x2 FILLER STRIP

2x3 LEGS HEIGHT TO SUIT

HORIZONTAL CORR. NAILING STRIP

1"x4"

1"x4"

10'

1/2x2x8 EXT. PLY.

2x3 FOR ALL FRAMING (STUDS AND RAFTERS)

1"x2" FILLER STRIPS ON OUTSIDE OF FRAME

FILON PANEL ROOF

GUSSET

4x4x10 CEDAR PLATE

HALF-LAPPED JOINTS

2"x6"x8" FLOORING

1"x2" NAILING STRIPS

3' ANGLE IRONS FASTENED TO PLATE WITH LAG SCREWS

GUSSET

8'

30'

6'-3"

BRICKS

ALTERNATE METHOD TO ANCHOR PLATE

GUSSETS GLUED AND NAILED AT FRAME JOINTS

4x4x8 CEDAR PLATE

ANCHOR BOLT

CONCRETE PILLAR

VENT

FRONT VIEW DETAIL

VERTICAL CORR. NAILING STRIP

1x4s FOR DOOR FRAME

6"

2'6"

5'

FILON PANEL

HORIZONTAL CORRUGATED NAILING STRIP

2x3s FOR DOOR

1x1s FOR DOOR STOP

PLATE

Before paneling; structure sits on a loose brick foundation, has a dirt floor.

Panels are cemented, then nailed with special washers to the corrugated strips.

Ridge cap consists of three overlapping lengths of the corrugated paneling.

mother earth, drive 3-foot-long angle irons into the ground at each outside corner and fasten them to the plates with lag screws. It may seem a gesture only, but they are a help. And still not assessable.

Systematize the framing by drawing a full-size pattern on two sheets of ½-inch plywood (use the ply later for the greenhouse tables along each side). This way, you have a jig for nailing all six frames. Make your miter cuts on a radial-arm saw (24 in all for the six frames), place them on the pattern and link the elements with the corner gussets, which are glued and nailed.

Mark the plates for the frames, temporarily brace them (or have a helper hold them) in plumb, then nail the ends to the plates. The nailing strips at the juncture of the wall and roof and along both sides of the ridge are trimmed flush with the outside frames.

The entire framework is now complete, with all nailing strips in place.

We used Filon corrugated plastic sheet which is delivered with Filon's own corrugated redwood nailing strips. The strips, which come for use both horizontally and vertically (for edges) are in turn nailed to the framework's nailing strips. Additional vertical filler strips, between the horizontal corrugated strips provided a finished appearance.

The Filon sheets are cut very easily with a crosscut saw. Use metal-cutting shears on the diagonal cuts, if you wish.

Before applying the sheets, a Filon sealant is applied to the horizontal corrugated strips. Readying the sheet for installation, a $5/32$ -inch pilot hole is drilled for each aluminum nail (the nails are used with neoprene washers). Position the sheet carefully, pressing it firmly into the sealant. Then drive the nails in far enough to squash the washer under the nailhead, producing a watertight fastening.

With all sheets in place, install the ridge cap—three overlapping strips of Filon nailed to the V-longitudinal filler strip—held with screws from below. A good, secure installation.

The interior layout is a matter of personal preference—a single table along each side or a single on one and a double on the other.

After sheathing, we installed a thermostatically-controlled ventilating fan at the far end of the greenhouse, a necessary item for dissipating extreme summer heat buildups.

Heating the greenhouse in winter is easily done with a small 1320-watt circulating type electric heater with thermostatic control. This unit, in my locale, can keep greenhouse temperature above freezing at all times. [S]

Greenhouse is 8 x 10 ft., framed in redwood and covered with Filon home greenhouse corrugated paneling.

Detail of gussets (tempered Masonite) which are nailed to the redwood framing.

Construction is simplified by making all six frames on a full-size ply pattern.

What's Cooking

Country Canning

Harvesttime is canning time, when the ripe produce from the garden and orchard is stored away to grace a winter table with summer's goodness. "Putting up" food used to be considered grandma's exclusive domain. Nowadays, though, canning is becoming more popular as people realize it's an economical way of feeding the family nourishing meals. And there is a special satisfaction in viewing a shelf full of home-canned produce.

Canning is easy, fun and, if you scrupulously follow directions, safe. Put up a few jars each week and save a little summer for the cold winter days ahead.

continued

ZUCCHINI-VEGETABLE COMBO

    2 lbs. unpeeled zucchini, sliced
    2 lbs. tomatoes, peeled, stemmed, cored, cut up
    1 c. chopped onion
    1 c. chopped green pepper
2½ c. water
    4 t. salt

In large kettle, combine zucchini, tomatoes, onion, green pepper, and water. Bring to a boil. Boil 2 to 3 minutes. Pack hot vegetables into hot, sterile jars, leaving ½ inch at the top. Add ½ teaspoon salt per pint. Cover with boiling vegetable liquid, leaving ½ inch at top of jar. Adjust lids. Process in pressure canner at 10 pounds (pints or quarts) for 40 minutes. Makes 8 pints.

TOMATO JUICE

    9 lbs. tomatoes, cut in pieces
    1 T. lemon juice
1½ t. salt

In large kettle, cook the tomatoes, covered, until soft, about 15 minutes. Stir often to prevent sticking. Force tomatoes through a sieve. Measure 12 cups of juice. Return juice to kettle and bring to a boil. Stir in lemon juice. Pour hot tomato juice into hot sterile jars, leaving ½ inch at top of jar. Add ¼ teaspoon salt to each pint or ½ teaspoon to each quart. Adjust lids. Process in boiling water bath (pints) 10 minutes; (quarts) 15 minutes. Makes 6 pints juice.

WATERMELON PICKLES

    7 c. watermelon rind, cut in 1-inch cubes
    ¼ c. pickling salt
    4 c. water
    2 c. sugar
    1 c. white vinegar
    1 T. broken cinnamon stick
1½ t. whole cloves
    ½ lemon, thinly sliced
    5 maraschino cherries, halved (optional)

Soak rind overnight in pickling salt and water. (Salted water should cover the rind.) Drain and rinse rind. Cover rind with cold water and simmer just until tender. Mix together sugar, vinegar, cinnamon, cloves and 1 cup water. Simmer 10 minutes. Drain. Add rind, lemon slices and cherries to spice mixture. Simmer until rind is translucent. Fill hot, sterile jars with rind and syrup mixture, leaving ½ inch at the top of the jars. Adjust lids. Process in boiling water bath (pints) for 5 minutes. Makes 2½ pints.

CORN RELISH

    8 c. corn, blanched and cut from cobs
    4 c. chopped celery
    2 c. chopped sweet red pepper
    2 c. chopped green pepper
    1 c. chopped onion
    2 c. sugar
    2 c. vinegar
    2 t. celery seed
    2 c. water
    2 T. salt
    ¼ c. all-purpose flour
    2 T. dry mustard
    1 t. turmeric

In large kettle, combine celery, red pepper, green pepper, onion, sugar, vinegar, celery seed, water and salt. Bring mixture to a boil; boil uncovered for 5 minutes, stirring occasionally. Blend flour, dry mustard, and turmeric with ½ cup cold water. Stir into boiling mixture along with corn. Again bring to a boil. Cook 5 minutes, stirring constantly. Loosely pack into hot, sterile jars, leaving ½ inch at the top of the jars. Adjust lids. Process in boiling water bath (pints) for 15 minutes. Makes 7 pints.

CANNED TOMATOES

15 lbs. tomatoes
 Lemon juice
 Salt

Select firm, fully ripened tomatoes of about the same size. Skin, first dipping tomatoes in boiling water ½ minute. Then dip quickly into cold water. Cut out stem ends. Quarter large tomatoes, use small or medium tomatoes whole. Follow directions below for either raw or hot pack. Makes 6 quarts.

Raw Pack: Pack tomatoes in hot, sterile jars, pressing gently to fill spaces. Leave ½ inch space at the top. Add no water. To each quart, add 1 teaspoon lemon juice and ½ teaspoon salt. To each pint, add ½ teaspoon lemon juice and ¼ teaspoon salt. Adjust lids. Process in boiling water bath (pints) 35 minutes; (quarts) 45 minutes.

Hot Pack: In large kettle, bring tomatoes to a boil, stirring constantly but gently. Pack hot tomatoes into hot, sterile jars, leaving ½ inch space at the top of jar. To each quart, add 1 teaspoon lemon juice and ½ teaspoon salt. To each pint, add ½ teaspoon lemon juice and ¼ teaspoon salt. Adjust lids. Process in boiling water bath (pints and quarts) 10 minutes.

PEAS AND ONIONS

8 c. shelled green peas
3 c. pearl onions

Cover peas and onions with boiling water; boil 5 minutes. Loosely pack hot peas and onions into hot sterile jars, leaving 1 inch at the top of the jar. Add ½ teaspoon salt to each pint. Cover with boiling cooking liquid, again leaving 1 inch at the top of the jar. Adjust lids. Process in pressure canner fat 10 pounds (pints) for 40 minutes. Makes 8 pints.

SUCCOTASH

4 c. shelled lima beans
6 to 8 medium ears sweet corn, cut from cob
4 c. water
 Salt

Wash and drain beans. Combine beans and corn in kettle; add water. Bring to a boil; cook 5 minutes. Pack hot vegetables loosely into hot, sterile jars, leaving 1 inch at top of jars. Add ¼ teaspoon salt to each pint. Pour in boiling cooking liquid, leaving 1 inch at top of jar. Adjust lids. Process in pressure canner at 10 pounds pressure (pints) for 55 minutes; (quarts) for 85 minutes. Makes 4 pints.

Before serving: Boil these vegetables for 20 minutes *before* tasting or using. If desired, add ½ cup light cream and 2 tablespoons butter or margarine to each pint of succotash; or add 1 tablespoon chopped canned pimiento.

SAUERKRAUT

5 lbs. fully matured cabbage, quartered, cored and finely shredded
3½ T. salt

Sprinkle salt over cabbage; mix well. Let stand 30 to 60 minutes. Firmly pack cabbage into room-temperature jars, leaving 2 inches at top of jar. Fill with cold water to within ½ inch of top. Adjust lids, screwing band tight. Place jars on shallow pan to catch brine that overflows during fermentation and curing. Keep cabbage covered with brine. If necessary, open jars and add more brine made by dissolving 1½ tablespoons salt in 1 quart water. Sauerkraut is cured and ready to can in 6 to 8 weeks. At that time, clean rims of jars, replacing any lids if the seal appears damaged. Screw bands tight. Set jars in water bath canner in cold water. Water should extend 2 inches above jars. Bring the water slowly to a boil. Process sauerkraut (pints or quarts) for 30 minutes. Makes 7 pints.

A Summer Creed

W. W. Argow

I believe in the flowers and their glorious indifference to the changes of the morrow.

I believe in the birds and their implicit trust in the loving Providence that feeds them.

I believe in the prayer-chanting brooks, as they murmur a sweet hope of finding the far-distant sea to which they patiently run.

I believe in the whispering winds, for they teach me to listen to the still, small voice within my feverish soul.

I believe in the vagrant clouds, as they remind me that life, like a summer day, must have some darkness to reveal its hidden meaning.

I believe in the soft-speaking rains, accented with warm tears, telling me that nothing will grow save it be fertilized with tears.

I believe in the golden hush of the sunsets, reflecting a momentary glory of that great world beyond my little horizon.

I believe in the holiness of twilight, as it gives me sense of the presence of God, and I know I am not alone. And whatever else I believe is enshrined in those abiding feelings that lie too deep for words.

Fragrant Roses of Yesterday

Louise Riotte

Old-fashioned roses—the kind that Grandma used to grow—are different from the hybrid roses we usually plant today. While they may not be as dramatically beautiful in form or color, they are far, far more fragrant.

Planting and care of the old-fashioned roses is the same as that of modern roses. Don't be frightened by a lot of complex rules concerning rose care. They are a hardy lot, the old-fashioned ones especially. Roses flourished forty million years before there were human hands to tend them; and they have even been found blooming in gardens abandoned for over half a century. You can grow the old-fashioned roses with your green thumb tied behind you!

Unlike the hybrid teas, old-fashioned roses are very hardy and will grow practically anywhere in the United States. This is particularly true of those descended from *Rosa gallica*. These roses, except for the autumn damasks, have one annual flowering and the ability to go dormant early and stay dormant through fluctuating warm and freezing weather in the spring.

Old-fashioned roses will grow well if you are careful of just a few things. 1. Buy only first-quality bushes. 2. Plant them with care in a sunny, well-prepared bed. 3. Maintain a regular dust or spray schedule. 4. Water and feed at correct intervals. 5. Remove spent blooms.

Opposite: Rambling roses grace a rustic fence near a country home. (Photo: Hampfler Studios)

Selecting a Site

Although roses are easy to grow, certain requirements are basic to every rose garden. Like most blooming plants, roses must have adequate sun—at least four hours a day. A service walk is also important in the rose garden. This permits the care of the plants and the cutting of blooms without stepping into the bed and compacting the soil. As with other plants, mulching helps retain moisture.

Moisture is as important to roses as to most flowers, but the rose bed must have adequate drainage. This can be best accomplished by raising the beds eight or ten inches and using a bordering material of wooden planks, bricks or stones. Roses prefer a good soil which is slightly acid (pH 6.5). If you are in doubt about the acidity of the soil, your county extension agent can give instructions for a soil analysis.

Roses can be planted early in a mild climate. If the winters are severe, however, plant as soon as the soil can be worked. Plant in peat pots large enough to accommodate the roots. When all danger of frost has passed, sink pot into the ground; the pot will soon disintegrate.

If there is a possibility of alternating frost after the roses are planted, mound the soil at least halfway up the canes of the plants. As the weather stabilizes, gradually and gently hose the hilled soil off the plants. This gives the roots a chance to develop and become established before hot weather.

There are certain plants that can be planted by roses that act as biological insecticides. The alliums (garlic, onions, chives and shallots) protect roses from black spot, mildew and aphids. The ornamental alliums, such as Jewel of Tibet, also serve this purpose.

Other plants which are beneficial to the rose garden include parsley to repel rose beetles, onions to guard against rose chafers, and marigolds which help keep away nematodes. Mignonette makes a nice ground cover, lupines increase nitrogen in the soil and attract earthworms, while geraniums prevent milky spore disease and repel the Japanese beetle. To improve spongy soil around the rose's roots, grow purslanes.

Roses, particularly the old-fashioned type, many of which grow into large bushes, should have plenty of room. Never plant roses with other plants which have woody, outspreading roots which may compete with roses for soil nutrients.

Preparing the Soil

Roses do well in all soils—whether sandy, clay, or in between—as long as there is good humus content. A little time spent in preparing the soil before planting will repay you many times over.

Spade the soil. As you spade, work in well-rotted manure or compost to two spades deep. If you are preparing a fairly large bed here is a good "recipe." For 100 square feet of bed area, mix the following ingredients into the top 14 inches of soil: 1 bale peat moss, ½ yard sand or sandy soil, ½ yard compost, 10 pounds rock phosphate, 25 pounds agricultural gypsum, ½ yard barnyard manure and 5 pounds complete rose food.

Inspect Your Plants on Arrival

Carefully look over your plants and, if possible, plant them as soon as you get them. If this is not possible, keep plants in a cool place well-packed in damp sphagnum moss; or heel them in, burying roots carefully in moist soil, covering most of the top. They can remain like this no longer than ten days.

Just before planting, place the roots, or most of the plant, in deep water. Soak for thirty minutes to one hour, or even longer if the plant is dried out.

Planting

Whether you plan to plant one rose or twenty, have the hole ready before removing the plant from the tub of water. Dig this hole about twenty-four inches in diameter and about ten inches deep. Shape some soil into a cone-shaped mound in the center of the hole. If soil is very dry, pour in a bucket of water and let it seep into the soil. Remove any broken or damaged roots from the plant; clip the ends from all large roots. Place the plant over the prepared mound. Cover roots to a depth of several inches

with soil crumbled to a fine texture. It is important that the rose be planted at approximately the same depth at which it grew in the field. Fill hole about two-thirds; then water.

After all the water has soaked in, finish filling hole. Remove all weak or broken canes and cut back the remaining canes to about six to ten inches. Cuts should be made on a slant just above an outside "eye." Water plant again in three days and continue watering weekly until good growth becomes apparent. Be sure to remove name label and place on a separate support. If you are making a large planting you may wish to make a plan on paper.

Feeding

If your soil has been well prepared and there is a good humus content, little or no fertilizer is necessary the first year after planting. When feeding becomes desirable, any rose food marketed by a reputable manufacturer will work well as an all-year feeding. Use as directed but remember that the food must be in solution before it can be assimilated by the roots. Water the bed thoroughly before feeding and again after. This will dilute the strength of the food so that it can be taken up without shock to the plants. This deep watering will also help carry the food down to the lower root area.

Watering

Roses like water and lots of it. If a rose is not doing well, it more likely needs water rather than food. If normal rainfall is not sufficient, give your roses about an inch of water each week. During dry weather an occasional watering from above is desirable; however, this should be done before late afternoon so the foliage will be dry by nightfall. Otherwise, spray directly at the base of the plant.

Top: Dr. W. Van Fleet
Middle: *Rosa Damascene Trigintipetala*
Bottom: *Gloire Des Mousseux*
(Photos, courtesy of Joseph J. Kern Rose Nursery)

Pruning and Care

It is in this area where old-fashioned roses differ from the more modern hybrid teas. Actually it is difficult to give specific rules; each old, rare, or unusual rose is an individual with different types and habits of growth.

Old, shrub, and nonhybrid roses should not be pruned in the spring as hybrid teas are since this would remove the canes which produce the greatest spring flowering. However, those roses which flower repeatedly, such as the hybrid perpetuals, should have weak growth removed, and they may be trimmed to shape. Pruning them is considered more a matter of shaping and thinning rather than cutting back. Removing spent flowers when they are in bloom will encourage the growth of new flowering stems. Among the hybrid perpetuals is *Arrillaga* with blossoms a creamy raspberry color. And the flowers when two-thirds open, are as big as medium-sized cabbages! This one is a showstopper.

Annual flowering varieties such as *Rosa damascena trigintipetala,* famous for making attar of roses, should be treated like flowering shrubs. Leave them alone and do not prune until *after* they bloom.

Some of the older roses such as *Fruhlingsmorgen* (Spring Morning) have long canes which arch over naturally because of their weight. Others have canes that grow straight up. These will bloom only at the top unless pruned or pegged. Ferdinand Pichard, a hybrid perpetual, is a fine shrub rose that responds well to "pegging," if you want it to be low and spreading. The beautiful double flowers are striped red and pale pink, or white, and the crisp foliage is lettuce green. Another candidate for this treatment is Waldfee, glowing red and spicily perfumed.

Arrillaga (Photo, courtesy Joseph J. Kern Rose Nursery)

Climbing American Beauty (Photo, courtesy Joseph J. Kern Rose Nursery)

Pegging is any method used to bring the canes into an arched or horizontal position. You may do this by hooking an eight- gauge wire over a matured cane and securing it in the desired position by pushing the other end of the wire into the ground. Or tie the canes in an arched position to stakes. This will cause flowering stems to grow all along the canes. Even two or three canes, arched over and tied to stakes, will make it possible to weave other canes among them, creating a delightful effect.

Fastening the canes to fencing, espalier fashion, is also very effective. After about two years it is good to remove a few of the old canes as new ones grow from the base of the plant.

If you want a bushy, many-branched plant, shorten the long canes by one-third *after the plant blooms.* Also, shorten lateral canes a few inches. You may keep this up until late summer, then leave the plant alone until after it blooms in the spring. A good example of this is the lovely pink moss rose, *Gloire des Mousseux,* which has one great annual flowering. The pink buds are enclosed by elaborately mossed and fringed sepals and the opened, rosy centered blossoms are delightfully scented. The compact plant has large, luxuriant foliage.

Why Grow Old-Fashioned Roses?

As Will Tillotson, a famous rose grower, puts it, "The new roses are for admiring, the old ones for loving." This is true, but they are also beautiful, easy to grow and durable. Many are not only completely hardy where winters are severe but also where summers are hot; and they are excellent for all sorts of landscaping effects.

The climbers, such as Climbing American Beauty and Dr. W. Van Fleet, make huge plants with abundant blossoms; and they will need little care, except to cut out old canes every few years. Belle of Portugal, a hybrid *gigantea,* actually grows an amazing twenty to thirty feet!

Yesterday's roses have many good qualities, but perhaps the greatest joy they give to their happy owners is fragrance, often very intense.

This is particularly true of the damask roses and of none more so than *Rosa damascena triginti-petala* which has one annual flowering. This rose is also known as Kazanlik, for it is grown extensively in the Kazanlik Valley of Bulgaria. It is the best rose for making attar of roses, and it's great for potpourri.

Here is a marvelous recipe for an old-fashioned rose jar:

Gather damask rose petals when rose is at the peak of bloom. Pack them in a glass jar which has a tight cover. Between every 2-inch layer of petals, sprinkle 2 teaspoons of salt. Add more layers of petals and salt to the jar each day until it is full. Keep in a dark, dry, cool place for one week. Then spread out the petals on a paper towel and loosen them carefully.

Mix the following ingredients thoroughly and mix well through the petals in a large bowl: ½ ounces violet-scented talcum powder, 1 ounce orris root, ½ teaspoon mace, ½ teaspoon cinnamon, ½ teaspoon cloves, 4 drops of oil of rose geranium. Add the following very slowly: 20 drops of eucalyptus oil, 10 drops bergamot oil, 2 teaspoons alcohol. Repack the mixture in the jar, cover lightly and set aside for 2 weeks to ripen. It will then be ready to distribute in rose jars.

Nature in the Country

The appreciation of nature is a secondary objective for many people. Large cities, paved sidewalks, and super highways alienate persons from the earth and their natural environment. But even the most dedicated city dweller must escape the concrete world for a refreshing, sanity-restoring encounter with nature. For ages naturalists have documented the wonders that can be revealed on a walk through the country. Painters and photographers have recorded the beauty and organic patterns of nature on canvas and film for those who are not fortunate enough to experience nature firsthand. But nothing is more rewarding to the spirit than communicating with nature on a personal basis. A keen, respectful eye will reveal many of the abundant lessons nature has to teach us about our world and ourselves.

"There are some who can live without wild things, and some who cannot . . . These essays are the delights and dilemmas of one who cannot" (from *A Sand County Almanac* by Aldo Leopold).

Aldo Leopold: The Naturalist's Naturalist

Ellen Hohenfeldt

No statement could more succinctly capture Aldo Leopold's character. A man of insight with an extraordinary perception of nature, he dedicated his life to the preservation of those wild things of which he speaks. In so doing, he left a legacy, not only of game preserves and wilderness areas which might otherwise have been lost forever, but of subtle and inspiring writings in tribute to nature.

Leopold's fascination with nature started at a very early age. From the family's big white house in Burlington, Iowa, he could look down and see the Mississippi River flowing lazily through wooded shores. Spring and autumn brought the flights of migratory birds along the Mississippi flyway, and he would rise each day with the sun in order to catch an hour's birdwatching before school. He has said:

> When I call to mind my earliest impressions, I wonder whether the process ordinarily referred to as growing up is not actually a process of growing down; whether experience, so much touted among adults as the thing children lack, is not actually a progressive dilution of the essentials by the trivialities of living. This much at least is sure: my earliest impressions of wildlife and its pursuit retain a vivid sharpness of form, color, and atmosphere that half a century of professional wildlife experience has failed to obliterate or to improve upon.

Without doubt, Leopold gained some of his early sensitivity to nature from his father, Carl Leopold. The elder Leopold was a dedicated naturalist who stopped his own spring duck hunting long before such hunting was prohibited by law; and he imparted to his eldest son a love for hunting which lasted throughout his life.

Leopold's love of nature was not limited to wild animals but included all of nature. Wood, for instance, which was necessary to Carl Leopold's furniture manufacturing business, was also a cause for concern. Speculation about the waste and possible extermination of certain trees must have been a topic of conversation in the conservation-minded household. Perhaps this is where young Leopold developed his first ideas about tree farming, a conservation practice now taken for granted but then unheard of. At any rate, it was in the U. S. Forest Service that Leopold took the first steps in a career of conservation.

With a Bachelor of Science degree from Yale in 1908, and a Masters Degree in Forestry granted the following year, Leopold went to work for the Forest Service. He was assigned to the Apache

National Forest in Arizona where he became a leader in the movement for game protection in the Southwest. Because of his lifelong love of hunting, he was unable to bear the thought of the extinction of wild animals in the area. He believed that the principles of conserving forests could be applied to the preservation of game. Like forests, animals could be encouraged to reproduce and also harvested as necessary. Later, he set these ideas down in a book called *Game Management* which is considered a pioneering work on the subject.

Leopold was at the forefront of the growing conservation movement. For some leaders in the movement, it was difficult to juxtapose progress and restraint; but Leopold never disdained the development of Arizona. In fact, he called it, "one of the most meritorious of occupations." The problem came, he realized, when more was lost through land development than was gained: when overdevelopment of the land resulted in erosion, dust bowls, or barren soil, then the benefits of progress was negated.

One of Leopold's contributions was the development of a philosophy of conservation and an ethical statement for naturalists everywhere. He called his concept of conservation and preservation the land ethic. According to Leopold, people could not separate themselves from their environment, but rather they must consider themselves part of the environmental whole. Therefore, any action affecting the environment must be studied "in terms of what is ethically and esthetically right as well as what is economically expedient."

The year 1924 brought Leopold out of his beloved Southwest to Madison, Wisconsin, where he served as Associate Director of the U. S. Forest Products Laboratory. In 1933, the University of Wisconsin created a position especially for him—Professor of Wildlife Management, the first of its type in the country. While in this post, Leopold sought to satisfy a lifelong desire—to have his own small piece of land with a hunting cabin. The answer to his dream was found in the form of a dilapidated chicken house turned cow-

shed. Cleaned up and weatherproofed, this cabin, in the heart of Wisconsin's sand country, became a weekend haven for the Leopold family. Here, Leopold wrote some of his best work which was published in 1949 by Oxford University Press under the title *A Sand County Almanac and Sketches Here and There.*

Sand County Almanac can be described as the diary of a nature lover. The sand country of Wisconsin was once an area of thick pine forests until the timber boom of the latter ninteenth century destroyed the trees. Leopold tried to repair the damage done by the logging firms by planting thousands of pines. In his *Almanac* he depicts, with sensitivity and insight, the subtle changes of the landscape according to the seasons and to the whims of nature.

It is for the flowing prose written here in the sand country that Leopold is best known. *Sand County Almanac* provides the reader with a very personal view of the way Aldo Leopold saw the world. It is the story of one man's intimacy with his environment. The following excerpt is a sample of that man's story.

The Geese Return

One swallow does not make a summer, but one skein of geese, cleaving the murk of a March thaw, is the spring.

A cardinal, whistling spring to a thaw but later finding himself mistaken, can retrieve his error by resuming his winter silence. A chipmunk, emerging for a sunbath but finding a blizzard, has only to go back to bed. But a migrating goose, staking two hundred miles of black night on the chance of finding a hole in the lake, has no easy chance for retreat. His arrival carries the conviction of a prophet who has burned his bridges.

A March morning is only as drab as he who walks in it without a glance skyward, ear cocked for geese. I once knew an educated lady, banded by Phi Beta Kappa, who told me that she had never heard or seen the geese that twice a year proclaim the revolving seasons to her well-insulated roof. Is education possibly a process of trading awareness for things of lesser worth? The goose who trades his is soon a pile of feathers.

The geese that proclaim the seasons to our farm are aware of many things, including the Wisconsin statutes. The southbound November flocks pass over us high and haughty, with scarcely a honk of recognition for their favorite sandbars and sloughs. "As a crow flies" is crooked compared with their undeviating aim at the nearest big lake twenty miles to the south, where they loaf by day on broad waters and filch corn by night from the freshly cut stubbles. November geese are aware that every marsh and pond bristles from dawn till dark with hopeful guns.

March geese are a different story. Although they have been shot at most of the winter, as attested by their buck-shot-battered pinions, they know that the spring truce is now in effect. They wind the oxbows of the river, cutting low over the now gunless points and islands, and gabbling to each sandbar as to a long-lost friend. They weave low over the marshes and meadows, greeting each newly melted puddle and pool. Finally, after a few *pro-forma* circlings of our marsh, they set wing and glide silently to the pond, black landing-gear lowered and rumps white against the far hill. Once touching water, our newly arrived guests set up a honking and splashing that shakes the last thought of winter out of the brittle cattails. Our geese are home again!

It is at this moment of each year that I wish I were a muskrat, eye-deep in the marsh.

Once the first geese are in, they honk a clamorous invitation to each migrating flock, and in a few days the marsh is full of them. On our farm we measure the amplitude of our spring by two yardsticks: the number of pines planted, and the number of geese that stop. Our record is 642 geese counted in on 11 April 1946.

As in fall, our spring geese make daily trips to corn, but these are no surreptitious sneakings-out by night; the flocks move noisily to and from corn stubbles through the day. Each departure is preceded by loud gustatory debate, and each return by an even louder one. The returning flocks, once thoroughly at home, omit their *pro-forma* circlings of the marsh. They tumble out of the sky like maple leaves, side-slipping right and left to lose altitude, feet spraddled toward the shouts of welcome below. I suppose the ensuing gabble deals with the merits of the day's dinner. They are now eating the waste corn that the snow blanket has protected over winter from corn-seeking crows, cottontails, meadow mice, and pheasants.

It is a conspicuous fact that the corn stubbles selected by geese for feeding are usually those occupying former prairies. No man knows whether this bias for prairie corn reflects some superior nutritional value, or some ancestral tradition transmitted from generation to generation since the prairie days. Perhaps it reflects the simpler fact that prairie cornfields tend to be large. If I could understand the thunderous debates that precede and follow these daily excursions to corn, I might soon learn the reason for the prairie-bias. But I cannot, and I am well content that it should remain a mystery. What a dull world if we knew all about geese! ⑤

From *A SAND COUNTY ALMANAC WITH OTHER ESSAYS ON CONSERVATION FROM ROUND RIVER* by Aldo Leopold. Copyright © 1949, 1953, 1966 by Oxford University Press, Inc. Reprinted by permission.

An Introduction to Backpacking

Michael Abel

All too often people take off on a backpacking trip with very little knowledge of where they are going. The results can be unfortunate.

Often a trip is ruined by bad weather, mosquitoes, impassable passes or a thousand and one other ills. Naturally, the sun will not shine every day and other impediments will arise to dim your enjoyment of the wilderness. Nevertheless, a little pre-departure planning can pay off handsomely. First of all, it is important to evaluate these factors: 1) Your physical condition, 2) Terrain, 3) Weather, 4) Transportation problems.

(1) Foremost consideration should be given to your *physical condition*. As the old expression goes, do not bite off more than you can chew. Try yourself out. Take a short (five to fifteen miles) weekend backpacking trip into familiar country.

Preparation of your body is as important as preparation of your equipment. A couple of hard weekends ''in training'' can pay off handsomely when the trail starts up the side of the mountain. You will feel better and perform better if you are in good shape.

Unfortunately, there is no shortcut to a good physical condition. Most people over twenty will find it necessary to start a daily regimen of exercise at least one month before departing on a major backpacking trip. Do not be afraid to exercise. There is nothing wrong with getting a few sore muscles, but do not strain your muscles. Work yourself into an exercise program gradually.

(2) *What is the terrain like?* What we are referring to here are the ups and downs of the trail.

As the saying goes: ''There are forty-mile hikes, and there are forty-mile hikes.'' I am familiar with forty-mile stretches of wilderness trail that can be covered in two days without too much trouble. I am also familiar with forty-mile stretches of trail which I would allocate at least five days to traverse. Why the great disparity? Is a mile not a mile? *No.*

On a well-graded flat or slightly downhill stretch, a good hiker can travel 2½-3 miles in one hour. On a slight uphill stretch a good hiker can travel about 2 miles per hour. On a very hard uphill trail at high altitude, a hiker is lucky to go 1 mile in an hour.

"In time you will realize that in the mountains the number of miles that you have traveled does not mean quite as much as the vertical ascents and descents that you have encountered."

Keep this in mind in planning out your hike. Obtain topographical maps and examine the uphill and downhill stretches of a trail that will be encountered along the way. Try to find out firsthand what it means to hike up 1000 vertical feet. In time you will realize that in the mountains the number of miles that you have traveled does not mean quite as much as the vertical ascents and descents that you have encountered.

Finally, there is no substitute for firsthand knowledge. A friend who has traveled over the same trail before is your best source of advice. Also, you should always consult with the local park rangers before setting out.

(3) *What is the weather going to be like?* This is not as absurd a question as it sounds. Naturally, it is not possible to predict the exact weather conditions in a given area weeks or even days in advance. Nevertheless, with a little good planning and luck, one can do a great deal to promote the enjoyment of a backpacking trip.

Three weather factors must be taken into consideration: snow on the ground, air tem-perature, and possibility of rainshowers.

If there is too much snow on the ground, it will be difficult if not impossible to cross over any mountain passes. For instance, 1971 was an especially bad year for backpacking in the northwest. Due to snow, most of the high mountain passes stayed closed until August. Some trails were never even opened officially. One can best avoid snowbound passes by planning a trip for August; however, in years of lighter snowfall one can easily cross the highest passes in June.

Next, check out the temperature conditions so that you will have the right clothes along. If the nights are especially cold, do not hesitate to bring along a pair of long underwear to keep you snug.

Finally, check out the possibility of rain. As a rule, weather fronts are uncommon in the western mountains during the summer months. Rainfall is usually the result of localized thunder-showers. Occasionally, however, a rain front will move through (this is most common in western Washington and Oregon). If you

"Also, do not hesitate to call up the park or forest ranger in the area you intend to visit."

are a fair-weather hiker like myself, you will maintain extra plans and maps for a hike in a different area.

As departure day approaches, stay abreast of the latest weather conditions and forecasts. Also, do not hesitate to call up the park or forest ranger in the area you intend to visit. Ask him for his latest weather reports. Find out how the snow levels are in the passes.

These people live in the area and work on the trails you will be traveling over. They are familiar with weather patterns and the snow levels. Telephone the ranger station nearest to your proposed trailhead and ask about the weather and trail conditions. They will give you better answers than the weatherman on local radio or television.

(4) *How are you getting there?* Most of us live in cities and either travel by bus or automobile. Rural areas seldom offer the public transportation facilities of a city, thus one most probable form of transportation to the trailhead will be the automobile.

While an automobile can get you to your trailhead quickly, it can also present you with a few problems. Paramount among these is what I call the "return liability factor." This is the matter of returning to your car at the end of your hike. There are at least two ways of accomplishing this:

1. Accept the alternative of backtracking to the trailhead over the same trail.

2. Plan a circular trip which takes you away from and back to your car on a trail which does not backtrack on itself. This is called a loop trip. With a few maps and a little time one should have little trouble finding a trail loop that will return you to a point at or near your automobile.

The opportunities for backpacking in North America are almost unlimited. We are fortunate that such vast areas of the North American continent remain available for wilderness recreation. We owe a tremendous debt of gratitude to our forefathers, who were prudent enough to set aside portions of the American landscape for posterity for us to treasure and enjoy.

Taken from BACKPACKING MADE EASY, by Michael Abel, Naturegraph Publishers, 1972, with kind permission of the author and publisher.

Elementary Mycology:
A guide to edible mushrooms

Nancy Weber

Some people mark the advance of the seasons by changes in the trees, others by the ever-changing panorama of flowers, or by the comings and goings of birds. A few curious souls classify the seasons by the mushrooms they find. To most people, mushrooms are curiosities to be passed by, whereas to others, mushrooms are prizes of great value in a contest of wits with nature. The fascination of mushroom hunting is not easily explained. It is a combination of the thrill of a scavenger hunt, the idea of something for nothing, the excitement of the pursuit of the unknown, the satisfaction of preparing a gourmet dish, and the joy of being out-of-doors.

Unlike most familiar plants, mushrooms are generally visible only during one phase in the life of the organism. Most of the mushroom plant is hidden in the soil, humus, or rotted wood and is composed of narrow threadlike filaments which form what is known as the mycelium or "spawn." The mushroom itself is a fruiting body produced by the mycelium, much as the apple is the fruit of the apple tree. Instead of seeds, mushrooms produce spores which reproduce and disperse the organism. The classification of mushrooms is based in part on how the spores are produced and their characteristics. Since the mycelium is seldom visible, the number of kinds of mushrooms living in an area cannot be ascertained except by finding the typically rather short-lived fruiting bodies. At different times of the year, different combinations of temperature and humidity stimulate the fruiting of different kinds of mushrooms. Thus, there is always the possibility of encountering the unexpected on a mushroom hunt.

Mushrooms grow in a variety of sizes, shapes and colors. Several thousand species occur in North America, but there is no complete catalog of all the known varieties from even a small part of the continent. Many species of mushrooms are inedible because of unpleasant flavors or textures, some are definitely poisonous, others are edible and good, and many have not been tested or reported on. Consequently, caution is needed when eating wild mushrooms. While there is no certain way to test the edibility of a mushroom other than eating it, precautions can be taken that will lessen the possibility of being poisoned. The first precaution is to use a reputable field guide or take a course in mushroom identification. The second is to learn the principal poisonous species in your area and avoid them.

The term "toadstool" is popularly (not scientifically) used to denote a poisonous mushroom. However, this distinction is not always clearcut; one person's mushroom may be another's toadstool. Each person must develop his or her own list of species that can be eaten and enjoyed.

Hunting mushrooms year round will provide ample reason to be outside during all but the coldest northern winters. The pleasures of mushroom hunting for the photographer, artist, curious hiker, or mycophagist (one who eats mushrooms) are numerous. Each season brings the possibility of encountering new forms, flavors and textures.

Spring

In spring, the arrival of warm weather and spring rains herald the arrival of the morel mushroom. The morels or sponge mushrooms are collected throughout much of the forested region of North America. The true morels have a pitted upper part (the head) which is hollow and borne on a hollow stalk. The white or big-footed morel (*Morchella crassipes*) is a favorite of mine. It often fruits in mixed hardwood forests, old apple orchards, and around the stumps of dead elm trees. Sometimes only a few fruiting bodies are found, but on good years they can be collected by the basketful.

Once you find these or some other interesting mushroom, the next challenge is getting them home in good condition. Wrapping each collection of each

with cold water and blotting the excess water will usually clear away any dirt or bugs. Morels are delicious sautéed in butter.

Summer

About the time morels are just a memory, and the urge to go exploring is getting strong, it is time to look for oyster mushrooms (*Pleurotus ostreatus*). The appearance of oysters marks the end of early spring and hints that summer is not far away. Growing on dead trees, especially hardwoods, their upper surface is smooth and varies in color from white to pale tan or grayish lavender. The underside has a series of structures that resemble the pages of a book held upside down. These thin structures are called "gills" and are covered with spore-producing

Oyster mushrooms (*Pleurotus ostreatus*)
(Photo, Dan Guravich)

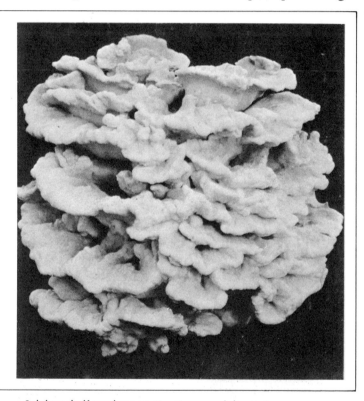

Sulphur-shelf mushrooms (*Laetiporus sulphureus*)
(Photo, Dan Guravich)

species in waxed paper and carrying the packages in an open basket is a good, easy method. Avoid plastic containers and plastic wraps if you have far to go, or if the weather is hot, since the mushrooms tend to deteriorate rapidly from the action of bacteria and yeasts. Store the booty in a cool place until time to prepare it.

Before cooking the morels, cut them in half longitudinally to get rid of any bugs so that a single cavity extends from the base of the stalk to the tip of the head. There is no need to soak morels in salt water before cooking; rinsing them under the faucet

cells and associated structures. The gills are whitish and extend from where the mushroom is attached to the tree to the outer edge of the oyster. Generally, no distinct stalk is present.

If a mature oyster cap is placed on a piece of white paper with the gills down and protected from drafts for a few hours, the spores will accumulate on the paper. This record of a spore's color is called a "spore print." In the case of the oyster mushroom, the spore print will be white or tinged lilac.

Oyster mushrooms are easily identifiable for beginning mushroom hunters. The flavor is distinc-

Morels in cross-section. Before preparing, these mushrooms should be cut in the fashion shown here to allow any insects that are inside to escape. (Photo, A. H. Smith)

Fruit of the hunt are found in the brimming basket of morels above. (Photo, Dan Guravich)

47

Chanterelles (*Cantharellus cibarius*) fruit in the forested areas of North America. (Photo, Dan Guravich)

The winter mushroom, or velvet-foot (*Flammulina velutipes*), fruits from fall to late winter when temperatures are above freezing for several days. (Photo, Dan Guravich)

tive: people seem either to like it very much or not at all. Frequently a large number of bugs will be found between the gills of this species, but a strong tap on the top of the cap is usually sufficient to dislodge them. Oysters may also fruit abundantly in the fall; this is one of the few mushrooms with two seasons.

Late Summer—Early Fall

By the time summer is well established, it is time to start looking for the sulphur shelf (*Laetiporus sulphureus*) which, during the summer and autumn, fruits on various types of wood. It is frequently found on oak or willow trees as well as on conifers. Like the oyster mushroom, the sulphur shelf typically lacks a stalk and forms what appears to be tiers of shelves. Instead of gills, the sulphur shelf has minute pores on the lower surface. The tender, young edge of each shelf is typically bright yellow, the older parts orange, and the underside yellow or occasionally white. The tender portions of the shelves are good eating, but inclined to become fibrous in age. As with all wild mushrooms, these should be cooked before being eaten. The firm texture of this species is a pleasant addition to casseroles, soups, or stews.

Another conspicuous summer and fall mushroom is the shaggy mane (*Coprinus comatus*) which appears in lawns, gardens, meadows, and along roadsides. When fresh and young, these are handsome mushrooms; but almost before your eyes, the edges of the cap may turn pink, then black, then start to drip a blackish liquid. This pattern of changes starts at the free edge of the cap and progresses toward the center until all that is left is a stalk supporting a few short, dripping, black spokes. Shaggy manes are definitely pick-and-eat mushrooms; nearly mature specimens left in the refrigerator overnight will be a mass of black juice the next day. When all parts of the cap are still white, however, it is edible. Some people get a slightly bitter aftertaste from shaggy manes, so individual testing is required. When the caps are sautéed in butter, they puff up a bit and turn a delicate golden brown; the stalks may require longer cooking.

Shaggy mane (*Coprinus comatus*) should be tested by individuals, since it may leave a bitter aftertaste. (Photo, Grant Heilman)

During the summer and early fall, the chanterelles (particularly *Cantharellus cibarius*) fruit in the forested areas of North America. The chanterelle or pfifferling is a justifiably highly rated edible mushroom which is sold in European markets. Imported canned chanterelles may be purchased at specialty shops at gourmet prices; however, with some attention to detail and good hunting, you can gather your own supply of this delicacy. The true chanterelle grows on the ground, often in patches; typically the fruiting bodies are not joined together. These relatively stout mushrooms have rather thick, blunt, narrow gills which are frequently joined by veins. (Worms also like chanterelles, so always check your mushrooms and discard wormy specimens.) Small holes in the stem or fleshy part of a fruiting body are indications that a worm, usually a small grub with a black head, got there first.

Chanterelles may be prepared in many ways. Since their flesh is relatively firm, they may be cut into thin slices and then deep fried; salted, these slices make good mushroom chips as a change from potato chips. Like most mushrooms, chanterelles may be preserved in several ways. Always use fresh, worm-free fruit for preserving. One of the easiest methods of preservation is to cook the mushrooms, then freeze them in their own juice in meal-sized packages. Drying is an effective method but requires a series of screens and a heat source which can be regulated so that the sliced mushrooms will dry in 12 to 24 hours. Once dried, the mushrooms may be stored in airtight bags or jars. Home canning is not recommended unless a pressure canner is used; mushrooms are non-acid and if improperly canned, the organism that causes botulism may develop.

Although most of the mushrooms mentioned so far are edible, some of the most striking wild mushrooms are poisonous. The best known poisonous mushrooms belong to the *Amanita* genus. Most members of this group of mushrooms typically have white gills which do not reach the stalk, a white spore deposit, and a layer of tissue called a veil which covers the young mushroom. As the young mushroom enlarges, this veil may break up in a variety of ways. It sometimes leaves patches of tissue on the cap and/or a cuplike structure at the base of the stalk or frills of tissue around the base of the stalk. Many members of this group also have a veil which extends from the stalk to the edge of the cap in young specimens and remains as a skirt around the upper part of the stalk at maturity. The deadly poisonous destroying angel which is pure white belongs to this group as does the fly agaric (*Amanita muscaria*). The latter species fruits in summer and autumn in woods across the continent.

The fly agaric is the mushroom usually portrayed on plaques, stationery, and napkins; and that is the model for many candle holders and Christmas ornaments. Characteristics of this species are the yellow orange to brilliant red of the cap, with the white, cottage cheese-like patches of veil material, the enlarged base of the stalk with ruffles of tissue around it, and the skirt around the upper part of the stalk. This beautiful mushroom causes a type of poisoning which is usually not fatal but which varies greatly in severity depending on the strain of the mushroom eaten and the condition of the person who eats it.

Winter

Even during northern winters, wild mushrooms can occasionally be gathered. The winter mushroom, or velvet-foot (*Flammulina velutipes*), fruits on deadwood, especially hardwoods, from fall to late winter when the temperatures are above freezing for several days. It is commercially cultivated in the Orient. The distinctive features of the winter mushroom are its white spore deposit; yellowish brown cap which is smooth and very slimy; and the stalk which, in mature fruiting bodies, appears to be covered with brown velvet near the base. Most people wipe the caps before cooking them. The main appeal of the winter mushroom is likely to reside in the time of year it can be collected rather than its flavor. This species should not be eaten raw. It contains a substance which might be poisonous if consumed in quantity but which is broken down by cooking.

In different parts of the country and at different times of the year, many different kinds of mushrooms make their appearance. Consider taking a closer look at the next mushroom you find—but be warned that such action could be dangerous! Everyone who pursues this fascinating study at one point took a first look. Many of us who paused for that first look are still stopping, looking, collecting and studying the wild and wonderful world of mushrooms. ⑤

*Leaves of three,
let it be.*

*Berries of white,
hide from sight.*

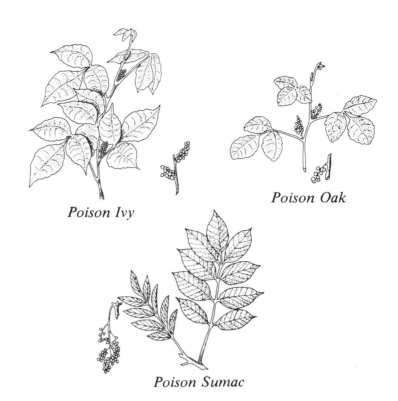

Poison Ivy

Poison Oak

Poison Sumac

The Pitch for Less Itch

Aileen Mallory

It's a beautiful day—perfect for tromping through the woods or cavorting down a country lane. Be careful as you traipse through the flora, however. Enough poison ivy may lurk beneath the wild flowers to make you itch for weeks.

Poison ivy is responsible for an estimated 333,000 lost workdays annually. It may cause only a week or two of itching discomfort; but in extreme cases, it's responsible for weeks of suffering.

The best way to avoid a bout with poison ivy is to learn to identify the plant and then keep away from it. The trouble is, it's not an easy plant to recognize. Generally, it has glossy, green leaflets which grow in clusters of three. (Children easily remember the jingle "Leaves of three, let it be.") The leaves may have smooth or saw-toothed edges; in autumn, they turn a brilliant orange or red before dropping off. The white, waxy berries stay on the stem throughout the winter.

Poison ivy often disguises itself by the position it assumes. It frequently grows along old fencerows and beside paths and roads; but it can even climb trees. Poison ivy might be a single bush, a sneaky creeper underfoot or a vine covering a wall as nonpoisonous ivy often does.

How It Does Its Dirty Work

How can such a pretty little plant cause such a big problem? Poison ivy contains urushiol, an irritant and sensitizing substance. It's in the ivy's sap, leaves, fruit, flowers, roots and bark, but apparently not in the pollen or wood. Tearing or bruising any part of the plant releases the toxic juice.

You need not come into direct contact with the ivy itself in order to have an allergic reaction. The sap can be carried on tools, pets or clothing. A dermatologist tells about an engineer who was extremely sensitive to poison ivy and knew it. He wisely brought a clean shirt, trousers and gloves to change into after he finished his surveying. He forgot, however, about his boots. Pulling his clean trousers over the dirty boots contaminated the inside of his pant legs. The result, of course, was a bad case of poison ivy.

If you think you're immune to poison ivy, don't be too smug. Botanists say it's doubtful that anyone is immune to it; some just appear to be. People who spend a lot of time in poison ivy country often acquire a degree of resistance. They never, however, acquire complete immunity.

Poison ivy's irritant can even be airborne; carried by smoke. Some of the worst infections occur in the fall when people are burning leaves that include poison ivy. Don't think of poison ivy only as a scourge of summer: remember, it is a pest for all seasons.

What To Do About It

If you believe you have come into contact with poison ivy, wash as soon as possible. Scrub the exposed areas of the skin with warm water and a mild soap. Lather and rinse several times. Then sponge rubbing alcohol over the area. A University of Penn-

sylvania study found that the poison penetrates the skin rapidly. Washing within five to ten minutes after exposure may lessen the infection in mildly sensitive people. If washing is delayed for an hour, even the least sensitive become infected.

Irritation usually begins a few hours (even several days) after contact with the plant; early signs are itching, redness and blisters. These symptoms are usually followed by elevation of temperature, restlessness, and considerable discomfort.

Once an allergic reaction has started, nothing much can be done to stop it. Soothing salve may relieve the itching but does nothing to shorten the course of the disease. Above all, poison ivy victims should try not to scratch the infected area, since the risk of infection is great.

Hot compresses and a zinc-oxide solution applied at brief intervals will help soothe small blisters on hands, arms and legs. If the reaction is severe—large blisters, severe inflammation or fever—see a doctor.

Contrary to a widely held belief, poison ivy is not contagious. You cannot "catch" the allergy from an infected person. Ⓢ

Tips on how to prevent a reaction to poison ivy:

1. Learn to recognize poison ivy and be constantly on the alert for it.

2. Carefully destroy the plants whenever possible. June and July are the best months for eradication. To get rid of poison ivy, remove all the root or the plant will return. Use caution with herbicides, however. Check with your county agent for the type required and instructions in using.

3. If it's impossible to avoid poison ivy, wear protective clothing. Put on boots, long trou-

sers, long sleeves and gloves. And remember —be sure the apparel has been washed since any previous contact with poison ivy.

4. Expose contaminated boots and tools to bright sunlight for several hours before using again.

5. Never burn poison ivy. The smoke can be just as poisonous as the leaves.

6. If you are frequently or seriously bothered by poison ivy, ask your doctor about the possibility of hyposensitization shots.

CLOSE-UP PHOTOGRAPHY

A NEW LOOK AT THE LAND:

Article and photos by Carroll Dale Short

You've got striking photos of barns, beehives, and basket makers. You've captured the colors of cidar apples, sorghum pans, and sage fields. Think you've pretty well exhausted the picture possibilities on your stretch of land?

Look again. There's a wealth of material as close as your fingertips.

That word *close* is the key. With a minimum of extra equipment (would you believe fifty cents worth, for a start?) you can photograph your world from a distance of inches. It's a thrill many camera owners, even the ones with all the flashy gear, will never know. Here's why!

A close-up, to most photographers, means the closest distance their camera will focus by itself. For most adjustable models, even expensive ones, that's about three feet.

To get the feel of what we're talking about, pick up your camera and watch your lens barrel closely, from the side. First set your focus indicator to infinity, the sideways 8 that's past the thirty or forty-foot marking. Now turn your focusing ring until it's set on the minimum shooting distance your camera allows.

See what happens? As you focus *closer*, the lens elements move *farther* from the film. So to get closer to your subject and still be able to focus sharply, you have to find a way to move your lens out still farther.

There are many ways to break the arm's-length barrier, but they all come under three categories: extension tubes, close-up lenses and "macro" lenses.

For the sake of simplicity, and our pocketbook's well-being, let's put aside the macros for now. They're lenses with specially made focusing systems that let you shoot from inches away without extra attachments. Mighty convenient, yes, but the price of the good ones begin in the hundreds and go up from there.

That leaves us with extension tubes and close-up lenses, each with their good points and drawbacks. Let's consider each briefly. You can decide which is right for you.

This bird was building a nest in the corner of a refurbished log cabin. I kept edging closer to his perching place, a foot or so at a time, while it was out gathering straw and bark for the nest. Eventually I was only a couple of feet away, with the camera on a tripod. An electronic flash, held at arm's length above the camera, supplied the light and froze any movement. Here it is the short duration of the flash pulse, not the shutter speed of the camera that matters. I was able to shoot at *f*/11 and 1/60 second on High Speed Ektachrome. (The 1/60 second was chosen because it is the speed at which that particular camera synchronizes properly with flash.)

Tubes go between the camera body and the lens. They're not glass, just hollow metal cylinders with fittings on the ends to tightly connect the lens and camera.

(Throughout, we'll be talking about the type of camera called a single-lens reflex, the kind with a series of mirrors that lets you view through the lens. Range-finder cameras, with their separate portals for viewing and shooting, aren't too useful for close-ups, regardless of how well they perform in a hundred other ways. The reason? They fall prey to the demon known as parallax, the slight difference in angles between what you see and what the film sees. When your range finder is inches from a honeysuckle blossom, the golden glory you're seeing on the viewing screen might be missed altogether by the lens.)

A set of extension tubes usually costs at least twenty or thirty dollars. But there are bargains to be found. Watch discount ads in the back of the big photo magazines, especially season clearances, and you might match the buy I got once—new extension tubes for . . . *three dollars?*

Extension tubes have no lenses to degrade the sharpness of your regular lens, so definition is fine. But they do have drawbacks. In the first place, you're obliged to screw an extra piece on and off your camera. Also, since this puts your lens farther from the film, the marked speed of your lens, its *f*-stop, no longer applies. These *f*-stops are figured with the lens nestled back in its infinity position, remember? If your camera has a light meter that reads through the lens, then it will compensate for the lag in light levels. If not, you've got some fancy figuring to do: inverted fractions, square roots and such.

Close-up lenses, on the other hand, are really just low-power magnifying glasses. They screw into the front of your lens, which makes them much simpler to use. But they do hurt the sharpness of your lens a bit—most noticeably at the edge of the picture and when you're shooting at large apertures. For the majority of situations, though, they're more than acceptable.

The first close-up picture I ever made was with a twenty-nine cent magnifying glass I bought at Woolworth's toy counter. (With inflation rampant, it'll probably cost you half a dollar).

Just as an experiment, I held it over the lens, put my eye to the finder, and moved back and forth until things—in this case, the bulging eyes of a handheld bullfrog—looked sharp. Distance, four inches. Picture quality, fine. And there's no exposure compensation to worry about, because your lens stays where it is.

Sure, there are screw-on close-up lenses made

Daylilies were shot with a #1 extension tube behind a 50mm lens. The exposure, by full sunlight, was f/11 at 1/125 second on Kodachrome 64, the smaller aperture chosen for the extra depth of field.

Depth of field, sometimes a handicap, was an advantage here because of the flowers' varying distances from the camera.

This coleus was photographed with a magnifying glass held in front of a 50mm lens of a single lens reflex 35. Exposure, by overhead sunlight, was about f/8 at 1/125 second on Kodachrome 64. The angle of the lighting emphasizes the texture of the leaf.

With the overall background a few shades darker than the rooster's front, this shot presented a problem for the meter. The exposure at the meter's suggested setting kept plenty detail in the boards, but made the rooster's face and breast too pale and washed out. Of a series of four bracketed exposures (at a half-stop, a stop, a stop and a half, and two stops *less* than the metered one), this one—a stop less—had the range of tones closest to what I was after. The light was cloudy daylight coming through an opening in the pen to the left. Exposure, with a 50mm and #1 extension tube, was f/5.6 and 1/125 second on Kodachrome 64.

The hat and boots, unlike the rough leaf of the coleus, needed to be photographed in softer light to hold the delicate shadings. Best light for such a purpose is when a thin film of cloud covers the sun. The exposure, with a No. 1 close-up lens on a 50mm, was at f/8 at 1/500 on High Speed Ektachrome.

for the purpose. Sure, they'll probably give better quality than my dimestore wonder. But I kept it for years, and didn't use anything else. Best twenty-nine cents I ever spent. Just try to hold steady, and remember not to shoot wide open if you can help it. The range of stops between f/5.6 or so and f/16 gives better results.

Now that the technical details are out of the way, what are we venturing out to shoot? Anything and everything. Just let your eye start homing in on tiny patches of color and texture you'd normally walk past without noticing.

Wild flowers, in all their million varieties, come immediately to mind. But don't overlook leaves, moss, mushrooms, fungus and the more prosaic weeds—such as dandelion and thistle. From the close-up perspective, even a common blade of grass can be intoxicatingly beautiful with a rainbow-hued drop of dew hanging from the tip, or encased in a spiky coat of frost.

Butterflies, dragonflies, frogs, fish (late afternoon sun glinting off iridescent scales can look like a fantasy landscape), turtles, snakes (preferably lethargic and good-natured ones), lizards, caterpillars—they're all frame-filling picture material, once you learn the mechanics of getting close.

As a matter of fact, you'll find interesting textures by the thousands: kudzu, sugarcane, gnarled roots, wheat, weathered wood, rusted iron, a relative's (or your own) embroidering and crocheting, the handwriting of keepsake letters, initials carved into a tree, wasp nests, barbed wire, gravestone lettering, tangled fishing line, worm spots on apples, borer holes in fence planks. The list is endless.

A few do's and don'ts, to help get the results you're after. Focusing is extra critical at such short distances because your depth of field is reduced also—that's the range of sharpness in front of and behind what you're focusing on. You'll probably get better pictures by abandoning your focusing ring altogether and moving your whole camera in and out until the subject is sharp.

And if you're using a slow film, the necessary small f-stops can lead you to dangerously shaky shutter speeds in low light. Then it's time to bring on some kind of camera support. Not necessarily a tripod, though—sometimes a stake in the ground or a knee to brace against can do the job. Tripods are fine, but they're sort of an encumbrance. And there's something about the exuberance of seeing close up that makes you leery of getting bogged down.

Another point to remember: in black and white, especially, the tones of the subject are in danger of merging—the foreground being lost against the background—unless you take steps to

Board with knothole was photographed by direct sunlight, coming in from above and to the side, to help emphasize the texture of the wood. With a strong magnifying glass on a 50mm lens, the exposure on Kodachrome 64 was f/8 at 1/250 second.

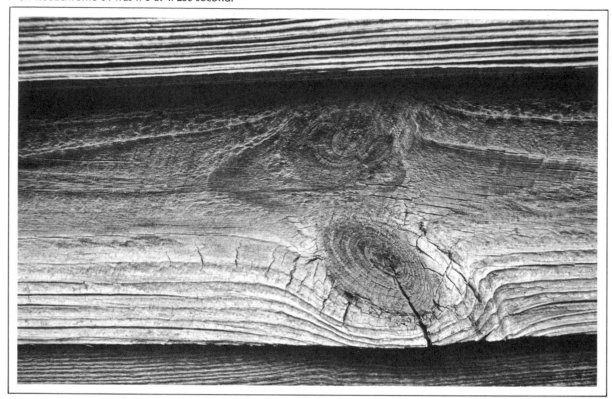

put dark subjects against light areas and vice versa. Black backgrounds are especially nice. I like them so much that I carry around a square yard of black velvet so I can have one whenever I want.

With predominantly light or dark backgrounds, though, there's a chance your exposure meter will read the main subject incorrectly. After a little practice, you can learn to compensate. Until then, make it a point to "bracket" your exposures, especially in color, like professionals do. After you've shot at what the meter advises, open up a stop, then two; close down a stop, then two. It's not haphazard shooting, only a way to make sure you'll have an exposure that's not just "usable" but truly gives the effect you envisioned.

Light comes in two varieties, harsh and soft. The harsh kind comes from an undiffused sun or from a flashgun. The soft kind comes from a cloudy sky, from shade, or from a flashgun bounced from a wall or ceiling.

Both kinds can make great pictures. Experiment until you can gauge the "feel" of the light, not just the amount of it. As a rule of thumb, soft light gives a quiet, ethereal mood. Harsh light, when it comes from the side at a narrow angle) pros call it cross-light) is best for emphasizing the texture of a surface such as bark, granite, or burlap.

When you shoot color, the temperature of the light is a problem (nope, it's got nothing to do with the day being warm or cold). Cool light tends toward blue and green hues; warm to the reds and yellows. The light on a cloudy day, in the shade, or just before sunrise or after sundown—all those are cool conditions, meaning your picture will have a tint of blue. On the other hand, the first hour or two after sunrise and before sunset is warm light—with a strong red-orange cast.

You can buy filters that balance the light to "normal," but some photographers often prefer the natural coloring .

After you get a taste of what close-ups can offer, you might want to specialize. Some hobbyists have built a photo collection around old jewelry, painted plates, wood carvings, needlework, wild flowers, insects, or the vanishing brand of old-fashioned woodwork found in crumbling houses.

Or you may just want to use close-ups as I do, to add extra impact to a group of regular photos: a screen-filling slide of a dusty butterfly wing, a wall-sized enlargement of a seed pod backlit by a summer sun. They can bring the viewer, and you, closer to the colors, shapes, and textures of nature, closer to the fascinating kaleidoscope of the land.

And isn't that what photography is all about?

Portrait of an American

JOHN JAMES AUDUBON'S greatest claims to fame and glory were the versatility of his talents and gifts, and the completion of his main ambition, the original elephant folio of paintings of 435 species of American birds, *a tour de force* which has never again been equalled in history.

Young Audubon had a spoiled and petted boyhood on an estate in France, early developing both a talent for drawing, and a love of the outdoors, natural history and birds in particular, which he could not control, and which motivated his entire life. When about seventeen years of age, he was sent to North America to take charge of a property near Philadelphia. He adopted his new country wholeheartedly. Here he met and married Lucy Bakewell, and began a series of commercial ventures with his patrimony, which took him to Kentucky in 1808 and to New Orleans in 1812. As Audubon could not restrain himself from continually hunting, shooting and drawing, all these ventures failed, until finally he had practically nothing left except a wife, gun, and the precious drawings of his beloved birds.

In the meantime his dream, to publish a series of paintings of every North American bird, had been crystallizing, and he determined to devote his time, talents and energy to the attainment of this goal, no matter what the cost. He was encouraged by his devoted and unselfish wife, who believed in his genius and a final triumphant success. For years Audubon led a truly remarkable life. Supporting himself by painting, por-

"When I think of these times, and call back to my mind the grandeur and beauty of those almost uninhabited shores ... that everywhere spread along the hills and overhung the margins of the stream, unmolested by the axe of the settler; when I see that no longer any aborigines are to be found there, and that the vast herds of Elk, Deer, and Buffalo which once pastured on these hills, and in these valleys, have ceased to exist; when I reflect that all this grand portion of our Union, instead of being in a state of nature, is now more or less covered with villages, farms and towns . . . that hundreds of steamboats are gliding to and fro, over the whole length of the majestic river, forcing commerce to take root and to prosper at every spot; when I remember that these extraordinary changes have all taken place in the short period of twenty years, I pause, wonder, and although I know all to be a fact, can scarcely believe its reality."

Audubon

traiture, and teaching drawing, in some incredible manner he always got where he wanted to go and attained all his objectives. He solicited subscriptions to his great work in the principal eastern cities, going back and forth to Edinburgh, London and Paris, most of the time leading a hand-to-mouth existence. In 1831 he made his famous expedition to the Florida Keys, the next year going to Labrador, then travelling through the southern states to the independent republic of Texas, always seeking out wilderness areas. In between trips he wrote the volumes of the text, and the whole work was completed in 1838 at a cost of about $100,000, the total number of sets issued being under two hundred, at $1,000 a set. The project had taken just about twenty-five years to complete, his wife's faith was justified, success and renown were his.

This success would have been impossible without the possession of qualities, many of which the world properly regards as magnificent. Audubon had enormous confidence in himself, inflexible determination, and the capacity of never admitting failure or becoming really discouraged. His physical endurance and energy were extraordinary, and some of his adventures required great bravery. His dealings with others were aided by a magnetic personality, he was remarkably handsome with beautiful eyes, and practised the arts of self-dramatization and salesmanship instinctively. The American Woodsman became a sensational success in the houses of the great and near great. Audubon's life has been described as a typical success story; he just could not be stopped. ⒼⓈ

Ludlow Griscom

From AUDUBON'S BIRDS OF AMERICA,
Introduction by Ludlow Griscom
(Copyright 1950 by the Macmillan Company)

THE NIGHT OF THE OWL

George H. Harrison

Barred Owl

The thermometer read zero as we stepped from the cabin porch. "This could be one of the coldest nights of the winter," I said to my friend Pete as we made our way across the front yard and down the road.

"It's a good night for owls," Pete answered.

"Yes, it's clear and it's February." I had to raise my voice a little to be heard above the crunching sound of our boots on the snow.

This walk was a ritual we have followed every night we've spent at our cabin in Hidden Valley, Pennsylvania. Our destination was an old park bench that overlooks some of the most beautiful wooded countryside I have ever seen. And under a full moon like the one we had that night, it is magnificent.

A few seconds after we reached the bench at the top of the ridge, the stillness of the night was shattered by a barred owl sounding its dog-like call from up the hollow: "hoo-hoo-hoo . . . hoohoo-hoohooaw."

Pete responded automatically with his own "hoohoo-hoohoo . . . hoohoo-hoohooaw," and immediately the owl answered him. I've heard this exchange many times during our years of bench sitting and it's always amazed me how much that barred owl sounded like Pete!

Suddenly, a second owl got into the act. This one was a great horned owl. Deeper and more resonant than the barred, the great horned gives out three, five or six uninflected hoots. "Hoo, hoohoo, hoo, hoo," echoed from the ridge above the barred owl's hollow.

So we had two owls. But that wasn't the end of it.

Almost on cue, a screech owl joined in the chorus with his mournful whinny or wail, running down the scale. Some screech owls call on a single pitch, but this one moved from high to low. And now we had three.

Our final entrant in the Hidden Valley Owl Choir was the most distinguished of all. His appearance on the moonlit stage nearly brought down the house . . . well, at least Pete and I were overwhelmed. The "too, too, too, too, too . . ." in a bell-like, mellow whistle, was the first saw-whet call I had ever heard. I was glad Pete was there to identify it, because I had never before heard anything like that, and I thought I knew my bird calls. So now we had four.

This was truly an exciting experience for us. Imagine four different species of owl, all singing at the same time on that one unforgettable night in February.

In spite of the zero temperatures, the calling of those owls was a sure sign of spring. All four were singing either to attract a mate or to defend a territory. At least one of them, the great horned, was already nesting.

The four owls we had singing that night all sang a different pitch.

The barred owl was a baritone, the great horned a bass, the screech an alto and the saw-whet a definite soprano.

Owls are to the night what hawks are to the daylight hours. Where the hawk leaves off, the owl begins. Together the two families of birds present a twenty-four-hour threat to many of man's enemies, particularly mice and rats.

Like turkeys or ducks, owls are easy to identify. Most members of the 130 species of owl in the world *look* like owls and nearly anyone recognizes them. They are large, soft-looking birds with huge heads and round, piercing eyes that stare straight ahead and give the owls a solemn or "wise" appearance.

Owls have several striking qualities, mostly adaptations to night

hunting, which make them unique. When most birds are searching for a safe place to sleep, owls are stretching and yawning and awakening for a night of hunting. Though not all owls are nocturnal, two-thirds are most active in late evening and at night. Their keen sight, acute hearing and almost silent flight make them masters of the night. In addition to binocular vision covering 70 degrees in a 140-degree field, they can swivel their heads around nearly 360 degrees for a better look behind them. By bobbing up and down, tilting or lowering their heads, they can also better judge distance.

Like many other birds, owls have dense, soft plumage, which makes them look considerably larger than they really are. These feathers are insulation—they pro-

Screech Owls (immature)

vide warmth during the cold of winter and ventilation on hot summer days.

Owls are not very fussy about their homes. Some nest in a hollow tree; others build a bulky stick nest in a tree, while some species use a grassy nest on or near the ground. A few species of owls will lay their white eggs at the end of an underground tunnel.

The largest and most powerful of North American owls is the great horned. It is big enough to attack and eat skunks and house cats. Most, however, will develop feeding habits based on the food available in the area in which they live. Where there is poultry, man and great horned owl may have serious conflicts. Sometimes it requires examinations of the pellets or castings of a particular owl to verify what it is eating. Owls swallow their prey whole, disgorging the indigestible portions in the form of a pellet. These can be used as positive evidence of what the owl has eaten from the analysis of the bones and fur or feathers. Many a maligned owl has been vindicated when its pellets or castings were examined.

The first of all the owls to nest, the great horned is sometimes found covered with snow while sitting on its nest incubating eggs. This species will often use abandoned nests of hawks and crows to lay its two or three white eggs, which take twenty-eight days to hatch. During the two months the young are in the nest, the adults are vicious protectors. I recall watching my father climb a tree containing the nest of a great horned owl. The adults nearly took his head off before Dad made a hasty retreat.

Barn Owls

Snowy Owl

Great Horned Owl

Happily, most states have stopped paying bounties on great horned owls. Though it is sometimes necessary to eliminate a particular owl which is killing poultry, there is no excuse for having a price on the head of every owl in the country.

The barred owl is also a large bird, almost the size of the great horned. It lacks the tufts of the great horned and displays a much milder disposition. Barred owls are rarely heard in cities, preferring deep deciduous forests like those around Hidden Valley.

The barred owl nests in a hollow tree, but like the great horned, will sometimes use the abandoned nest of a hawk or crow. In the Everglades they have been found nesting on the ground. Two to four pure white eggs are laid, and in three to four weeks the blind young hatch. They remain in the nest for well over a month.

Although it is large, the barred owl limits itself to rather small prey such as frogs and lizards, with mice being its major source of food.

Our third caller on that cold February night, the screech owl, doesn't screech at all. It emits a wavering, eerie, ghostly sound that carries for long distances and causes some superstitious people discomfort. There are those who believe that if a screech owl lands on a house, someone inside will soon die.

It certainly does land on houses. It is the only owl that is commonly found in the city. As a boy, I recall hearing a screech owl call outside my bedroom window.

Sometime during that same period of my youth, I had a pet screech owl who loved to perch on my shoulder and rode there as I walked to school, to the store, or wherever. He was considered quite an oddity by my peers. Fortunately,

he decided that the wilderness was better for him and one day he left, never to return. Perhaps he was the same fellow who serenaded me with that weird song as I tried to sleep.

The screech owl is the smallest owl with horns. These horns, or tufts, are not its ears as is commonly believed, but are merely ornaments. Like other owls, their real ears are openings under their head feathers.

One of the most distinguishing features of screech owls is their ability to go through two plumage phases—a red and a gray. They mate with no regard for color, and the color of the youngsters is not necessarily determined by that of the parents.

The screech owl is guilty of killing a large number of songbirds as well as mice, insects, crayfish, spiders and reptiles.

Cornell University discovered that the screech owl is very important to the balance of the songbird population. One researcher calculated that if a single pair of robins were permitted to breed without control, their offspring would increase the population by over 15,000 birds in five years.

Preferring a nesting cavity, the screech owl will also nest in a manmade nesting box about the size of those built for squirrels and sparrow hawks. They lay their four to five white eggs in March and care for the owlets in the nest until they are about one month old.

Smallest of the group, the sawwhet owl rounded out the chorus with its high-pitched call. The sawwhet gets its name from one of its sounds which is like that made by the sharpening of a saw blade.

It may also be the tamest of all the owls, and can be touched or picked up while roosting. Because of this unusual trust in man, it has often become man's victim.

It, too, nests in a cavity, such as an old woodpecker hole.

The bird is so small that it is often preyed upon by larger owls. In one incident, the leg band of a saw-whet was found in the regurgitated pellet of a long-eared owl only two days after the saw-whet had been banded.

Hearing four different owls at the same time may not excite everyone as it did Pete and me, but anyone interested in the outdoors can appreciate our experience.

Had we been able to see and hear everything within five miles of the bench that night, we might have noticed more species of owl.

Since we were in farm country, we knew there must be a family of barn owls nearby. Sometimes called "monkey-faced" owl, the barn owl, with its white, heart-shaped face, can be mistaken for no other. The most common owl in the world, it is found on every inhabited continent.

The barn owl, however, would not have added much to the owl chorus, for its common call is a hissing sound, often uttered while in flight. Its other call, a rasping scream that pierces the night, is frightening to many people who hear it.

Another species we always look for in winter is the snowy owl. During what is known as an "owl year," snowy owls find food scarce in their native tundra country and must migrate south into the U.S. It is during these winters that we see the big white day-hunting (diurnal) owls sitting on a fence post looking for an unsuspecting field mouse.

The burrowing owl, also diurnal, is a bird of the prairies and desert. It is a small brown owl that uses tunnels of prairie dogs and other mammals for its nest.

The best known desert owl is the elf owl which often nests in a hole in a saguaro catus. I remember sitting patiently with my father all night at a saguaro cactus ready to take the bird's photograph as it brought small desert creatures in to feed its youngsters.

Long-eared, short-eared, spotted, great gray, hawk, boreal, whiskered, flammulated, pygmy and ferruginous owls complete the list of those found in North America. Many of these latter species are rare or secretive and are seen infrequently.

But whether they are nocturnal or diurnal, large or small, hole-nesting or ground-nesting, owls are extremely interesting birds. They first caught the attention of man because of their "wide-eyed" appearance. And, more recently, because of their special adaptations to night hunting.

But now we need to be concerned about the protection of owls. Like so many wild creatures, these magnificent birds have been hurt by loss of habitat and the introduction of poisons to the biosphere. We must give our attention to preserving natural habitats for the benefit of these birds . . . and for man, too.

An elf owl makes its home in a saguaro cactus. (Photo: Bruce Coleman)

The slaughter of eagles in Wyoming, disclosed in 1971, brought increasing public attention to the plight of America's national bird. Many scientists believe that pesticides, suspected of causing eggshell thinning, are the primary peril to the species, but loss of habitat and direct destruction by man through shooting and poisoning, even electrocution by powerlines, also have contributed.

Opinion of April 23 stated that the "Secretary is required to inquire into place and time regarding taking" and interpreted the Act as addressed to "serious eagle predation which resulted in economic hardship to limited areas, and not simply normal predation . . ."

The Wyoming killings became national news in May, 1971, with the discovery in Jackson Canyon of more than 20 eagles that

EAGLES:
OUR DYING EMBLEM

Population estimates of eagles are hard to come by, but perhaps there are 12,000 to 15,000 golden eagles and 2,000 to 3,000 bald eagles in the United States, excluding Alaska. Only about 300 members of the southern race of bald eagles are believed to remain, and this species is on the endangered list.

Although population estimates vary, there is no disagreement on one thing: the figures are going down.

Congress became concerned with the possible extinction of the bald eagle as early as 1940. The Bald Eagle Act of that year forbade the taking of bald eagles or their feathers except under special permit. It provided for fines of not more than $500 and imprisonment of not more than six months, or both. The preamble to the legislation proclaimed the bald eagle "no longer a mere bird of biological interest but a symbol of the American ideals of freedom."

The Bald Eagle Act was amended to include golden eagles in 1962, but livestock interests, fearing heavy losses of young lambs, succeeded in obtaining important exceptions.

By 1969, the Department's policy was becoming more restrictive. A Solicitor's

autopsies at Patuxent Wildlife Research Center and the University of Wyoming indicated had been poisoned by thallium—a deadly chemical not used in the Fish and Wildlife Service's predator control programs since 1967.

An investigation conducted by the Service's Special Agents in cooperation with State officials resulted in a $674 fine, on State charges, being paid by the rancher involved.

In the meantime, rumors persisted that hundreds of bald and golden eagles had been shot from aircraft in Colorado and Wyoming. Pilot James Vogan broke the story publicly in testimony on Capitol Hill, in return for immunity from Federal prosecution. Evidence gathered by Service Special Agents confirmed the occurrence of a mass eagle slaughter, and prosecutions were begun on December 14, 1971.

By may, 1972, eight defendants had been charged on a total of 429 criminal counts of killing bald and golden eagles by gunfire from a helicopter. Six defendants pleaded guilty to the unlawful killings. They were fined a total of $4,200 and placed on

probation for terms ranging from six months to one year. The two remaining defendants, one of whom was later killed in an auto accident, were never convicted.

Congress meanwhile, with enthusiastic support from Interior, acted to increase penalties under the Bald Eagle Act. An October 23, 1972, amendment to the statute increased the penalty for first violations to a fine of up to $5,000 and imprisonment for not more than one year. Second or subsequent offenders would be liable for up to $10,000 and two years in jail.

Service Special Agents then turned their attention to the illegal commercial traffic in eagle feathers and parts. As the popularity of Native American craft objects increased during the early 1970s, a lucrative commercial market was developing for eagle feathers, talons, beaks—even feet and bones. By 1974, intelligence reports indicated that several thousand eagles were being killed each year to satisfy the commercial demand for the feathers and parts used to manufacture Indian curios.

In April, 1974, Special Agents seized over 40,000 eagle and migratory bird feathers in Oklahoma, citing twenty-four individuals for selling in violation of Federal law. Then, on December 5, 1974, over sixty individuals in ten States ranging from Ohio to Oregon were arrested or cited for selling protected bird feathers. This latter raid was the largest of its kind in the history of the Fish and Wildlife Service.

The Bald Eagle Act provides for the religious use of eagle feathers by Native Americans, but expressly prohibits sales or other commercial activities. The overwhelming majority of the individuals cited in these raids were non-Indians.

The protection of eagles from illegal commercialization is, and will continue to be, one of the top enforcement priorities of the Fish and Wildlife Service.

The Service has other programs devoted to the preservation of the country's eagle population.

Patuxent Wildlife Research Center is studying pesticides and has developed facilities where propagation of the northern and southern races is underway. Eight national wildlife refuges in the southeastern United States have bald eagles nesting on them.

The Service also is conducting an inventory of remaining eagle nesting sites to determine which ones would be suitable for acquisition as national wildlife refuges, using funds provided by the National Wildlife Federation.

Two locations appear as leading possibilities: an area below Fort Randall Dam in South Dakota which attracts up to 200 bald eagles in the winter, and another area below Keokuk Dam on the Mississippi River near Hamilton, Illinois, which provides habitat for 75 to 100 bald eagles. ⑤

Culver Pictures, Inc.

The Wit and Wisdom
of
Mark Twain

I confine myself to life with which I am familiar when pretending to portray life. But I confined myself to the boy-life out on the Mississippi because that had a peculiar charm for me, and not because I was not familiar with other phases of life. I was a soldier two weeks once in the beginning of the war, and I have shoveled silver tailings in a quartz mill a couple of weeks, and acquired the last possibilities of culture in that direction. And I've done 'pocket-mining' during three months in the one little patch of ground in the whole globe where Nature conceals gold in pockets— or did before we robbed all of those pockets and exhausted, obliterated, annihilated the most curious freak Nature ever indulged in. There are not thirty men left alive who, being told there was a pocket hidden on the broad slope of a mountain, would know how to go and find it, or have even the faintest idea of how to set about it; but I am one of the possible twenty or thirty who possess the secret.

And I've been a prospector, and know pay rock from poor when I find it—just with a touch of the tongue. And I've been a silver miner and know how to dig and shovel and drill and put in a blast.

And I was a newspaper reporter four years in cities, and so saw the inside of many things; and was reporter in a legislature two sessions and the same in Congress one session . . . and I was some years a Mississippi pilot, and familiarly knew all the different kinds of steamboatmen—a race apart, and not like other folk.

And I was for some years a traveling "jour" printer, and wandered from city to city—and so I know that sect familiarly.

And I was a lecturer on the public platform a number of seasons and was a responder to toasts at all the different kinds of banquets— and so I know a great many secrets about audiences—secrets not to be got out of books, but only acquirable by experience.

Now then; as the most valuable capital or culture or education usable in the building of novels is personal experience I ought to be well equipped for that trade.

I surely have the equipment, a wide culture, and all of it real, none of it artificial, for I don't know anything about books.

—*Mark Twain*

Prose and quotations from the works of Mark Twain published by Harper & Row, Publishers, Inc. and reprinted by permission.

From MARK TWAIN HIMSELF by Milton Meltzer, Copyright © 1960 by Milton Meltzer. With permission of Thomas Y. Crowell Company, Inc.

Mark Twain says...

Training is everything. The peach was once a bitter almond; cauliflower is nothing but cabbage with a college education.

As to the adjective, when in doubt, strike it out.

He was as shy as a newspaper is when referring to its own merits.

The universal brotherhood of man is our most precious possession—what there is of it.

Prosperity is the best protector of principle.

By trying we can easily learn to endure adversity. Another man's, I mean.

Everyone is a moon, and has a dark side which he never shows to anybody.

When in doubt, tell the truth.

Truth is stranger than fiction, but it is because fiction is obliged to stick to possibilities; truth isn't.

Truth is the most valuable thing we have. Let us economize it.

It is easier to stay out than get out.

Always do right. This will gratify some people, and astonish the rest.

October. This is one of the peculiarly dangerous months to speculate in stocks. The others are July, January, September, April, November, May, March, June, December, August and February.

The Bettmann Archive, Inc.

The Artistry of Richard Sloan

Richard Sloan is a native of Chicago who now lives in Shreveport, Louisiana. For a number of years he has been engaged in the creation of a series of fifty 22″ x 28″ paintings of North American birds.

Sponsoring this ambitious project is Nature House, Inc., an organization whose aims combine both art and nature. Nature House is headquartered at Griggsville, Illinois, but works with art galleries across North America displaying and distributing the works of art by Nature House sponsored artists. In Griggsville, the galleries are located in remodeled railroad cars, part of some thirty railroad cars in Purple Martin Junction, an extensive education complex.

Because of its emphasis on knowledge, Nature House chooses its artists according to unusually high standards. It was with these criteria in mind that Richard Sloan was chosen as a Nature House artist.

Throughout the early years of his career, Richard Sloan pursued a number of jobs to support himself and his family while he developed his wildlife art skills. By the late 1960s he was well known in the Great Lakes area for his magnificent bird paintings, particularly those of the birds of prey. He was also known as an experienced zoo keeper and an ardent conservationist on behalf of the birds of prey.

CAROLINA WREN
Thryothorus ludovicianus
(following page)

The Carolina wren is the largest species of wren east of the Rocky Mountains. In all of the United States and Canada, only the 6½-inch-long cactus wren of the southwestern deserts is larger. The Carolina averages 4¾ inches in length; that's ¼ inch longer than the Bewick's wren and ½ inch longer than the house wren.

Historically a bird of the southeast, it has extended its range northward very slowly. It is a nonmigratory species and does not tolerate extremely cold winters well, but it still has managed to move into the midwest and middle Atlantic and is occasionally seen elsewhere in New England and the Great Lakes region.

This is a shy bird, but curious. If you try to approach it, you will have little success: it will stay artfully hidden just ahead of you and even though you may hear its song you will not see it. But if you remain still, chances are this energetic little bird will approach you in an effort to satisfy its own curiosity.

During this period, Nature House conducted a continent-wide search for an artist to create a series of bird paintings. The paintings were to be very realistic in order to be of educational value; the artist was therefore chosen on the basis of the detail, authenticity and lifelike qualities of his work.

In order to learn more about particular species, Sloan traveled and studied throughout much of North America and the area surrounding the Caribbean, and his horizons extend farther each year. The result of his travels and dedication is a series of bird paintings—now nearing completion—that is one of the most important series of this century.

Each of the paintings is being reproduced in a limited edition so that the benefits of this series can be widespread. Or, you may collect 31 of the reproductions in *Wings Upon the Heavens*, a book which combines the beautiful Sloan prints and inspiring accounts of woodland, meadow and backyard bird communities. This richly bound, superbly illustrated gift book is available directly from Ideals Publishing Corp. or through your local bookstore. Or use the order blank at the back of this book.

Richard Sloan's pioneering series has paved the way for similar projects in the fields of animals and flowers by other Nature House artists and captured the attention of nature art enthusiasts from coast to coast. And as for Richard Sloan, there seems to be no limit to the contributions he will make to America's natural art heritage in the years to come. Ⓢ

BOBWHITE
Colinus virginianus
(following page)

The bobwhite is a member of the quail family, and when persons in the eastern half of the United States and Canada refer to "quail," the bobwhite generally is the bird to which they refer.

The bobwhite is popular. Rural residents have long cherished its familiar "bob-bob-white" or "ah-bah-white" call, given with the last not highly pitched and strong. Farmers like this species because its diet consists largely of weed seeds and insect pests such as grasshoppers, cotton boll weevils, army worms and cutworms. It also eats large quantities of grain picked up from fields after harvest, but this is not considered harmful to farmers' economic interests.

Bobwhites are perhaps best known as game birds. The explosive way in which a "covey of quail" bursts from cover when flushed has startled and thrilled human observers for countless centuries, and has also made these little birds much sought after by hunters. This species has been so heavily hunted that it is protected by law and can be hunted only in a limited season.

On the Farm

As our life becomes more technological, traditional methods of production change. On the farm, investments in machinery have lead to greater productivity and efficiency, a necessity for modern food demands. Likewise, the family farm has become a memory to some people. For others, such as the Amish, who have fought in courts for their rights to educate their children and drive horse-drawn buggies on the roadways, tradition remains the same. In either case, the expansive fields and invigorating air create a beauty and a peace no matter what period of time or sophistication. *Country Scene Digest* takes you into the country for a glimpse at contemporary farms and families who still have a strong foothold in tradition.

Antique Butter Mold

I came across a butter mold, one day,
Engraved with scalloped edge and sheaf of wheat;
A trademark from the past—the settler's way
Of signing home-churned butter creamy sweet.

I marveled; though the housewife baked the bread,
And spun the wool to make her family's clothes,
Created patchwork quilts for every bed
From scraps of bombazines and calicoes,

Although the husband cleared and tilled the land
And worked from dawn to dark to make things go,
Yet someone took the pains to carve by hand
This tool to print a golden cameo.
Upon a pound of butter, worked with care
To grace with beauty ordinary fare.

Darlene Workman Stull

Joy

There's never a rose in all the world
But makes some green spray sweeter;
There's never a wind in all the sky,
But makes some bird wing fleeter.

No thrush but may thrill some heart,
His dawn light gladness voicing;
God gives us all some small, sweet way
To set the world rejoicing.

John W. Scott

Late Summer Rain

The late summer rain vanished
As quickly as it had come,
Leaving behind a vapor world
Full with the scent of dampened earth.

And a pale sun took a last look
At the day through clouds,
Suspended in the stillness
Above a distant steeple.

Charlene Slocum

Rainbows Across the Farm

Cattle in the pasture,
Sheep grazing by the hill,
And a rainbow arches distance
With geometric skill.
From golden sheep to golden cattle
Curves this arc of vibrant light,
And its vibrant shadow glistens
From a cloud the hue of night.
Another arc of color
Lies across the flooded land,
Sapphire, amethyst and ruby,
Made from common loam and sand.

Men may lose their innate vision,
Men who work the soil,
For vision dies a victim
Of unremitting toil.
The radiance of the rainbow
Transforms both flesh and sod,
And thus renews the farmer's faith
In the omnipotence of God.

Laura Coffin

Country Charm

In a crowded maze of city thoroughfares
As noise of horns and sirens rend the air,
I miss the peace a quiet country night
Provides without an artificial light,
Where only rays from lamp and candle gleam,
And from the dome of heaven, the moon's pale beam.
How pleasant the nocturnal symphony
Of insect orchestra in minor key!
And, from afar, a lonely partridge cry
Commingles with the river's lullaby
Of soothing calm. How well do I recall
The charm of childhood years. But most of all
I miss the plaintive song of whippoorwill
That came when shadows fell on bush and hill,
And gentle winds blew scent of honey-musk
From fields of clover-bloom in gathering dusk.

Donalda von Poellnitz

I have been asked
(by those inexperienced in country life)
what it's like to live on the land,
                away from millions of people,
                miles from anywhere.
How can I explain
        the freedom of open spaces,
        the exultation of seeing earth
            and sky meet,
                touch?
The quietness
    privacy,
    soft, low sounds of the country
I will cherish forever.
I will not forsake you, rural land.
(and you're *not* miles from anywhere.)

Cheryle Van Pelt

Summer Reverie

Give me a golden afternoon
Where white clouds roll on high
And stand like castles towering
Against the summer sky.
Where the sun is warm, and grass is green
With breeze as soft as spring,
And trees nearby that rise on high
With warblers as they sing.
The lullaby a brooklet makes,
On twinkling gravel rill,
While spinning dreams; it almost seems
That time itself stands still.

D. A. Hoover

This Small Lad

He's quite a little actor,
A tricyle is his tractor.

The porch is his cornfield;
To him it's almost real.

A cardboard box his plow, that
Grandma's closet did endow.

Through a long day, this small lad,
Works as hard as his farmer dad!

Beverly Ann Hoffeditz

Fading Memories of The Family Farm

Jay Scriba

Someday soon the old family farm will be nothing but a dark stain in the leached clay of somebody's cornfield. There will be nothing for the archeologist but the caved in brick wells, with the rusty Galena pumps fallen in time's burial. For the moment, though, the locust grove still rises like a green island, with the weather-beaten clapboard house sagging in a thicket of ragweed and tansy . . .

On our last visit, the only sign of recent human habitation was in the smokehouse, where Aunt Grace's patched chore sweater still hung on a nail, just where she left it when the weariness of eighty-five years forced her to "rent a little place in town."

She was the last of the old folks, still living on a little eighty acre farm which, even in the 1940s, was run with kerosene lamps, a horse-drawn corn plow and cobs burned in the kitchen stove. When we visited during summer vacations, there were still

trunks in the attic, left from the family's immigrant trip from Sweden in the 1880s.

For a restless town boy, nothing could match the thrill of a couple of July weeks on the old farm. You awoke to crowing roosters, opening an eye to sun streaming through the cracks in the green shades. Even the bedding was different . . . a patchwork quilt over a rustling corn shuck mattress and embroidery on the feather pillows (smelling richly of the hen house).

The aunts and uncles, of course, had been up since dawn, milking cows, watering chickens, digging into the lard crock for pre-fried pork sausage patties, pungent with pepper and sage. There was a smell of Swedish pot coffee, a sound of soft farm talk from the kitchen. Sometimes the milk on our oatmeal was still warm and foaming from the cow.

What to do first? Uncle Charley was hoeing among the sweet corn and cucumbers, stopping now and then to file a bright edge. Later he would be puttering in the garage, where a Kentucky rifle still hung on the wall, over a collection of license plates dating back to 1914.

Aunt Grace was pumping one of the old Galenas, filling the smokehouse trough with cold water to cool the milk, butter and cottage cheese, fresh from the back of the kitchen stove.

Aunt Mary had put on a sunbonnet and stretched silk stockings over her arms to protect them from brambles on a blackberrying expedition to Burton's woods. (One of several dark, grape tangled, oak and hickory groves left from the great clearing after the Civil War. "Indian groves," Uncle Charley called them.)

For a start, we generally went off on our own, out to the barnyard to pump the pig and horse troughs full, eager to pat a snuffling mare on her velvet nose. The little pigs were warier, standing stiff legged and alert, set for playful, squealing flight at the wave of a new straw hat.

We might go into the corncrib in the new red barn to shell a few ears in the racketing hand sheller. Or we might climb into the heaped wheat in the grain bin . . . the most comfortable lounging cushion in the world . . . and chew a handful of kernels until they became a chaffy gum.

For heart-pounding excitement, we visited the hog house, where a surly five-hundred pound brood sow in the shadows made the place seem as menacing as a lion pit. ("Hey, you, get in there and she'll eat you to the bone!") There was also an ornery cow that Uncle Charley had named W.F.M.S. . . . for Women's Foreign Missionary Society . . . who would charge you like a ring bull. One Leghorn rooster was mean, too, an immensely haughty creature, the epitome of that description of a young sport heading for a dance as "steppin' out like a rooster in high oats."

Through the rest of the morning we might ride on one of the big horses while Uncle Charley plowed corn, clinging desperately to the fly netting as Big Jack shook his hide to dislodge a horsefly. The thing to do was grip hard on brass collar balls and never look down.

Then it would be noon, with Aunt Grace ringing a cowbell. Time to go to the rain barrel, swat the wash pan hard to drive down the swarming mosquito wigglers and wash up, maybe sticking your cowlick under the icy pump water. (The wooden pump deck stood among moss, wild mint and the purple flowers of gill on the ground.)

Dinner was substantial, with dark slices of smoked ham down from the attic, bowls of mashed potatoes with cream gravy, watermelon pickles, spiced peaches, iced tea, a firm flaky slice of cherry or apple pie. (Always by 11 a.m. a pie cooling in the kitchen window.)

After the pie there was time for a nap on the creaking porch swing, next to the sweet honeysuckle, or in the hammock, next to the truck patch (gooseberries, currants, chives, asparagus, a gourmet's dream of fresh vegetables).

The ninety-degree afternoon heat might find us with an oil can, filling the cups on a dilapidated corn planter, mower and other machinery in the implement shed. We would hunt eggs by the hour in the tangled goldenrod and jimsonweed, sometimes returning in triumph with whole clutches.

By four o'clock it was time for coffee and a slice of pink iced angel cake. Aunt Mary would be back with a milk pail full of glistening blackberries. Uncle Charley would tell Aunt Grace that the wind had shifted west and that it was "darkening up" . . . a signal for everybody to get out and shoo the half-

wild Plymouth Rock hens into a dozen weathered lean-tos.

As farmer readers have already surmised, the old folks seldom saw anything larger than a five dollar bill. But what is poverty when there are bushels of potatoes in the root cellar and flitches of bacon hanging in the smokehouse? The milk and eggs always provided enough for a new pair of "gum boots," a pledge to the church, a quart of vanilla ice cream from the supply store. (Mixed, on Sunday afternoon after the croquet game, with homemade root beer to make "black cow" sodas.)

Evening came with a flight of hundreds of crows, beating for a roosting woods beyond the sleepy river. You began to hear farmers calling their hogs, Ben Osborn's "Whoooeeeee!," burly Levi Holst's bawling "Wheeeeaaaaww!" There was a great

squealing rush of pigs as Uncle Charley banged corn ears into a metal bushel, poured slop into the wooden hog trough. Then it was time for milking, with the white streams ringing in the pails, the one-eyed farm cats creeping in for their enameled pan of frothy largesse.

We would hang on the Dutch barn door, watching the shadows slant over the miles of cornfields, listening to the slow creak of the vine-covered windmill. Sometimes we turned the crank on the milk separator, winding it to a high whine.

Supper was in the soft dark, under a fake Tiffany kerosene lamp with an irresistible glass bead fringe. For a while we would sit on the lawn with Uncle Charley, smelling the hot hay wind while he picked fat ticks off his tail-thumping "shepherd" dog. Aunt Grace had already begun to yawn before she put on her reading spectacles and sat down with the crossword puzzle or her worn Bible. Half an hour and she began to snore, not a nerve twitching in the peace of her tired soul. By now Uncle Charley, who lived in town, had bumped his Model A down the grassy lane, leaving the locust grove steeped in quiet and the beep of katydids.

Nobody would set an alarm clock in a country-side full of boastful roosters. By nine o'clock a strange, delicious weariness made it easy for even a fidgeting boy to unlace his tennis shoes, put aside his copy of *Black Beauty* or the *The Bobbsey Twins at the Farm*.

It wasn't until years later that we realized how lucky we were to have savored the good, simple people, the last years of a pioneer pocket in the American Middle West.

Reprinted from THE MILWAUKEE JOURNAL, June 6, 1971.

Pennsylvania Barns

R. J. McGinnis

If there is any doubt about who wore the pants on early American farms, a look at the old-time barns will quiet the doubt. Into the barn went the bulk of the family savings and the profits from the cattle and grain. The house might be a box with partitions and the spring a weary trip with a bucket, but the barn had to be the newest, the biggest, and the handiest of all barns in the countryside. Anything was good enough for the women; the house, for the men, was only a place to eat and sleep. The barn was for the cattle and the crops, and only the best would do.

Barns have always been an avenue of self-expression for the farmer. They have satisfied his yearning for beauty and his desire to project himself into the material things around him. The best American barns combine a harmonious blending of beauty and utility found nowhere else in the world of rural building design. Like every form of art, barn architecture grew; it did not spring full-blown from the brain of some carpenter, but, little by little, evolved from simple beginnings to the masterpieces which still stand as monuments to the creative ability of unlettered country craftsmen.

The first barns were built of logs and were small because the farms were small. As more land was cleared, the barns grew in size, and as wealth accumulated, more money went into making the barn solid, enduring, and a thing of beauty. Craftsmen through the years perfected their skills and designs.

It was in the Pennsylvania Dutch area, in Lancaster, York, and surrounding counties, that barn building flowered, bursting into full bloom during the first half of the nineteenth century. Incidentally, this was one of the rare areas where the houses kept pace with the barns in design and sturdiness. The thrifty Dutch pioneers liked the creature comforts and they were sociable. They built homes to accommodate a host of relatives and friends for their famous Sunday dinners. The pioneer Pennsylvania farmer dug a cave out of a hillside and shored up the opening with logs. In the dark interior were stalls for his cow and his horse, and possibly a small storage bin for grain. His straw and hay he stacked outside. A split rail fence enclosed a small barnyard.

As he cleared more land and his livestock increased, he used the logs from his clearing to build a larger and more pretentious structure. The roof was covered with hand-split shingles and the doors were planks sawed by an "up and down sawmill." The hinges for the doors were made of strap iron hammered out by the local smithy. If the farmer was a sensitive man he used hinges and latches of forged iron in decorative shapes. There was a mow overhead for hay and a central driveway where he stored his cart. The cows and horses had separate stalls on either side of the driveway.

On his third round of barn building, the Pennsylvania farmer bethought himself of a permanent structure, one of brick or stone and good, stout timbers that would last out his life and the lives of his grandchildren. He used the materials native to the district, limestone and kiln-dried brick, and oak, walnut, and chestnut. He hired experienced stone masons and carpenters, but when the timbers were joined, his neighbors came in for a barn raising. The frame of the barn went up in a day, and was followed with feasting.

About the middle of the nineteenth century a standard design had developed. Variations from then to the present were either elaborations or adornment. Size varied to fit the needs of the farm, and there were modifications to conform to the lay of the barn lot or the whims of the owner. Serving as they did the same type of general farming, housing the same kind of livestock, and storing the same kind of grain and feed, these modifications were minor.

The typical barn was set against a slope, which provided a natural ramp for entry into the driveway on the second level. This is the "bank" barn, common everywhere. The ground level accommodated the horses and livestock. There were from one to several rows of stalls, pens, a feed room, and perhaps a harness room. This level was entered only at one end, the other being against the ramp or hillside. There was an overhang from the second level to protect both man and beast from inclement weather. There were passageways among the stalls and pens; hay was dropped from the mow directly to the stables through a door or chute. Many of the later barns had root cellars which extended beyond the stalls into the hillside. The side driveway between the mows on the second floor was used as a threshing floor and to store machinery, which was taken out when the granaries and mows were being filled. The potato and turnip cellars were sometimes filled from a trap door in the floor of this level. Large doors, which extended from the ground to the eaves, could be opened to give free access to any part of the threshing floor.

Timbers, up to a foot square, were hand-hewn, mortised, and fastened together with stout pegs. The walls of the stables were of stone, rarely of brick, and extended above ground level on all sides. These masonry walls were sometimes carried upward on the ends of the famous stone and brick end barns. If there was a plentiful supply of stone on the farm, or if a man wanted to build for the ages, he constructed his barn entirely of stone, and labored to contrive timbering of the same durability. The original roofs were usually split shingles, but being the perishable part of the structure, most of them have been replaced by metal, slate, or fabricated shingles.

Refinement and adornment reflected the personality of the owner or the builder. There were elegant cupolas, which served both as ventilators and as decoration; windows with scrollwork to match those on the dwelling; arched doorways, and fancy designs in brick and stone; paint, usually red, often with a white trim; and hex marks, to ward off bad luck to man and animal and keep away the ever-present threat of fire.

When the hex marks were first placed on barns, they were true symbols of the owner's belief in the supernatural, and a genuine effort to placate the forces of evil, especially witches. Later, they appeared on many barns because the owner thought they added a pleasant touch. To many people, no Pennsylvania barn would be authentic without a hex mark.

The brick end barn is the rarest of all types of Pennsylvania barns and is generally regarded as the masterwork of the early barn builder. Virtually all of them are found in the rich farming region of southeastern Pennsylvania; there are a few across the line in Maryland. Most of them were built by the Amish and Mennonite descendants of German and Swiss emigrants.

They were notable for the geometric designs built into the brick work of the two ends and were usually larger than the average barn, and cost a small fortune for those days. Few have been built since the mid-nineteenth century.

The grilled designs built into the brick work served a double purpose — they are highly decorative and they provide light and ventilation. The functional purposes of the designs are so well disguised by their good taste and proportion they seem to be there for their own sake and do not intrude their practical purpose upon the barn's appearance.

The designs were formed by laying the brick in such a way that openings the size of the end of a single brick formed the pattern. There is no evidence that the open work resulted in structural weakness. Some brick end barns 150 years old show no signs of sagging or weakness in or near the designs. A few rare builders incorporated designs in stone end barns, the designs being in brick set in the stone.

By the middle of the nineteenth century barn architecture and design had been brought to a high state of refinement. Farm magazines devoted pages to comment on barns, and there were barn designers and experts in every community. One of the best farm magazines of the period, the *Pennsylvania Cultivator*, published a complete description of what was known as the Switzer barn, a design which closely followed the typical layout of the period. The description of the barn is prefaced by a bit of boasting, easily forgiven when one understands the pride with which Pennsylvanians viewed their fine structures. Here are the *Cultivator's* own words:

However much before us in Agricultural Improvements generally, the Farmers of the States North and East of us may perhaps be, we claim for Pennsylvania the distinction of being the only State in the Union in which the building of good, substantial, convenient and spacious BARNS is understood and practiced. Properly speaking, in other States, *they have no barns*—they don't know what a real good barn is—a stable or collection of

stables, sheds and out-houses being their makeshift substitutes for them. This is a little singular, but it is nevertheless true. A journey through New York and New England, will confirm our remarks. There is hardly a real barn to be seen. Evidences of plenty there are, and of excellent farming. You see good houses, beautiful shrubbery, admirable fences, clean and smooth fields, splendid cattle, plenty of *hay* and *grain stacks*—and lots of sheds and stables; but *no barns*. They will have to come into Pennsylvania, and take pattern from some of our mighty bank-barns, looming out in the horizon like double-decked men-of-war beside sloops, or like churches beside log huts. As in our war vessels, so in our barns also, we have both *single* and *double-deckers*, the latter being tremendous affairs, that would make our eastern brethren open their eyes in astonishment. Below we present the floor plan of one of the *singledeckers*—a most superb new Bank Barn, called a "Switzer" barn, which was recently erected upon the farm of August O. Heister, Esq., on the Susquehanna about three miles above Harrisburg. The engraving was made by Lowe, of Philadelphia, from a Daguerreotype by Barnitz, of Harrisburg.

Dimensions.—We expected to obtain from the architect of this barn, Mr. Isaac Updergrove, a specification of its dimensions, etc., but have not received it, so we must do for the present with a brief and less detailed description. It is one of the best and most convenient barns on the Switzer plan, in this vicinity. It is about one hundred feet in length, by about sixty feet in width, and proportionately high. It is built on a small hill side, so that the front or barn floor is on a level with the ground; while the hill is dug away and the stables placed beneath. The rear of this stabling is likewise on a level with the ground, though some ten feet below the front level. The cut presents this rear view only. As will be perceived, the barn has an *overshoot* of seven feet, the stone wall being brought out flush the entire width, which is an improvement. The walls are eighteen inches thick, and rise ten feet up to the front level.

The cost of this barn was about $1,500. It is weather-boarded on the outside—painted white—furnished with ventilators, lightning rods, and every improvement.

This, briefly, is the description of one of the best kind of Pennsylvania barns, and one of the best of the kind. We shall give other plans, from time to time. ☐

about the amish

In 1693 a clergyman, Jacob Amman, withdrew from the Mennonite religion because he believed in a more rigid code of church discipline. He gave his name to a religion and a way of life that flourishes to this day among the Plain People . . . the Amish.

The Amish migrated from Europe, mostly from Krefeld, Germany, in the early eighteenth century, to the area which is now Germantown, Pennsylvania. Because this region was originally settled by the Dutch, the Amish are often referred to as "Pennsylvania Dutch."

Binding all Amish people together is their religion, one that demands much and returns to them a life rich with religious fulfillment. Church for them is home. They do not believe in building churches as we know them. Instead, they alternate services in homes of members of the congregation.

For the Amish, home is still the center, the framework and the foundation of their lives. Generations may go by without a member of the family traveling farther than fifty miles from home. The Amish children would delight anybody with their carefree games, charming mannerisms and rosy-cheeked faces. To see a group of these children is to see their parents in miniature, for both children and adults wear the same simple style of clothing. A distinguishing mark of an Amish woman is her white prayer cap, worn at all times according to the Biblical admonition that a woman "that prayeth or prophesieth with her head uncovered dishonoreth her head" (I Corinthians 11:5).

Photos opposite:
William Allard (Bruce Coleman)

Amish Farming

Amish farming has not changed much in the past thirty years. The Amish use simple machinery for their work and tend to stay away from the newfangled contraptions of their non-Amish neighbors. Yet they are the epitome of good farming and run prosperous farms that are both bountiful and beautiful.

Horse-drawn equipment is the standard means of working the land, so the farmer's livestock consists of draft horses for pulling as well as driving horses for transportation. The number of animals depends on the size of the farm. An eighty-acre farm will support five or six draft horses and two driving horses, while ten draft horses and four driving horses are average for a farm of over two hundred acres.

Amish farmers have recently begun to use diesel-powered tractors for some of their work, but they are by no means converting to the use of modern farm machinery.

While they do use a tractor for such operations as threshing and grinding grain, the work is still shared by neighbors who join the farmer in his field for a hard day's work. Young men of school age also help the family until they are old enough to acquire farms of their own. The noontime lunch is a congenial affair served by the family women.

Within the last fifteen years, Amish farmers have started to use balers and corn pickers. No, they haven't changed their ways entirely—both pieces of equipment are drawn by horses. But a small motor is used to operate the machinery itself.

The horse shares the barnyard and farmyard with chickens and hogs, although these are not numerous unless they are the farm specialty. Hogs are also a part of the farm life but, like chickens, are not kept in large numbers unless they are a farm specialty. Sheep, too, are sometimes raised, primarily to keep the farmyard neat and clean.

In addition to large farms run for the family's livelihood, each farm sports a garden that is the woman's responsibility and provides for the family.

The Amish want nothing more than to lead a humble and holy life. They ask nothing more than what they can produce themselves, so they have kept to the farm and lived a simple life of the soil.

The Golden Cows of the Big Spenders

John C. Vitale

DURING THE FIRST DECADE OF THE TWENTIETH CENTURY, when elegant living and overwhelming splendor where the calling cards of the rich lords of industry, the ranking status symbols of the moment were the blooded Jersey, Holstein and Guernsey cows. Such cows as Johana Pieterje Artis Craemelle, with names suggesting Broadway rather than the pasture, were the toast of the day, filling the thoughts and emptying the purses of the great money lords.

Dr. William Seward Webb, a Vanderbilt-in-law, was one of the first of the big spenders to establish blooded cows as a symbol of wealth. He had a passion for fine Jerseys and Guernseys and began raising blooded stock on his luxurious Shelburne farm in Vermont. Quartered in the best style that money could provide, Webb's herd provided butter for the dining cars of the Vanderbilt's New York Central railroad. To assure proper respect for the butter, a printed card listing the names of the Shelburne farm herd was placed at each table of the dining cars. Few passengers, despite their sophistication, failed to be impressed and found great pleasure in eating butter produced by such an aristocratic herd.

However, despite his leadership in the direction of making cows a status symbol extraordinary, Mr. William Seward Webb was only the first of a long line of big spenders who established cows as debutantes in the society of farms. Charles M. Schwab, for one, having spent nearly $1,000,000 on a blooded herd, followed the path to a new world of prestige created by Webb. Once, after he had acquired a name as a breeder, he created a sensation equal in the newspapers to a jewel robbery by offering his guests a choice between vintage champagne or milk. "They both cost the same," he boasted.

Understandably, after this sensation, cow collecting became the new passion of the money

At one time the calling cards of the rich lords of industry were blooded animals such as the Guernsey (opposite page) and Jersey (above) cows. Entire herds of the animals were purchased for as much as $1,000,000.

tycoons. No sum of money seemed too great to acquire a choice cow or bull. For example, railroad tycoon William H. Williams paid $15,000 for a single Guernsey. Later, he spent $25,000 for another superior beast placed on the open market with the name of Shuttlewick Levity. Then Williams, without blinking his financial eye, purchased a bull, Langwater Eastern King, for $35,000.

Left: Passengers traveling on the New York Central railroad were impressed by the fact that butter served aboard the train was the product of the aristocratic herd owned by Dr. William Seward Webb.

Photo opposite: The Holstein cow was among the favored three breeds of animals that were so highly prized for their blood lines.

20th Century Limited

Williams's passion for his herd, however, was real and outstandingly unpretentious. The one-time chairman of the board for both the Wabash and Missouri Pacific railroads regularly visited his prize herd. Although the farm was located in Lyon Mountain, New York, Williams boarded his private Pullman once a week and made a personal tour of the farm. Moreover, when away on business, he used the telephone to keep in contact with the farm. Each night, without fail, he called the superintendent of his herd and discussed, long distance, the problems of the day.

In the early 1930s, the name of James Cash Penney of retail fame became as prominent in the world of cows as that of William H. Williams. Penney, who spent more than $1,000,000 collecting a herd of blooded dairy cows, established himself as a leader in breeding prized cows without match. His Hopewell Junction farm, located in New York, was a model of cow collecting on a grand scale. Numbering up to 1,000, the Penney herd was quartered with such elegance that visitors to the farm were frequently reminded of being aboard a yacht rather than inside a series of barns. Proud of this image, and feeling that he was extending a service to the farms of America with his collection, Penney ruled over his numerous branch stores from a desk crowned befittingly by a bronze bust of Foremost—the sire of his first herd.

To such men as J. C. Penney, *Fortune* magazine, standing as a critical judge of the time, gave this message: "The landed lord grew rich on his acres and bought a town house for pleasure; today's industrial lord grows rich in the town and buys a country place for his pleasure. The landed lord was rich because he had cattle. The industrial lord has cattle because he is rich."

Nevertheless, despite the charge leveled by *Fortune*, such names as Webb, Schwab, Williams, and Penney will live beyond their span of years, and give an added luster to any discussion on the great art of collecting a prize herd of dairy cows. For, to the world at large, these cows, collected, bred, and loved by the giants of industry, will always be remembered as the golden cows of the big spenders. ⑤

The family cow, that foster mother of America, where has she gone?

Today she is attended by technicians in spotless white coats and has become a milk factory with no personality and no function except to produce milk high in fat and large in quantity.

The Family Cow
R. J. McGinnis

The family cow, as she was known down through the years, was a symbol of family life, the hub around which the little world of the small town and the farm revolved. Those of us who cared for her, and subjected ourselves to the iron discipline of milking and feeding her and bedding her twice a day, 365 days a year, know that we got something from her besides the milk and butter curds.

We undoubtedly have a better milk supply since the family cow's demise, and we have a sounder and more efficient dairy economy. But there was something about the family cow that made up for her lack of high production.

When Bossy went, she went quickly. I milked a family cow and I'm not an old man, but it appears I may well have milked a family cow about as recently as any family cow milker, because between the time I sold my herd and went away to school and the day I returned from World War II the family cow faded away.

When my family moved to a small town south of Des Moines in the early thirties, our family cow provided a family of five with all the milk we could drink, and we drank a great deal. We had a little bench-type separator and Mother made cottage cheese and creamed it and we ate this by the ton, mixed with grape jelly.

From the cream we made butter, and we used plenty of that. Father had all the buttermilk he wanted, and he loved the stuff. When my herd was at full strength—three milkers, three resters and a calf, I sold raw milk in gallon buckets on a nice little route. I delivered every day on a bicycle, hanging the little covered buckets on my handlebars. It was legal; it was profitable; and some of the time it was fun.

But Bossy's contribution in dollars and cents is not what I miss, although she made a very real contribution, at two bits a gallon, to my high school and college expenses. It is the friendship of the cows them-

Grant Heilman

selves, the management practices (some strange, indeed) through which farm animals were adapted to small-town living, and the way in which daily chores contributed to the growing up of boys, that come to my mind when I think of Molly, Polly and Sue.

All of our cows were characters. I've talked to other ex-family cow people and all of their cows were characters, too.

We probably had a dozen cows from the time we bought Molly for eighteen dollars at a community sale until I sold the noble Frieda to pay my first year's college tuition. Yet, I can remember every cow by name, what we fed to each one, how much milk they gave, how many calves they had and when, and the sex of each of these and their names. Everything around our place had a name, even the turtle that lived in a hole under the kitchen.

I can remember winging home from school after Mother called the principal to report that Susie had broken down the fence around our little lot and eaten Mrs. McClellan's grapes. Not just once—often. That was why we finally sold her at the community sale.

Then we got Dolly. Dolly calved a month early and I found her bull calf lying in the cold mud. He was worth $1.50 for veal and nothing whatsoever for any other purpose. Still, it was a victory when he revived under the stove in the kitchen.

But Molly, perhaps because she was my first venture, was always my first love in spite of her wanderings. She was a rangy beast, covered all over with red hair, and she had a great voice, clarion-clear, full-throated, with fine tone and character. She bellowed at the slightest provocation.

I thought the world of Molly but Father thought differently. We traded her for a smaller, more settled type, with less voice and greater power of production.

Our next animal was Polly. Like Molly, she broke out all the time. We sold her for beef and got Frieda.

95

Frieda's acquisition marked a new peak in our cow business. All through the Susie-Polly-Molly era, we'd dreamed of some day having a really good cow. Near town was a dairyman with an excellent herd. We'd visited there often. He announced a dispersal of his herd and I wasted no time in getting out to his place. Frieda was a standout—four-year-old, well built, of good mixed blood and fresh.

The dairyman wouldn't sell her ahead of the sale—she'd been advertised and he said it wouldn't be honest. But he did do one thing—he promised me he'd sell her first, and at that kind of sale big buyers frequently didn't get warmed up until well after the sale had started.

I had $85 in the bank and drew a cashier's check for all of it. When the bidding opened I started boldly.

Bidding went to $80 all too quickly. This was to have been my limit, for trucking her home would cost $4 and I wanted some lunch. But we soon passed the $80 mark—in 50-cent and finally 25-cent bids—and I kept going. Unbelievably she was struck off to me at $84.25. We walked home—four miles, in the dark, with rebellious Frieda on the end of a rope.

Roughage, not grain, was the biggest feeding problem in the handling of a town cow. Each fall I cut sweet corn fodder from every garden in our end of town and carted it home on a coaster wagon. You can get a whole shock of sweet corn fodder on a wagon if you tie it on right.

Saturdays I worked all day for a load of hay. It mattered little how much a day's work was worth or what hay was bringing—you pitched hay for a farmer and then brought the last load home. I'd take the horses back on Sunday morning.

To house the cow, I spent hours insulating the old carriage shed with cardboard cartons and rigging plumbing from old gutters. This contraption led from the pump near the house to the barnyard, where it emptied into a sawed-off barrel.

You hear tales about milking in the dark by the light of an old kerosene lantern, morning and night every day all winter, and milking outdoors morning and night all summer. I did all those things.

For pasture, we either staked out the cows in the wide ditches along the highway or rented pasture from elderly ladies who lived on the edge of town.

There were two lovely ladies—one a widow and the other a spinster—who had pasture for rent. They, too, had cows. Cows are gregarious and thrive on company. Town cows get lonely. They wear themselves out bawling and patrolling the fence, leaning methodically on every post, and making very little milk.

I used to walk to pasture and milk there rather than drive the cows back and forth. Feed was served in a dishpan. It was up to the milker to finish milking before the cow finished eating and walked away.

Modern dairymen would scoff at a cow eating melon rinds, leftover salads, potato peelings, overripe fruit, pea pods, corn shucks, spaghetti, etc. We fed garbage. One of our cows, Susie, liked meat.

This mixed diet didn't seem to offset the flavor of the milk much. We used our milk raw, but we used it very quickly. Milk was also kept scrupulously clean, not by modern standards, but by my mother's. Mother said she could see germs with the naked eye. When she poured the warm milk through a cheesecloth strainer, about all she got out were the frogs and the flies. But it looked clean and tasted fine.

We did have trouble with wild onions. In a big dairy, one cow with off-flavor milk probably doesn't affect the whole bulk-milk tank. When the herd is just one cow, and that cow is filled with wild onions, the milk is fit only for onion soup.

When a cow became mournful, we turned to *Bailey's* for the needs. *Bailey's Cyclopedia of Agriculture* isn't well known today, but we couldn't have done without it. It consisted of four giant tomes and covered just about everything that was known about husbandry. Many of *Bailey's* theorics have since been disproved, but I suppose even a modern cow would respond to a good dose of salts, and *Bailey* prescribed salts for almost everything.

Bailey's also spoke of what to do with a high molar. One of our first cows, Bessie, had such an infliction. It pained her and she wouldn't eat—not even molasses. I got her mouth propped open with a short broomstick and filed the tooth down with a wood rasp. It never bothered her again, thanks to *Bailey's*.

I wonder now why we never had leptospirosis, or brucellosis, or acetonemia, or hemorrhagic septicemia, or for that matter, aftosa. In later years we tested for TB, but we had few major health problems which we didn't cause ourselves with poor feed, poor hay, or irregular hours.

Milking and tending the cow were round-the-clock, round-the-year business. Up every morning before dawn all winter, to feed and milk, home for milking, feeding and bedding every night. Strangely enough, it wasn't unpleasant. There was always a half-hour of peace and quiet, morning and evening, to plan a day's work and to go over what had been done or learned or missed. I used my chore time to think, to conjure up football plays, to memorize parts in the school plays and to practice debate. Cows liked to hear me sing; at least they never complained. How often have I wished, since I have grown up, that I had a half-hour in the morning and a half-hour every night when I could depend on being alone and unbothered.

Chores seize on a boy and won't let go. I have little sentimentality about the good old days nor do I set great store in the adage about giving a boy a cow to keep him from crime's door.

I won't say that the youngsters today are headed straight for hell because they haven't got a family cow. She came from whence no one knows; she played her little part; and now she's gone. Bless her memory. Ⓢ

Around the House

For many persons who enjoy the activity of household work there are projects that can be undertaken to bring a piece of the country inside. Even for those who do not care for housework the necessities can be made more bearable. The chores a household demands often become dull through routine. By trying new and economical approaches to clean a stain or brighten a bathtub you will get surprising results, and you may escape the ordinary drudgery. Creativity always enhances the surroundings of a home, and family and friends will appreciate the effort made in keeping the setting attractive. When entertaining, colorful applications to the living room will please your guests, and special homemade treats will have friends asking for your recipes. While the outdoor work continues, the household can be enhanced with a freshness all its own.

Country Pinafores

Darlene Kronschnabel

The crisp look of the old-fashioned ruffled pinafore apron is right at home in the country kitchen or on the patio.

Here is a trio of charming pinafores just in time for spring and summer entertaining. All are made from one basic pattern; the trim is up to you. Plan to color coordinate your pinafore and visit the sewing notions counter in your local variety store. You will find an inspiring selection of bright trims to give your pinafores a colorful country look just like grandmother wore.

Materials

4 yds. 44″ material (broadcloth, seersucker, poplin, lightweight cotton, gingham, etc.)
2¼ yd. rickrack or trim, as desired
Tissue paper for making pattern
Fine point felt-tip marker
Masking tape
Dressmaker's pencil

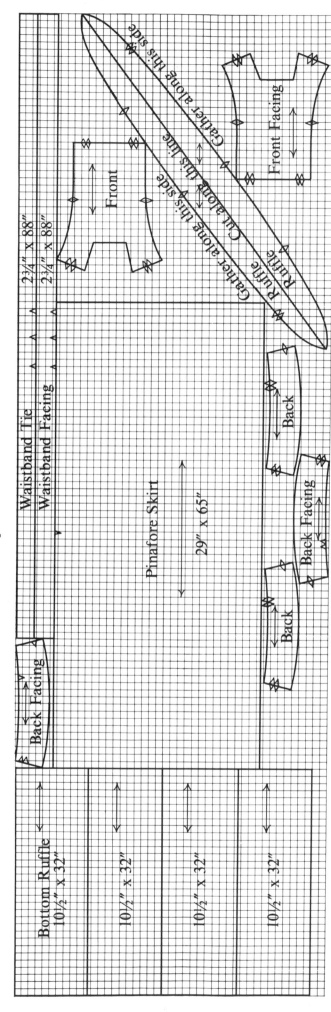

This represents 4 yd. of 44 in. material

1 square = 1 inch

Front

Front Facing

Gather along this side
2¾" x 88"
Cut along this side
2¾" x 88"
Gather along this side
Cut along this side

Ruffle

Ruffle

Waistband Tie

Waistband Facing

Back

Back Facing

Pinafore Skirt
29" x 65"

Back

Back Facing

Bottom Ruffle
10½" x 32"

10½" x 32"

10½" x 32"

10½" x 32"

Cutting

Transfer pattern to tissue paper. Cut out the pattern and lay it on the material as shown in the cutting guide. Cut out pattern and transfer all pattern markings to the pieces. Note: All pattern pieces have a ⅝" seam allowance.

Top

Sew front to back at shoulder seams. Press seams open. Turn under ¼″ of straight side of ruffle and stitch. On the other side of ruffle, sew a double row of long gathering stitches, ⅛″ apart. With right sides together, pin ruffle to back and front, matching dots and adjusting gathers to fit. Baste. Repeat for other ruffle.

Sew front facing to back facing at shoulder seams. Press seams open. With right sides together, pin facing to front and back at neck opening and at sides, matching dots. Stitch through all thicknesses, leaving lower edges free.

Reinforce corners at neck opening. Trim seams and clip corners and curves. Turn top right side out through shoulders. Press.

Waistband

With right sides together, pin front and back to waistband-tie, matching dots and being careful not to twist back straps. (The front should be six inches away from the back on the waistband.) Baste.

With right sides together, pin waistband facing to waistband. Beginning at dot, stitch waistband and facing at bottom of ties, ends, and top, leaving waistband open between dots. Turn right side out and press.

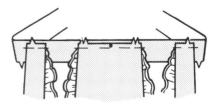

**Basting front and back
to waistband**

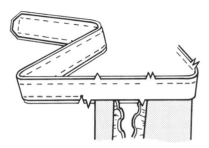

**Stitching around
waistband and tie**

Skirt

Sew pieces of pinafore ruffle together making a long narrow strip. Press seams open. Finish lower edge and sides of ruffle with a narrow hem. Sew a double row of long gathering stitches ⅛″ apart, along top edge of ruffle. With right sides together, pin ruffle to skirt, matching center seam of ruffle to center front of skirt and having hemmed edges of ruffle 1¼″ from sides of skirt.

Turn under ¼″ on sides of skirt and stitch. Then press under the remaining 1″, turning it over the ruffle seam on the bottom, and stitch. Sew a double row of long gathering stitches along top of skirt. With right sides together, matching center front of skirt and waistband, pin skirt to waistband, adjusting gathers to fit. Keep waistband facing free. Stitch. Press seam toward waistband. Pin waistband facing over skirt seam and slipstitch. Press.

Trim pinafore with desired decorative trimmings. [s]

APPLIQUÉ ROSE PILLOWS

Darlene Kronschnabel

Roses, roses, everywhere! Country gardens are filled with roses of all colors and sizes from early summer to late fall. Fragrant roses were the favorite flowers in early American gardens too. Perhaps that is why Colonial homemakers adopted the decorative flower as the central motif in their needlework and quilts.

The ever-popular "Rose of Sharon" is considered a quilting classic. Some claim a Biblical source from the Song of Solomon for this delightful pattern. Early quilters copied the flowering tree-like rose in traditional patterns using pink, white and green calico with yellow rose centers. To quiltmakers this design, with many variations, became symbolic of constant and enduring love.

There are other rose patterns, too. Ones with wreaths, leaves, and sometimes just a single large rose. There were bright red roses and dainty yellow ones growing in country gardens and they, too, were transferred into colorful appliqué patterns.

Appliqué rose blocks were designed for quilts, but they also make charming pillows. Each can be created in an almost endless variety of color and arrangement with your individual touch. The machine appliquéing makes these pillows quick and fun to make.

Directions follow.

Materials Needed (for each pillow)

Knife-edge pillow form, shredded foam for stuffing, or inner pillow*. Sturdy material for pillow front and back, plus scraps of nonfraying fabric for flowers, buds, stems and leaves of the same general type of fabric. Select fabric of the same weight. (Yardage given based on 45-inch fabric)

Matching or contrasting thread, as desired
Ruler
Scissors
Straight pins
White or brown wrapping paper to make pattern

*Filling: To make your own inner pillow: Finish the appliquéd pillow cover. Turn inside out and measure carefully. Then sew an inside pillow ½ inch smaller than the decorative cover. Use unbleached muslin to give a firm, yet soft body to the completed pillow. Fill this inner form with poly-fiber filling. Stuff the muslin pillow into the appliquéd casing and carefully slipstitch the opening.

GENERAL DIRECTIONS

Using a large sheet of white or brown wrapping paper, rule off 1-inch squares. Make sure you rule off as many squares as the diagram shows. Then enlarge pattern by drawing in the same lines as in the corresponding square of the diagram. Cut out pattern pieces. Transfer individual pattern pieces to either fine sandpaper or heavy cardboard. Cut out each pattern piece exactly for a perfect fit.

Place your pattern pieces on wrong side of fabric. Carefully trace around each piece with a soft lead pencil. Cut out material.

Working with the front, determine center by first pressing flat, fold in half, then in quarters. Press. Following creases, position all flowers, buds, leaves and stems in place, overlapping each piece slightly.

Secure flower pieces by pins or fusible webbing. Zigzag around edges with close satin stitch with matching or contrasting thread.

Assembling Pillows

With right sides together and edges even, pin finished pillow front to back. Leaving ½-inch seam allowance, sew around edges, leaving an opening large enough to insert a pillow form. Carefully clip corners and turn right side out. After turning, be sure to push all corners out. A knitting needle works fine to help bring out sharp corners. Insert inner pillow form or stuffing. Slip-stitch opening. Fluff, and your pillow is ready to use.

Note: **Each square equals ¼″.**

Pattern A: Two pieces plain material 14½ inches square for front and back, ⅛ yard green for leaves, two shades of pink fabric, ⅛ yard each, to make four flowers and centers. Follow general directions.

Pattern B: Two pieces plain material 21½ inches square for front and back, ⅛ yard each green for leaves and small print for flowers, 9½-inch square scrap of red for center flower, small yellow scrap for center flower. Follow general directions.

Pattern C: Two pieces plain material 18½ inches square for front and back, about ⅛ yard green print for leaves and ⅛ yard each of pink print and pink plain for flowers, a small yellow scrap for center, about 25 inches of matching green bias tape for stems. Follow general directions.

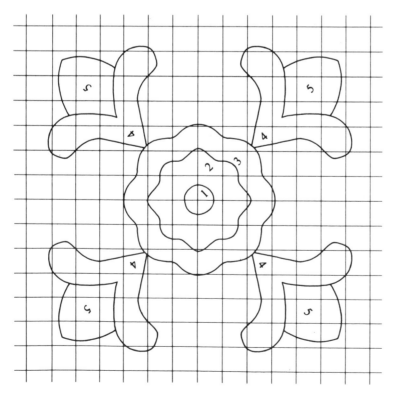

Pattern D: Two pieces of plain material 14½ inches square for front and back, about ⅛ yard each dark green, yellow and small print material. Follow general directions.

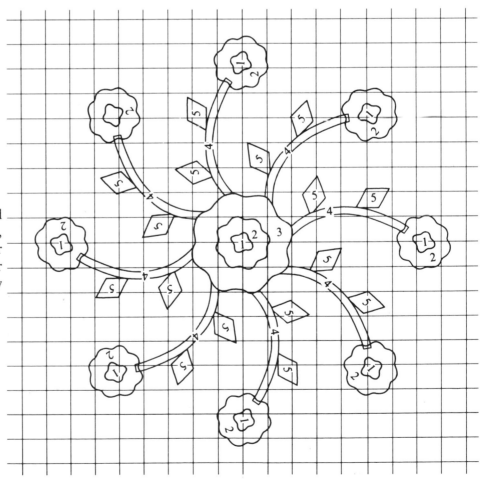

Pattern E: Two pieces of plain material 14¼ inches square for front and back, about ⅛ yard each dark green for leaves, yellow and yellow print for flowers. Follow general directions.

Pattern F: Two pieces of plain material 16½ inches square for front and back, about ⅛ yard each brown print for stems and leaves, and small print for flowers, scraps of red and yellow. Follow general directions.

The Country Doctor

R. J. McGinnis

A product of an early Midwest medical school, he came to our little village in the hills of southern Ohio and hung out his shingle. His name was Alonzo Adams, and he was in his mid-twenties. He grew a beard, and people were soon calling him "Old Doc," a name he carried for sixty years.

He was the first doctor in our part of the country. Before he came we got along with a midwife, home remedies, and prayer. We survived.

Men were kicked by horses and laid low by falling trees; they cut their toes off with axes, froze their fingers and ears, and were poisoned by contaminated water and unrefrigerated foods; they were bitten by snakes, got rheumatism from exposure, and suffered from gastric troubles brought on by lack of proper food, but somehow they got well again.

The cure for all ills was the brews and potions passed down from ancestors, and the old reliables, castor oil, Epsom salts, and arnica. They used whiskey and a wad of tobacco for disinfectant. Sulphur and molasses, fol-lowed by dandelion greens and sassafras tea, were sovereign spring remedies for phlegms accumulated in the body during the winter. Most ills were worn out, or they wore out the victim.

When a doctor came to a community he was promptly challenged by these home remedies, and Old Doc never quite conquered them. Naturally, he was called only when old home remedies failed and, of course, for accidents. He had to be wise and patient in substituting science for the bark of the sassafras root. He soon learned that he could not be a person, for there was really no place in the community for a person of his mythical and actual gifts. He was both at the top and the bottom of the social order, more important than the banker in time of trouble, less important than a hired hand when it came time to pay the bills. He was more an institution than a person, and few thought of him as a man with the emotions of an ordinary person. Old Doc observed the vows of his calling faithfully. What he knew about the private lives of the people in his community would have sent most of them to jail. They took their intertwined spiritual and domestic problems to him along with their ailments, and found a wise counselor.

His fee for a house call was two dollars when he came to our community, and when he died sixty years later his fee was still two dollars. A house call might take him two blocks down the village street on a pleasant summer afternoon; it might take him twenty miles into the country in the worst blizzard of the winter.

While Old Doc practiced his profession without the multitude of scientific refinements we have today, he did surprisingly well with his simple drugs and tools. He was a good diagnostician of the mind as well as the body, and was not above psychological tricks if he thought they were needed. He regularly sold, for a dime a bottle, "the best cure for sore throat in the country." It was a six-ounce bottle of common salt solution, colored red, and was used as a gargle. If asked what it was, Old Doc lowered his voice mysteriously and said, "Sodium chloride and H_2O."

He was versatile, too. He pulled teeth, examined the eyes for glasses, and occasionally ministered to a sick cow or horse. His favorite remedy was a vile mixture of quinine, iron, and strychnine, which he called Q.I.S. Sometimes calomel was substituted for the strychnine. It was a sort of shotgun mixture good for most anything that came along, could do no harm, and tasted vile enough to satisfy the most rabid hypochondriac. Most of the emergency surgery was performed in the field or on a kitchen table. His surgical kit contained a saw, two or three scalpels, a pair of forceps, and a needle with a length of catgut.

He might have laid by a fortune, for he never had time to spend money, if he collected only a modest percentage of what was owed him. The grocer and the hardware store were paid when the hogs were sold in the autumn. Old Doc was paid out of conscience money. He rarely collected his five-dollar fee for the birth of the first child; it was only after the second came along that the embarrassed father paid his old bill. He was paid in odd ways, too. The very

poor were the best pay, for they put a bag of potatoes or a couple of fat hens in the boot of his buggy when he left, and often at Christmastime a ham or a barrel of apples came his way on a bill he long since had written off. He never billed his creditors. He never married; never no time for courting.

Joe Wilson, some thirty-five years old and a well-to-do farmer, went to Old Doc for a birth certificate. He wanted to take his family to Europe and needed records for his passport. Old Doc looked up his records, wrote out the certificate and handed it to Joe. "How much do I owe you?" asked Joe. It was then that Old Doc came as near as he ever had come to dunning a creditor. "You don't owe me anything for the certificate," he said, "but you're not paid for yourself yet. Your father forgot the item when you were born."

Old Doc's sole heir was a nephew in Pittsburgh. His biggest legacy was six ledgers recording three score years of service and more than $100,000 in unpaid bills, some almost sixty years old. He left also a modest house in the village, 120 stony acres and an old farmhouse two miles out, and three old horses.

He kept two horses in a stable back of his home, a light cart for summer use, and a staunch, closed buggy for the bad season. People said he wore out a horse a year galloping over country roads in a sea of mud to bring a baby, or tie up an artery. His horses and the stable were cared for by the village dolt, Henry Carr, who slept in a room in the stable and was always on call. When Old Doc died, Henry got his bank account—$325.76.

Old Doc passed away during the peak of a flu epidemic. It was not the flu that took him, but at eighty-six, two days and nights without taking off his clothes and with no food except coffee was too much for his aging heart. He came in early one morning, fell asleep in his chair in his office, and never awakened. He has the finest marble monument in our cemetery, put up by his faithful friends who never thought to pay him in life, but opened their purses when he died. His funeral was the largest in the history of our village. Ⓖ

A Household Hint . . .

Great-grandmother's *Household Hints* is more of a treasure than any of the new cookbooks in my library today. The writing is quaint and the sentence structure would spell despair for grammarians.

Some of the recipes are great. I have tried them. Others call for ingredients I have never heard of and so I am forever asking my mother's generation. I am fortunate enough to have known my great- grandmother and her daughter, my grandmother, but I was too young then to care about what went into their magic dishes. Mama can help me somewhat, but she and I agree that it would take Solomon to unriddle some of them.

The most mystifying and intriguing are listed under "Handy Household Hints." Here are a few of them. See how many of the ingredients you recognize and the methods you understand.

The hand-sewn book containing the recipes of my great-grandmother and her neighbors is falling apart, but I cannot bring myself to have it rebound any more than I can correct her English. Most of her concoctions end with: "Let stand . . ." so I think I shall follow her directions.

Let It Stand

June Masters Bacher

SOOT STAINS: Soot falling from open chimney can be swept up without a heap of trouble by sprinkling lavishly with salt at first, then sweeping.

TO CLEAN KID GLOVES: A good-sized piece of light-colored flannel, some laundry soap and sweet milk. Put glove on, put flannel over finger, moisten by merely dipping in milk, then rub on cake of soap and apply to glove. Rub toward ends of fingers, changing flannels as it becomes soiled, being careful not to get the flannel too wet or let gloves dry on hands.

CLEANING FLUID: One gallon deodorized benzine, one ounce chloroform, one ounce ether, two ounces alcohol, one ounce oil of cologne. Do not breathe.

VARNISH AND PAINT: Use turpentine on coarse goods; on fine goods, alcohol. Sponge with chloroform if a dark ring is left by turpentine. Stay away from fire.

TO WASH EASY: Put over the boiler with one-half or two-thirds full of water. Cut up two tablespoonfuls of paraffin and one-half bar of lye soap and melt in a quart of water. Let boil up and add this to the water in the boiler. Wet the clothes, wring out and soap dirty places. Put in and let boil twenty minutes, stirring once in a great while. Take out and rub on a rub-board, rinse in seven waters and hang on line or barbwire fence to dry.

TO CLEAN WOOL: To five cents worth of soap bark add one and a half pints of water. Boil half an hour and strain. Brush goods and spread out smooth. Apply warm liquid with flannel cloth to right side, pressing on wrong side until dry. Will make old look new unless it felts.

FOR CLEANING BATHTUBS: Wipe with moistened cloth with kerosene. It will disappear completely.

FOR CLEANING SILVER: Take a pound of whiting and pour one quart of boiling water, stand aside until cold, then add one tablespoon turpentine and ammonia. Shake and stand away until wanted.

TO GIVE STOVE A FINISH: A teaspoonful of pulverized alum mixed with stove polish if you have some and it will be quite permanent.

FURNITURE POLISH: Half pint benzine, four ounces Golden Japan, three ounces linseed oil, three ounces carbon oil. Rub on hard.

TAR: Soften the stains with hog lard, then soak in turpentine. Scrape off carefully with a knife and rub gently until dry—no matter how long it takes.

SOOT STAINS: Rub spots with dry corn-meal before sending them to the wash pot.

MILDEW: Soak in a weak solution of chloride of lime for hours; rinse if the water is cold. If it stays there, wet the cloth and rub on soap and chalk mixed together, and lay in the sun; or try buttermilk or lemon and lay in the sun.

GRASS STAINS: Rub molasses on the spots, then wash the garment to remove the molasses.

WOODEN BATHTUBS: If they go to stave, instead of filling them with water which sure will go stagnant, just paint them with glycerine. The wood will not shrink until the glycerine dries and that may not happen for months. If it does just do it again.

GOOD SOAP: Good soap for those who do rough work like tending fires and sifting ashes is made by melting good soap and stirring in Indian meal until it is thick, then adding one teaspoonful of tincture of benzoin.

TO EXTERMINATE MOTHS: An ounce of gum camphor, one shell of red pepper, macerated in eight ounces of strong alcohol and strained. Sprinkle furs and wrap them in sheets.

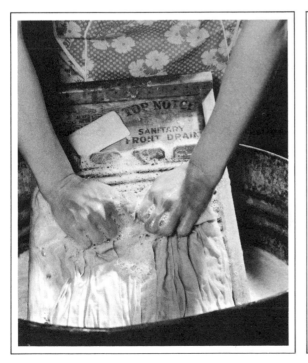

What's Cooking

Homemade Ice Cream
Darlene Kronschnabel

Homemade ice cream is never old-fashioned. One of the best treats on any hot summer afternoon is a frosty dish, piled high with rich, creamy, homemade ice cream. The summer ritual is dear to most of our childhood memories. It is not hard to recall the hand-cranked ice cream freezer churning and clanking out the cooling treats on hot afternoons or the happy anticipation of licking the cream-laden dasher.

Ice cream making is too enduring to neglect. It is still a summer thrill to churn out the silky smooth ice cream in the shade of a sun-warmed back porch.

Interestingly, ice cream is not an American invention. It is a romantic world traveler with its precise origin unknown. However, homemade ice cream is an American invention thanks to a New Jersey hostess, Nancy Johnson. In 1846, she devised a crank and paddle, freezer-in-a-bucket machine that allowed the average homemaker to make the dessert with ease. The principle of ice cream making has not changed.

Most modern ice cream freezers are electric powered; but hand-cranked models have been rescued from attics, dusted off and work as well today as they did a generation ago. Purists claim the best homemade ice cream is produced by churning a cream or custard-base mixture in a hand-cranked or electric ice cream freezer, using ice and rock salt.

Ice cream is a favorite American dessert, if not the world's. Rich and creamy, it is a great treat as is. However, it is also delectable over, in, and under an appealing assortment of baked apples and pears, hot gingerbread, applesauce, spice or pound cakes, crushed berries, pies, fresh, frozen or canned fruits and sauces.

Directions for Freezing Ice Cream

Most ice cream freezers come with a set of general instructions; and for best results follow these. Be sure to read all the directions and get acquainted with your freezer before starting to make ice cream.

For the best ice cream in any freezer, use only the best ingredients. Be sure each is heated and cooked as recommended in the recipe. Prepare your cream or custard base and chill before using.

Wash the freezer can, dasher and can top in hot sudsy water. Rinse, dry and chill.

Insert the dasher in the can. Pour cooled mixture into cooled freezer can filling only ⅔ to allow for expansion. Assemble the can cover and turn the dasher stem to be sure it turns freely. Place the assembled can in the tub, making sure it rests in proper position on the stud in the bottom of the tub and following freezer instructions. Begin churning.

Alternate layers of crushed ice and rock salt until the tub is filled. Add about 1 cup water to the tub to start the ice melting. (You will need about 16 pounds of crushed ice and about 3 cups of rock salt to fill a 4-quart freezer. If you cannot find rock salt, use coarse kitchen salt, sometimes called Kosher salt.)

Freezing does not begin until the ice melts enough to cause the water to flow from the overflow hole. Never let the hole become clogged. During the freezing period it will be necessary to add additional salt and ice as needed to keep the can covered.

Allow the freezer to churn until the motor slows or stops, about 20 to 30 minutes. (Disconnect electric freezer as soon as it stops to prevent motor damage.) If using a hand-cranked model, the process is finished when the crank becomes too difficult to turn. The ice cream mixture will be the consistency of whipped cream or soft mush.

Remove the dasher and pack down the ice cream. Place a cork in the hole in the can cover. Replace the cover. Remove the can from the tub, dry, and freeze ice cream in food freezer until firm, at least two hours.

CHOCOLATE ICE CREAM

1 qt. milk	2 c. sugar
1 c. cocoa	1 qt. heavy cream
1 c. light corn syrup	1 T. vanilla
5 eggs	

In 2-quart saucepan, combine 2 cups of the milk, cocoa, and corn syrup. Bring to a boil over medium heat, stirring constantly. Cool. In a large mixing bowl, beat eggs until foamy; gradually beat in sugar. Add cocoa mixture. Stir in remaining 2 cups milk, cream and vanilla. Chill. Churn-freeze. Makes about 1 gallon.

BLUEBERRY ICE CREAM

2 pts. fresh blue- berries	2 c. heavy cream, lightly whipped
1 c. sugar	1 c. evaporated milk
⅛ t. salt	

Mash berries and cook with sugar over medium heat, stirring constantly, for five minutes. Press berries through a sieve. Cool. Add salt, cream and evaporated milk to the berries. Churn-freeze. Makes 2 quarts.

PEACH ICE CREAM

2 eggs	2 c. heavy cream
1 c. sugar	2 c. milk
1 T. vanilla	2 c. peeled, pitted and
½ c. condensed milk	mashed fresh, very
	ripe peaches

Beat eggs and sugar together until very creamy. Add vanilla, condensed milk, heavy cream and milk. Churn-freeze to a mush. Add peaches and continue to churn-freeze until firm. Makes 2 quarts.

STRAWBERRY ICE CREAM

1 qt. crushed straw-	3 c. heavy cream
berries, sweetened	½ t. vanilla
to taste	⅛ t. salt
2 eggs	3 c. milk
1 c. sugar	

In a large mixing bowl, beat eggs until foamy. Gradually add the sugar, beating until thickened. Add milk, cream, vanilla and salt. Blend in fruit. Chill. Churn-freeze. Makes about 4 quarts.

VANILLA ICE CREAM

1½ c. sugar	4 eggs, slightly beaten
¼ c. flour	4 c. heavy cream
⅛ t. salt	1 T. vanilla
2 c. milk	

Combine sugar, flour and salt in a large saucepan, stir in milk. Cook over medium heat, stirring constantly, until mixture thickens and boils 1 minute. Cool slightly. Stir half the warm mixture slowly into beaten eggs in a medium-size bowl. Stir egg mixture back into saucepan. Return to heat and cook over medium heat, not allowing it to boil. Cook 1 minute, stirring constantly. Pour into large bowl. Stir in cream and vanilla. Chill at least 2 hours. Pour mixture into a 4 to 6 quart freezer can; freeze, following directions of your freezer. Makes about 2 quarts.

ICE CREAM SAUCES

STRAWBERRY-RHUBARB SAUCE

1 c. fresh rhubarb, cut into ½-inch pieces
1½ c. sliced, fresh strawberries
⅓ c. sugar
Red food coloring, if desired

In 1-quart saucepan, combine rhubarb, 1 cup strawberries and sugar. Boil 5 minutes. Remove from heat. Add remaining ½ cup strawberries and red food color, a few drops at a time, to desired color. Chill. Makes 1¾ cups.

COFFEE CARAMEL SAUCE

Melt, over boiling water, one 14-ounce package vanilla caramels and 3½ teaspoons instant coffee. Stir in 2 teaspoons light corn syrup and 2 tablespoons half and half. Serve hot. Makes 1 cup sauce.

PEANUT SAUCE

Combine ½ cup butter, 2 tablespoons flour and 1 cup water in a saucepan. Cook until slightly thickened, stirring constantly. Add ¾ cup chunky style peanut butter. Stir to blend. Remove from heat. Stir in 2½ cups sifted confectioners' sugar and blend until smooth. Serve hot or cold. Makes 3 cups sauce.

CHOCOLATE SAUCE

¼ c. butter	⅛ t. salt
2 1-oz. sq. un-	¾ c. light cream
sweetened	½ t. vanilla
chocolate	
1½ c. sugar	

Melt butter and chocolate over very low heat. Add sugar and salt gradually, blending well. Mixture will be very thick and dry. Gradually stir in cream. Cook 5 to 6 minutes to dissolve the sugar. Remove from heat and add vanilla. Serve hot or cold. Makes about 2 cups.

Wind and Weather

The weather plays an integral, and often confusing, role in the life of every person; but nowhere are its sudden changes and seasonal characteristics more carefully observed, respected, and clearly understood than in the country. A farmer's dependence on favorable weather to provide him with food and a livelihood compel him to look long and hard at the climate. This resulting awareness allows him to harness the weather to water his livestock, crush his grain, and provide electricity to economically improve his way of life. Weather is an unpredictable phenomenon; but to best understand its force, a constant effort must be made to go beyond the technical forecasts and casual, fleeting observations, and go out to the country where the weather must be contended with and depended on every day of the year.

GRANDPA'S SKY ENGINE

Article and photos by Grover Brinkman

Several centuries have rolled by since a bulky wooden windmill, brought from Europe in a sailing ship and erected at America's first permanent English settlement at Jamestown, Virginia, disappeared, evidently rotted away. The date of its erection was about 1622, inaugurating more than three and one-half centuries of "harnessing the wind" for power.

Although the windmill seemed to be vanishing from rural America, the recent energy crisis has at least temporarily halted its demise. Momentarily, it is being given a second look.

The windmill is free power, not depending on fuel oil, gasoline, coal or propane, or any type of electrification. Whether or not it makes a vigorous comeback remains to be seen.

No more than a handful of windmills remain in the Midwest, Colorado and Kansas, the Texas Panhandle, Nebraska's sandhills, Florida's back country, the Dakota and Oklahoma plains, but new ones are appearing on the skyline.

Harnessing the breeze kept these windmills operative to water livestock in areas where electricity was not available. The past decade saw electricity come to the most remote areas, and the windmills seemed useless. But the energy crisis has brought many of them back into operation.

In many areas of the nation, windmills have been standing idle, black skeletons of rusting steel against the sky, moving slowly to extinction. Many have lost their windwheels. On others, television antennas have been mounted. But the towers are not going down anymore. They just might be needed, owners say.

When electricity came to rural America through the REA in 1930s, it sounded the death knell for the farm windmill. The machine that doomed the old oaken bucket and the village pump itself seemed a sudden outcast. But now it has a stay of execution.

Perhaps it is all for the best. Why should something that is free not be utilized? The windmills that stand today are poignant reminders of the late 1800s and early 1900s when life in rural America was much slower paced.

The heyday of the windmill spanned half a century or more. At its peak, sales ran into the millions, with more than six million wind machines manufactured yearly for rural America. At least twenty companies competed in the manufacturing field.

For less than $100, a purchaser could erect a windmill over his deep well and forget about pumping water. There usually was enough breeze to turn the oblique vanes. The fan-shaped tail kept the vanes facing the wind, and soon a soft purring of water sounded in the cattle trough. A float arrangement stopped the pump when the tank was full, so water was not wasted.

Today many a senior citizen remembers the windmill on the farm of his youth, the cacophony of sound that was a reassuring symphony as the vanes rotated merrily in a stiff wind. The tower, reached by a shaky

This windmill might be familiar to you. It is on a movie and television set near Old Tucson, Arizona.

Photo on preceding page: This new windmill in a Nebraska park, continues the tradition of Grandpa's wind machine.

This windmill in western Kansas is the only source of water for these cattle.

metal ladder, was always a good vantage point when one of the lambs got lost or a colt didn't come home from pasture. Junior soon learned to climb to the tower in his derring-do.

Unlike an internal combustion engine, or an electric motor, the windmill ran free of cost. Or almost free. An Illinois farmer, remembering his windmill, said it served him for more than forty years, and the only cost was the oil used on the bearings. Some of the windmills were victims of storms, but only a few; it was a very rugged machine.

The windmill came to America from Europe with the first colonists. Once here, American ingenuity soon improved it. The canvas sails used in Europe's mills were soon replaced with wooden vanes. Later the wooden vane gave way to more rugged metal.

Daniel Halliday, a Connecticut mechanic, invented the prototype of today's windmill. But it took a minister, the Rev. Leonard Wheeler, a missionary to Indians on a Wisconsin reservation, to fashion the hinged tail which kept the wheel facing the wind. In 1888, LaVerne Noyes brought out the first all-steel windmill. His invention at first was scoffed at. But within a few years he had most of the market cornered.

The windmill boom that followed did not dim until President Franklin D. Roosevelt's New Deal brought REA electric current to rural America. Soon electric wires spread to farm homes, no matter how isolated. The windmill was doomed, along with the walking plow, the grain binder, the wall telephone, the milk can, and hundreds of other items now listed in the category of nostalgic antiques, primitives or collectibles.

But today, with an acute energy crisis staring at us, the windmill just might come back. History does repeat itself. In its day it was a colossus; it helped millions of farmers and ranchers; and it even took an active part in the building of the first railroads.

Remember, the wind is free, and unless our entire weather balance is disturbed, it will never be in short supply. [S]

History at its most picturesque . . .

Water Mills

Beth Huwiler

The water mill is one of the most charming and widespread relics of early American culture. If you travel through the countryside, particularly in the East, you are likely to see an occasional mill nestled beside a rippling stream. Although the years may have halted the spinning of the wheel and spread moss over the adjacent building, you can still get a sense of the activity that once made the mill the hub of its community. In fact, it was not uncommon for towns to be charted around mills; we recall this

today by the number of towns with "Mill" as part of their names.

Water was one of the cheapest and most efficient sources of power in the New World. So it is not surprising that water mills provided power for a variety of purposes—from sawing lumber to tanning hides. But the first mill erected in a community was likely to be a gristmill, and this was the mill most essential for the settlers' survival. For bread was the staple of their diet, and it was the gristmill that ground grain into flour.

Of course, mills did not originate in America. They go back to prehistoric times—the times when men first began grinding grain for bread. Archaeologists have discovered primitive mills—simple stone slabs—that ground grain more than nine thousand years ago. These forerunners of modern mills usually consisted of two stones rubbed together, the grain between them. After a time, the bottom stone would begin to wear away, leaving a hollow in the center that made the process more efficient. Soon millstones were made with a hollow in the bottom stone.

From these early mills developed several more sophisticated inventions that also involved a simple rubbing action. One is the mortar and pestle, for centuries the mark of the apothecary shop. Another is the saddle mill, so called because the bottom stone was shaped like a saddle. In both mills, grain was placed in the center of the bottom stone; as it was ground, it fell down the side depressions. After a time, people began putting a hole in the center of the top stone so that grain could be added more easily. For many centuries, these simple mills provided all the flour that was used.

Photo opposite: Pat Powers

Several hundred years before the birth of Christ, rotary mills were invented. They, too, consisted of two stones. The large stone on the bottom stood still while the top stone revolved to crush the grain. This type of mill was called a quern. The first querns were operated by hand; but over the years, as they were made larger and larger, they became more difficult to operate. For a time, the needed power was provided by slaves; but when Constantine became the first Christian to rule the Roman empire, he outlawed slave labor. The use of slaves persisted for a time; but eventually people resorted to other means of operating their mills.

The most obvious method was animal power. But it was not long before people realized that animals, too, could be put to better use and that other sources of power were available if they could

be harnessed. The most obvious source was water, and it was the Romans who invented the water mill. The use of these mills grew after slave labor declined, and as the Romans conquered foreign lands, they brought their knowledge of mills with them. In Britain, the water mill was readily accepted, and it soon became a common sight in the English countryside.

In lands either very dry or flat, the water mill could not be used. The windmill was an independent development which the European Crusaders found in the Holy Land. Returning to their native lands, they brought the idea with them. It was adopted in countries where water mills were impractical—lands like Holland, where the windmill has become a trademark. But where water was available, it was a more reliable source of power than the wind; so the water mill was preferred.

The type of mill used depended on the type of water power available. There are three basic classifications of water mills with wheels, classed by the way in which water was used to turn the mill wheel. With an overshot wheel, the water flowed over the top of the wheel which was the most efficient method, because it used the weight of the water to make the wheel turn. But it could only be used where there was a waterfall or hill. An undershot wheel used the speed of the water rushing past the bottom of the wheel to turn it. It would be used wherever there was a rapidly flowing stream, but it was not very efficient. The third type of mill used a breast wheel, turned by the mass of water against the middle of the wheel. Although it was more efficient than the undershot wheel, it required a dam and lock to store up sufficient water to turn the wheel. Not surprising, the most popular place to build a mill was on the hillside where a simple and efficient overshot wheel could be used.

The first colonists in the New World, like everyone before them, came upon the problems of how to grind their grain to make flour. The first people in a region often used stone slabs, much as primitive peoples had in the past, because they did not have the equipment or time needed to erect more modern mills. Some settlers built homemade hand-cranked mills; these were able to provide enough flour for a single family living in an isolated area. But as the population increased, it became practical to build mills powered by wind or water, depending on the terrain of the area. In the first section of the country to be colonized, the East, there were plenty of streams and hills, so water mills were usually built. These are the mills that we see today. Although historians believe that the first gristmill in the American colonies was a windmill, it did not take long for water mills to predominate.

There were refinements in the milling process throughout the nineteenth century. Water continued to be the major source of power until the invention of the steam engine; and stones were used to grind the grain until the mid-1800s. At that time Americans adopted a system invented in Hungary, that of crushing the grain between iron rollers. Successive runs through the rollers reduced the grain to a very fine flour. In the process, the iron rollers generated heat which destroyed some nutritional value, but the time saved was financially beneficial. This method retained only the central portion of the wheat.

The use of iron rollers could have signalled the end of the era of stone-ground grain which had lasted nine thousand years. With the recent emphasis on health and natural foods, however, people rediscovered the value of traditional methods. Stone grinding generates less heat; thus resulting in a more nutritional flour. In addition, people now believe that the bran and the germ, which commercial methods tried to eliminate as much as possible, are important. Thus, many health enthusiasts are returning to stone-ground flour and meal.

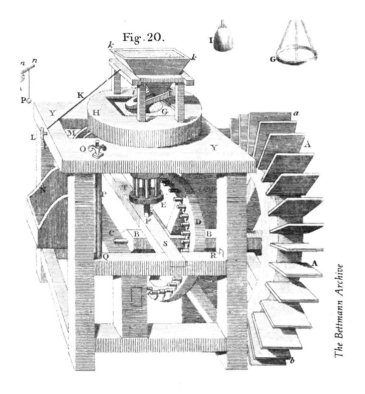

The Bettmann Archive

The combination of this increased attention to nutrition and a growing desire to explore our country's past has led to the restoration of some of the old, traditional mills. In addition, new water mills are being built—including replicas of old mills—which are occasionally built of materials salvaged from mills no longer in use. It is possible in many states to tour these mills, view the traditional milling process, and at the end of the tour buy some stone-ground flour or meal. The bread you bake with flour ground the old-fashioned way might not taste any better than bread made with store-bought flour—but chances are it will. Maybe it's the added nutrition, and maybe it's the magic of doing things the traditional way, the country way. It could be the best bread you've ever eaten. Ⓢ

Early Weather Forecasting

J. Holt Byrne

Our forefathers were perceptive people. They planted crops by the signs; they planned the next day's work by the look of the sky; they pretty well knew in April and May what the summer would bring; and if a picnic were being planned—that, too, was scheduled by the signs.

Man has always lived close to the weather; and down through the ages, he has naturally collected a lot of weather lore. In the murky past, few people could read or write so these bits of weather wisdom were put into easily remembered doggerel and proverbs.

Some of these sayings are almost as old as man himself. In the book of Job it is written: "Out of the chambers of the south cometh the storm and cold out of the north."

Dr. Edward Jenner took many of these old sayings and proverbs and wove them into a sort of poem that goes:

Last night the sun went pale to bed,
The moon in halos hides her head,
The boding shepherd heaves a sigh,
For see! a rainbow spans the sky.
Hark how the chairs and tables crack,
Old Betsy's joints are on the rack;
Her corns with shooting pains torment her,
And to bed untimely send her.
Loud quack the ducks, the peacocks cry,
The distant hills are looking nigh;
How restless are the snorting swine!
The busy flies disturb the kine,
Low o'er the grass the swallow wings;
The cricket, too, how loud he sings!

How fiery red the sun doth rise
Then wades through clouds to mount the skies.
'Twill surely rain—I see with sorrow,
Our jaunt must be put off tomorrow.'

And no matter what you may think of Dr. Jenner's meter, many of the signs are as true today as they were then. It has long been known that air pressure affects both birds and insects. Before a storm the air pressure is high and both birds and insects fly close to the ground. This in turn affects the swine and kine (cows) as the insects come in greater lots to plague them.

The morning sun usually casts a rainbow on clouds to the west, clouds that will generally bring more rain; but the afternoon rainbow would be cast on clouds that had already passed to the east and are beyond us. So came the doggerel:

Rainbow in the morning,
Sailors take warning.
Rainbow at night,
Sailors delight.

Christ, when asked for a sign from the heavens, said "When it is evening, ye say, it will be fair weather for the sky is red. And in the morning, it will be foul weather today, for the sky is red and lowering."

Today, meteorologists point out that a red sunset indicates there are no clouds for a long way to the west; therefore, the next day is likely to be clear. On the other hand, a red morning sky will follow a muggy, fogless night, a condition that so often precedes the storm.

"Rain before seven, clear before eleven." That

was a favorite of our forefathers and it is still heard today. They were usually right, as few summer rains that start in the cool early hours can survive the rising temperature of the day.

There were other signs that told whether the day was a good one to air the quilts or make a trip to the berry patch on the hill.

When the dew is on the grass,
Rain will seldom come to pass.
Or
When the grass is dry at morning light,
Look for rain before the night.

Up in the mountains, the old-timers used to say: "When the ridge has cap it will rain in six hours." Put into verse, this doggerel of centuries said:

When the clouds are on the hills,
They'll soon come down by the mills.

But the old sayings don't always agree. For instance, most people associate the north with cold. "The north wind doth blow and we shall have snow." But another one says: "When the wind is in the northwest, we find weather at its best." "When the wind is in the south, the rain is in its mouth." "Wind from the northeast is good for neither man nor beast." "Wind in the west suits everyone best."

Our forefathers related the weather to next year's harvest for, as surely as death and taxes, the weather controlled their future and well-being. "Water in May is bread all the year," or "Thunder in spring, your barn will fill," and "A cold April the barn will fill," make sense. Thunder means rain and water to be stored in the ground for the long months

ahead. A cold April means that the fruit will be held back and not killed by frost that usually follows unseasonable warm weather.

The Indians said: "when the moon is in its house, it will soon rain." They were speaking of a ring or halo; and since such acts of nature are usually caused by ice crystals, the ice does indicate rain.

Another bit of doggerel which said the same thing went like this:
If the moon shows a silver shield,
Be not afraid to reap your field;
But if she rises haloed round,
Soon we'll tread on deluged ground.

Usually these signs are correct for a white moon shining like a silver shield could mean nothing but a cloudless and dry atmosphere. A red moon indicates high humidity, a state of affairs that often goes before a blustery, rainy spell.

But if all these signs fail, there are others by which we can foretell the storm:

"Old sinners have all points of the compass in their joints and bones," or "A coming storm our corns presage, our aches will throb, our hollow teeth will rage."

And don't try to laugh these signs off as old wives' tales, for scientists have found that such ailments are particularly sensitive to changes in temperature and barometer readings. So if you have a trick knee or some remainder of an old injury, be your own weather prophet without leaving your chair.

However, you're reminded that "In dry weather, all signs fail."

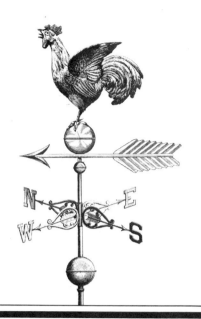

WEATHER VANES

Joseph W. Daniele

Rooster weather vane on top of a schoolhouse.

The vast popularity of weather vanes in New England is the result of changeable weather and long winters. New Englanders have seen hail, wind, rain, snow, lightning and sunshine all in one day. Early settlers and seamen were dependent upon the weather and erected vanes to help forecast, as best they could, the possible conditions ahead.

New England winters found many men with little to do but mend tools and equipment around the home, farm, or port. There was plenty of time for carving and whittling. Many times the creative object of this spare time was a silhouette for a personal weather vane.

Most homemade vanes were made of wood, while the metal vanes were the work of professional whitesmiths, blacksmiths, or coppersmiths. Local artisans constructed vanes in their slack periods and offered them for sale to the townspeople. Occasionally a special order was placed for an unusual style or symbol, such as the huge grasshopper ordered for the Boston Farmer's Exchange, or the dove vane for Washington's home; but for the most part, the majority of household weather vanes were built by early Americans for themselves along common basic lines.

These common lines were a flat silhouette cut from a board or piece of tin in a shape well-known and liked by its maker. The more creative workers sought a third dimension effect in the vane symbol. One prerequisite for a weather vane is that a fair amount of flat surface must be offered to the wind in order for the vane to turn. A pointer or arrow was sometimes used to show direction as well as offer a central "anchor" point for some vane symbols. The cardinal points, North, South, East and West were placed in fixed positions for quick reference to the compass heading of the wind.

Weather vanes were and still are excellent forms of folk art. Some were created in excellent detail while others offer only a rough shape. Some vanes are as large as fifteen feet across, while others measure a mere fifteen inches. All of the old vanes tell us something about early America and the men who made them.

Like great paintings, vane symbols should invoke a personal feeling. Behind each design is a special history and folklore, often as important as the vane symbol itself. It becomes part of the vane and gives us a personal tie to our early American ancestors who lived in a time when men made things for themselves and were pleased with the beauty and utility of the result.

Modern colonial style homes and newly built "Early American" churches exhibit some excellent rooster weather vanes. The church rooster began with an eleventh century papal decree instructing every church to display a rooster from its highest point. Since the common barnyard rooster almost universally functioned as the poor man's alarm clock, it could be readily accepted by all men. For Christians, the rooster was symbolic of the part the fowl played in the betrayal before the death of Jesus. The high flying rooster would, therefore, be a constant reminder that man should not betray himself and that redemption was always obtainable. Secondly, the rooster's crow at dawn was the first call to morning prayers. With church influence, the rooster became the most widely used symbol for early European weather vanes. During the Reformation, the rooster went the way of the new church in Europe.

The horse has long been a favorite model for artistic works from recorded history to the present time. The Greeks used the horse in temple carvings, in relief or in full body. The image of a good horse sent the colonist's blood racing, much as a sleek new automobile excites modern man. Early Americans had an intense sporting instinct, and horse racing was a popular event enjoyed by both owners and spectators.

Horses were important to people in the Colonies in many ways other than racing. Men who didn't have them walked; those without work horses tilled the soil as best they could. Horses have been displayed in all gaits, shapes and sizes, with the Morgan and Hambletonian breeds

In addition to the "Wedercock," the eagle is a popular weather vane symbol.

used most often. While to most people one horse weather vane looks much like any other, the creators would give names to their art or model the weather vane symbols after famous horses of the time. Ethan Allen, Dexter, Smuggler and Dan Patch are a few of the more famous horses used. The vane motifs were most often cut from flat boards or tin plate by individual makers while professionally made vanes were often made of flat, heavy steel plate or cast full-bodied. It mattered little whether a flat-cut vane looked like the namesake, only that the maker or owner felt it did. This personal aspect of weather vanes is not present in modern reproductions.

In the animal world, horses were just one of many symbols used. The pig, dog, fox, stag, deer, lamb and prize bull were also used to grace weather vanes.

The choice of a symbol was often regional; for instance, the use of maritime symbols in the Eastern seacoast towns. Many different fish were used, including the cod, mackerel, tuna, or swordfish. However, New England's favorite was the whale. Complete with harpoon for a pointer, the whale fought the fierce winds of coastal New England, a perfect maritime symbol.

The sailing ship rivaled the whale as a weather vane motif. Ships were used with or without sails, fully rigged and often highly detailed. These ships have sailed

The Bettmann Archive

Fire engine motif weather vane, circa 1880

The Bettmann Archive

Angel weather vane made of
gilded metal, circa 1840

through torrential storms, calm fair weather and blinding northeasters, their courses determined by the prevailing mood of "downeast" winds. Herman Melville said, "Whenever I feel a damp, drizzly November in my soul . . . I take to the sea." Those landlocked fellows who could not take to the sea sat and carved ships; and as they worked, their imaginations wandered with the trade winds to every foreign port of the world.

Some ship vanes are over twelve feet long, while others barely cover twelve inches. Some have a full set of sails; some are in port with sails tightly lashed to the spars; and some others have only the spanker sail set to give surface to the vane. Many of these model ships are fashioned after famous ships of the line, but the majority are rough interpretations of New England clippers.

Throughout American history,

sailing ships have had a universal appeal to boys and men who still react to the majesty of a trim sailing vessel. Ship weather vanes transfer the romance of the sea to land.

Because of its universal acceptance, the "Wedercock" has become a favorite American symbol. Thousands of different styles and breeds of birds have been used. Some of the oldest New World weather cocks were made by Shem Drowne, with three of his original vanes still in use today. Remarkable that these symbols have been exposed to all kinds of weather for over two hundred years and are as good today as the day Shem made them.

Although the rooster is one of the most popular vane symbols, many other birds are used depending upon the personal choice of the maker or owner.

The king of birds, the American

bald eagle, became prominent during and after the Revolution. Once our young country decided upon the eagle as a national symbol, workers were quick to incorporate its form into useful objects, weather vanes included. Nowhere else does the eagle look so majestic as atop a high spire, soaring against the blue sky. In this respect the American eagle has been shown in every shape, position and manner—as important in displaying patriotic pride as in telling wind direction.

The goose as a vane symbol found its development along the flyways of annual migration where it has always been a favorite hunter's target. Geese show some human qualities such as mating for life. Sometimes the mate of a downed goose will return only to fall prey to the hunter. It is sad that faithfulness should be paid back in such a way. Goose hunters who

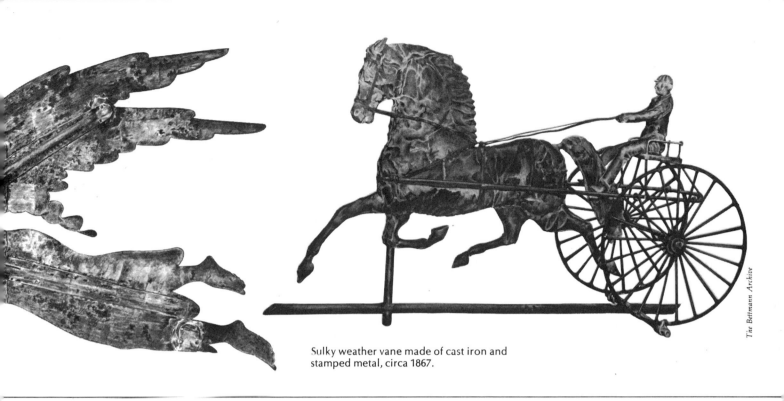

Sulky weather vane made of cast iron and stamped metal, circa 1867.

The Bettmann Archive

carved wooden decoys also carved larger versions to be used as weather vanes.

The ring-necked pheasant is used as a vane symbol inland, or "up-land," as it is called in hunting circles. Again, the personal choice of the creator or maker is the governing factor. The peacock, swan and stork also have reached the heights of vane spires. A hospital in Northhampton, Massachusetts, has a huge stork displayed over the roof of its maternity section.

One of the most unusual bird vanes is the dove weather vane designed by George Washington in 1783 for his Mount Vernon home. Washington's dove holds an olive branch in its beak, symbolic of his intentions.

Washington seems not to have cared if the weather vane worked but only that the symbol of peace be made and displayed. In Washington's letter to his workmen he stated, "The bird need not be large, for I do not expect that it will traverse with the wind." Along with his design, Washington issued instructions for fixing the cardinal points and the painting of his vane symbol.

"The spire must have that (color) of black, the bill of the bird to be black, and the olive branch in the mouth of it must be green . . . Great pains must be taken to fix the points truly; from North, South, West, and East. One way of doing this may be by Compass being placed in a direct north line on the ground at some distance from the House by means of which a plumb line, the point (North) may be exactly placed."

The rooster was not the only medieval symbol used on early American weather vanes. Heraldic banners as weather vane symbols came directly from Europe during the same period. Heraldry is often traced as the root of such transplanted folk art forms as carved eagles, trade signs, and weather vanes. Thirteenth century noblemen carried banners with their family crest or symbol into battle or tournaments. The same banners fluttered from castle turrets or were mounted outside of country inns when these knights traveled. The cloth flag became a metal banner which would traverse with the wind atop churches and buildings, both public and private.

One of the most unusual banner vanes is still in use today, high over Christ Church in Shrewsbury, New Jersey. This banner vane was erected in 1702 and contained a crown over the banner to pay honor to King George II who ruled from 1727 to 1760. This church is now acknowledged to be the only church in America still directly under the British Crown. During the Revolution, all royal symbols came under attack and the Shrewsbury crown was often the target of Colonial sharpshooters. However, eighteenth century muskets were not very accurate and the best the marksmen could do was nick the crown a few times. The crown and banner are still there, a highly prized possession of the congregation of Christ Church.

Americans, once they began moving toward self-rule, turned the imagination of man created wondrous beings never seen by human eyes. One of the most interesting and often repeated vane silhouettes is that of the archangel, Gabriel. This angel has been used in many forms but always in flight and with his eternal trumpet poised for use. Many churches were fond of using Gabriel as their inspirational symbol and reminder of the hereafter.

vane symbol.

The sign of an Indian against the sky does not always mean disaster despite a "bad press" from many writers. True, the early settlers and the Indians did clash, but their disputes were often intensified by Old World countries who were at war with the Colonials or their ruling agents in Canada who used Indians as part of their armed forces. Had it not been for Chief

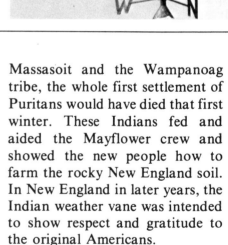

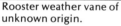
Rooster weather vane of unknown origin.

This weather vane and the one on the right are homemade.

the banner into a patriotic symbol by placing patriotic slogans of Liberty, Justice, Freedom, or Equality upon the flat surface.

Banner weather vanes vary from very simple flat surfaces cut from sheet metal or wood, to very complex series of scrolls, curves, involutes and embellishments. The early American flag and a carved wooden "Columbia," complete with a flag over her shoulder, could be considered the very ultimate in banner vanes.

Symbolism is very real to weather vane designers. The very height at which it is displayed suggests that the vane should be at home next to the sky and wind, soaring in the mysterious unknown. Mythical figures found substance in wood and metal, as

One antique "Gabriel" weather vane achieved national fame as the main motif for a seasonal Christmas stamp in 1965, portraying the idea of "peace on earth" on millions of Christmas cards and letters.

Gabriel was not the only mystical being used as a weather vane symbol. The Roman goddess, Diana, in full figure and standing upon a golden ball, is now on display in the Philadelphia Museum of Art. At one time, this thirteen-foot goddess of the moon, woods and wild creatures stood poised with bow and arrow seeking the ever-present winds from Olympus. A strange figure to rule over an urban fief of steel and brick. However, Diana is more artistic than functional, more a mode of exterior sculpture than a weather

Massasoit and the Wampanoag tribe, the whole first settlement of Puritans would have died that first winter. These Indians fed and aided the Mayflower crew and showed the new people how to farm the rocky New England soil. In New England in later years, the Indian weather vane was intended to show respect and gratitude to the original Americans.

Artistically, the American Indian with bow and arrow lends itself perfectly to the weather vane intention; the poised arrow, ready for flight, points in the direction of prevailing winds.

One of the oldest Indian weather vanes was made by Shem Drowne in 1716. Colonials told their children that this Indian shot his arrow toward the sun every noon, and often small children gathered in front of the Royal Governor's house to see the magic performed. They, of course, were always disappointed. But undaunted, the children would appear another day to stand and watch, just in case.

In modern times, the old Indian weather vane motif has been taken down from its high perch and hung out much like tavern or trade signs. Many archery clubs have used the Indian vane silhouette as their organizational standard.

While all weather vanes have certain appeal, one of early America's favorite vane silhouettes is the huge grasshopper made by Shem Drowne in 1742 for an artistic crown to Faneuil Hall in Boston. Some historians claim this symbol has an heraldic meaning, being connected with the Royal Exchange in England. Other authorities link the grasshopper to an early friendship formed between young Shem and Peter Faneuil, long before Faneuil became a man of means. Whatever the reason, Americans have come to regard this grasshopper as a patriotic symbol; perhaps because Faneuil Hall housed so many Massachusetts patriots before and during the revolution.

When Drowne was making this large weather vane, Boston's youngsters flocked to his small shop to see the "bug" take shape. Sam Adams, then a student, was one such viewer. Folklore has it that Benjamin Franklin, while on a trip to Europe, proved his identity by describing this golden bug, which sat ready to leap across Boston town. This story has been told many times with different important personages in place of Franklin. As with most folk tales, it contains more myth than truth. However, such stories enhance interest in folk art objects. Drowne's hopper was such an object.

Weather vanes, starting with the "Tower of the Winds" in 500 B.C., have always been popular. It doesn't matter if the building is a huge edifice of steel and brick costing millions, or a small single family home. The vane becomes an extension of its owner, projecting his choice and desires as the crowning touch to his building. It becomes a more personal expression when the vane is made by the owner himself.

In modern times, many valuable weather vanes have been moved inside buildings to protect them against theft. The theft of antique weather vanes, apparently a big business, presents a double mystery. First, how are the vanes, located high in the air on scanty rods obtained? Does a daredevil climb the dizzy heights, or does the theft occur by air, via helicopter? Either way, the means and cost involved stretch the imagination. Secondly, what does one do with a large weather vane symbol? Public display is dangerous, and no reliable concern would be connected with stolen property. However, the fact remains that many old vanes have disappeared from their spires, much to the disappointment of owners and viewers alike.

Often a home owner displays a vane symbol as a wall decoration, enjoying its shape, color and uniqueness as an object of art. Small vane symbols are used in clusters.

Weather vanes atop buildings are often ignored until attention is drawn to them. Perhaps the hustle and bustle of living has restricted our view, and we don't turn our eyes upward often enough. In this respect, it is perhaps well that vanes have been moved to the interiors of museums and homes where we are more apt to see these objects which remind us of a time when a man had the desire and took the time to cut and shape a beautiful silhouette whose functional purpose was to tell him what he probably already knew—which way the wind was blowing. [S]

The horse was a very popular model for weather vanes.

The same cloud system that produces hailstorms may develop a vicious tornado like this one approaching a farm home. (Photo, courtesy of the U.S. Air Force Air-Weather Service)

The Beauty and the Beast in a Cumulus Cloud

K. D. Curtis

At first, the cloud was beautiful and serene, displaying all the fluffiness and brilliance of freshly fallen snow. With ever increasing height and full-blown curves, it billowed into the otherwise clear sky. No one suspected it could turn into a brutal killer. To most folks it was only a thunderhead.

Such a cumulus cloud brings great beauty to our skies. But, once altered, it can also bring pounding rain, shredding winds, ear-splitting thunder, arsonous lightning and devastating hail.

Flights into clouds by airplanes specially fitted with complex meteorological and electronic equipment, plus radar studies, have yielded additional facts on the physics of cumulus and storm clouds. Still, there remain mysteries to challenge students of weather.

The cumulus starts life at the top of an almost vertical updraft of moisture-laden, hot air, often generated by a warm summer day. This invisible updraft, called a thermal, is the delight of glider pilots. These thermals boost sailplanes skyward swiftly; and once aloft, these silent craft can zoom merrily from beneath one single cumulus to another. Birds by the thousands also joyride these buoyant thermals; and youngsters' kites fly easily atop them. There is considerable sorcery, however, connected with a cumulus, as meteorologists will explain.

Cumulus clouds can form anywhere. Commonly, in our country, they drift over relatively flat land. "During the warm months in the United States, large areas of warm, maritime tropical air frequently are sucked northward over the Mississippi Valley by a strong Atlantic high pressure region over water at about eighty degrees, which is cooler than the inland soil," explains Robert Fisher, an authority on weather with the U.S. Air Force.

"This moisture-laden air, as it flows over millions of acres of heated inland soil, rises and forms clouds. The Atlantic-centered high may push maritime tropical air as far as the inland Rockies where violent storm clouds may form. In the nearer Appalachian mountains, thunderstorms may also be born."

A main, or centering, cumulus cloud begins building with the birth of a cloud "droplet." This airborne moisture is so minute that it takes a million to create a raindrop. Droplets are so tiny and so light that they are not easily pulled earthward by gravity.

Born at the relatively warm surface level, these invisible cloud droplets move skyward atop thermals being drawn by the cooler air of a high cumulus. As they encounter layers of cooler air, these droplets begin giving off the heat that they acquired on the ground. They condense into a visible vapor —cloud material. This new cloud formation gives off more heat which in turn intensifies the upward air movement (the uplift may reach 6,000 feet per minute). This upward movement sucks up still more moist air from below.

As the cumulus propels dazzling banks of vapor, huge and beautiful, into the azure sky, it becomes a complex structure. Floating along tranquilly, it may transport tons of succoring rain. Or . . . converting itself sneakily into a cumulonimbus formation, it may bludgeon to death thirsty crops with its brutal hailstones.

The cumulus base begins at about 1,600 feet. With every 1,000-foot increase in altitude, the rising air cools about five and one-half degrees. Thus, though the air may register seventy degrees on the ground, at 10,000 feet, inside the newly-born cloud, it may be a chilly thirty-two degrees.

"At 20,000 feet, a frigid zero degrees may exist," meteorologist Fisher explains." And since cumulus clouds may vault upward 30,000 feet or even higher, a so-called supercooled upper region, more intensely cold than zero, is not rare even on a hot summer day."

At these higher altitudes, the air is so supercooled that the now cold updraft is stalled and thwarted. The top of the cumulus

A sailplane (or motorless glider) soars happily, uplifted by benign and safe thermals which have developed these beautiful cumulus clouds. It is only when cumulus formations shift into cumulonimbus that danger of hail and damaging windstorms becomes a possibility. (Photo, courtesy of Schweitzer Aircraft Corp., Elmira, N.Y.)

develops a flat, anvil-shaped, somewhat shredded cap—and a cumulonimbus (or storm cloud) has formed. The nimbus cap on our cumulus contains moisture drops now frozen into ice crystals. Just why these droplets have not frozen earlier, at, say, that 20,000-foot "zero belt," no one knows for sure.

Low, ragged, darker clouds may profane the base, once gleaming and graceful, of the original cumu-lus. Merging with other clouds may occur. The once serene cumulus may now contain turbulent, fast-moving updrafts and downdrafts. Large, swiftly falling raindrops—often formed by the collision with smaller, slower-moving droplets—may become negatively charged with electricity as they plummet towards the cloud base. Those drops sustained near the cloud's crest retain their positive charge. More mysteriously, the negatively charged drops, by their proximity to the ground, induce a positive charge at the earth's surface. Indeed, the ground level now becomes a gigantic electrical condenser or capacitor.

Suddenly a spark arcs between the negatively charged raindrops and the positively charged ground. Lightning has been created. For a dazzling moment, the air is scorched with a bolt of more than 25,000 degrees and the thunder of

The fair weather clouds at left have transformed into the potentially dangerous cumulonimbus formation below. (Photos, courtesy Atmospherics Inc.)

A once beautiful fair-weather cumulus cloud has altered itself. A shredded, cirrus-type formation, frigid with ice crystals, is beginning to form near the top. This may be a prelude to cumulonimbus storm clouds. An automatic rain gauge is nearby to record the amount of rain. (Photo, courtesy J. M. Schaffer & Son, Baltimore, Maryland.)

that awesome thrust is heard.

Now the devil's brew thickens in the highest, supercooled cloud area. Ice crystals may form about dust particles or other sublimation nuclei. In three to five minutes, an ice crystal will grow to .005 inches. It will enlarge by colliding (coalescing) with cloud droplets and fusing. Large raindrops may exist near the base of a "feeder cumulus" (a cloud destined to merge with the main cumulus). These may also become hailstone centers or embryos.

As one writer explains, "the madness that is a swift and violent hailstorm begins with the rise and fall of raindrops within this cumulonimbus thunderstorm as these drops are heaved up and hurled down by interior turbulent currents. As insane vertical blasts (some reach 200 mph) roar inside 'chimney channels' of 200 to 300 yards in diameter, the storm moves horizontally at about 50 mph."

One of these trapped raindrops can shoot ten miles up, and freeze around a core of dust, or it may acquire a layer of snow. Some hailstones have frozen around pebbles, leaves, twigs, nuts and insects sucked up into the clouds by buffeting currents. With slackening current-thrusts, the frozen drop will now descend to another less cold segment where it becomes sodden. Quickly, it is rocketed upward again—and accumulates more ice, grime and snow layers.

This yo-yo action continues until the raindrop becomes a many-layered ball of ice. The new hailstone might be spherical or cone-shaped, or even resemble a spike, a disc, a quartz crystal or a pyramid.

Ultimately, the stone becomes too heavy to be lifted anymore—and it plunges to the ground, a dangerous instrument capable of causing injury and death to anything it hits.

Almost every area within America has experienced part of the annual one-quarter-billion-dollar hail damage. Man is now attempting to tame the maverick cumulus cloud by treating it chemically.

Presently, one hail-suppression theory is that the lower regions of certain cumulonimbus clouds have relatively few "cores" or nuclei, amid an abundance of moisture. Hence, larger-sized "frozen raindrops"—the prelude to large, dangerous hailstones—form.

At around 12,000 feet, or below twenty-five degrees, lies the cloud segment where cloud seeders hopefully inject artificial nuclei (or raindrop "cores") to trigger rain while preventing hail. They know that at 15,000 feet, nucleation will begin naturally and produce whatever precipitation form destined to fall.

The National Center for Atmospheric Research explains the cloud-seeding process: "Seeding this super-moist cloud segment with millions of silver iodide crystals causes smaller frozen drops to form around the crystals. These tiny hailstones melt into beneficial, harmless rain when they fall to the earth."

Perhaps, one day that fluffy, graceful cumulus so high in our peaceful sky will be robbed of its hail producing possibility by mere man. Then, the thing of beauty will remain so. ⑤

Yesterday and Today

Memories are most meaningful when there is pride and dignity in the past, in one's heritage. This pride is felt to a degree in every person; but, perhaps, it is most strongly evident in the lives and customs of country folk. Cultural heritage is an essential ingredient of the country fairs and festivals in nearly all American communities. These events call attention to the time when the family was a self-sufficient body that relied only on a few skilled individuals for outside services. The professions of these rugged craftsmen have been developed, perfected, and maintained through generatons; and the quality of their craftsmanship is unsurpassed in our fully automated society. That this fact is recognized is evident by the nostalgic interest pervading this country, and in the widespread appreciation of antiques. The past intrigues, and the quality of products and life from long ago is impressive because of the pride and dignity in our heritage.

Portrait of an Artist

John Slobodnik

On these pages, COUNTRY SCENE DIGEST is proud to present the works of one of our favorite artists, John Slobodnik. We think John has that rare talent—the ability to capture on canvas all that is warm and good in human nature. His characters are appealing because they are the good people we know today or remember fondly from childhood.

We hope you agree with our assessment of John's artistry and will enjoy a glimpse into his background.

John Slobodnik wanted to be an artist from the time he was able to hold a pencil. At the age of four, he was filling every available scrap of paper with drawings until his mother finally ran out of places to hang them.

As he went through school, teachers were quick to recognize the boy's ability and encourage him to develop his talents. While still a teenager, he decided on a career as an illustrator.

Instead of seeking formal art training, John entered George Williams college near Chicago to pursue a liberal arts degree. In his spare time, he studied the works of great American illustrators such as N.C. Wyeth, A.B. Frost, J.C. Leyendecker and Norman Rockwell, whose influence is apparent in his paintings.

John finds inspiration for his subject matter everywhere. "I love to paint the people around me in the homespun American interest settings in which they actually live," he says.

Much of his work is done from live models. He scours his neighborhood searching out just the right characters for his paintings, much as a movie director looks for the right actor to cast in a role. He has used relatives and sometimes even

Gratitude

The Old-Fashioned Featherbed

himself as a model. Neighborhood dogs and cats have also been immortalized on his canvases.

John uses models for his inanimate subjects as well. Calendars, old butcher's scales, kitchen utensils—all are painted from the actual articles. This often necessitates a trip to the antique shop, but John feels the added air of realism is well worth the trouble.

The end result of these details is a perfectly believable picture. If you find a smile stealing across your face when you look at John's work, don't be surprised— it's a common reaction when you spy the butcher shop where your mother sent you for pork chops, or backstage at your own grade school Christmas play.

But our lasting memories lie with people, and when we turn to his characters,

"The Christmas Program"

"Scoot to the Butcher"

that's when the smile turns to a grin. Maybe they remind us of our own friends and relatives, or even of ourselves as we used to be. We see kindness and humor in the twinkling eye of the comfortably plump grandma making up the old feather-bed. Devout thankfulness as well as anticipation play on the features of a young boy at Thanksgiving grace.

These are the scenes John loves most to record in his paintings, for it is his belief that such little moments add up to great meaning in our lives. "As an illustrator, I want to create an awareness of the apparently unimportant moments in all our lives that can slip by unnoticed, taken for granted."

John Slobodnik is an artist in love with people. Perhaps that is why he paints them so well. He sees no basic difference in the way people were and the way they are today. "Although the clothes we wear and the cars we drive have changed radically since the turn of the century, I believe people are essentially the same on the inside.

"Love is still the greatest force on earth," he says. When we look at his paintings, we have to agree. [S]

The Kutztown Folk Festival

Each year during the week of July 4, the Pennsylvania Dutch hold their eight day Festival at Kutztown, Pennsylvania. The festival was founded thirty years ago by three professors from Franklin and Marshall College in Lancaster for the purpose of perpetuating the customs, folkways and down-to-earth practices of their ancestors. Early development, however, was slow; and for many years it was just a local country fair.

In the early fifties the fair caught the attention of the nation; and city folks—craft enthusiasts, students and countless summer travelers—came in droves, causing problems. Facilities were inadequate; food sometimes ran out; and attractions, such as the craft stalls, were crowded while the people strained to see and hear.

It took persistence, determination and the joint efforts of scholars, craftsmen, artisans, farmers, cooks, demonstrators, teachers, parents, grandparents, and children-growing-up to keep it going and to try for a better Festival each year. It also took the vision and energy of its farsighted manager, a young Pennsylvania Dutch lawyer from Lancaster, to turn the Kutztown Festival into a rewarding experience rich in culture, entertainment and hearty fun.

From every state in the Union, thousands return to Kutztown year after year. Some come to view the hundreds of handmade quilts, others to talk with artisans and craftsmen. Some to watch Amish pageantry, others to eat the good food. Still others come to dance the lively dances on the hoedown stage; but there are always the vast numbers who come to see everything!

One of the Festival's most outstanding attractions is the food. "Cooking for the Lord" occupies the energies and skill of hundreds of the Pennsylvania Dutch. For over a quarter of a century, headquarters for family-style meals has been the Windsor Castle food pavilion. For three generations, families from Zion's United Church of Christ have worked twenty-four hours a day during the Festival's run to give thousands of hungry visitors all they can eat of fried chicken, baked ham, potato filling, string beans, *snitz un knepp* and pot pie.

There are specialty stands, too, sprinkled throughout the thirty-four acres, offering snacks and between-meal pick-ups of shoo-fly pie, fennel cakes, cherry fritters and corn-on-the-cob for those not willing to sit and stuff.

The Festival family is large and composed of warm, giving folks, recognized for the bigness of their hearts, and their devotion to church, family and country. They boil soap, pitch hay, thatch roofs and demonstrate the old culture in chaffing, corn shelling, cider making, vegetable dyeing, quilting, candle-dipping, pottery, fraktur and much more.

Professor Phares Hertzog, who is youthful beyond belief for his ninety-five years, is the "youngster" of the Festival family. In addition to being the snake man who milks his creatures before fascinated

continued

A happy Festival participant displays a quilt she has made.

Children stand in line to shell corn.

Hex signs are a common sight in Pennsylvania. This Pennsylvania Dutch girl adds to the charm of this symbol of her culture.

This expert candle dipper is a popular attraction at the Festival.

Quilts, quilts and more quilts! An amazing display of quilts is usually a part of the festival.

audiences, he also sings in dialect with the Heidelberg Band, does tricks with knots and relates tall tales from his pioneering work with the Boy Scouts of America.

Many other members of the Kutztown Festival Family are distinguished—all in different ways. Three generations of the "bee people" (the Breiningers of Robesonia, Pennsylvania) daily expound on the food, household and medicinal values of beeswax and honey, for centuries a staple on Pennsylvania Dutch farms.

Lester Breininger and his wife, Barbara, are also outstanding potters. Last year the Philadelphia Museum of Art chose as a permanent collection the Breininger's "Combed Dot" redware pattern plates which are fashioned after traditional Pennsylvania German wares of the late eighteenth and nineteenth centuries.

The term Pennsylvania Dutch includes many cultures; and the austere Mennonites, Dunkards and Amish are not the majority, but rather the minority. Actually it's the "Fancy" or "Gay" folks, largely of Reformed and Lutheran upbringing, who make up eighty percent of the Pennsylvania Dutch. Because they are of the world, they are the ones who perpetuate the customs and beliefs of their German ancestors. The Gay Dutch were the ones who organized the Kutztown Festival back in 1949; and through this consuming endeavor over the years, have strengthened and enriched the traditions of their own lives.

Old World traditions blend with those of the New World on the Fourth of July. This is a special day during the Festival as craftsmen, pageant personnel, exhibitors and visitors, led by the Heidelberg Band, parade around the Commons. Thus, they recreate the patriotic celebration as carried out a century ago in every small town and hamlet in the Pennsylvania Dutch country.

Kutztown, said a New York lady visiting the Festival for the fifteenth time last summer, "is a special celebration which takes me back into history and reaffirms my beliefs in the goodness of people and the strength of our Republic."

It's that way for many and, not-the-least, for the Pennsylvania Dutch participants themselves. Ⓖ

Among the many crafts demonstrated at the Festival are handmade brooms, toys, pottery and handpainted plates. The lady in the photo on the middle right is preparing cabbage for sauerkraut, one of the many traditional dishes offered.

Cookie cutters are a popular item and much in demand at the Kutztown Folk Festival.

The Lure of Tinsmithing

Lester Breininger

Speak of "tin" and many people think of something cheap, lowly, or poorly made and disposable—like the 50,000,000,000 tin cans Americans use and throw away each year. Actually one should say "tinplate." Tin by itself is of little use although it is of great value in alloys and plating. Consider this description from a 1798 encyclopedia:

> Tin—Stannum, Jupiter—is an imperfect or base metal distinguished from other metals by the following characters; it is white which verges more to the blue than the silver, the most fusible, the least ductile, unites with most metals but renders most of them very brittle, and has a smell particular to itself, which cannot be described. Tin is beat into fine leaves and may be extended between rollers to a considerable surface. Tin sheet is used in various arts, is commonly about 1/600th of an inch, but can be extended twice as much. Looking glasses are foliated or tinned with this plate.

As very little tin occurs in America and practically none in the east, England happily supplied the colonists with finished tinware. At first sheets of forged charcoal iron were dipped in a vat of molten tin. This gave a very desirable material. Later "tin" is rather flimsy with a very thin coating on steel.

By the early 19th century, numerous native craftsmen were busily engaged in the production of tinware of all types. Since the tin-plated thin iron sheeting was rather strong, easy to manipulate, and light in weight, it became ideal for coffeepots, teapots, kettles, sconces, milk dippers, pudding and cake molds, candle molds, match boxes, measures and funnels. If certain areas required more strength, as in the case of the rims of funnels and some handles, iron wire was imbedded in the piece. Scraps of tinplate often wound up as cookie cutters.

Cartloads of finished tinware were peddled throughout the countryside. The tin peddler and tinker was usually a very welcome visitor as he brought news as well as new kettles and he could mend old ones on the spot.

While hand-crafted coffeepots and cookie cutters—folk art in tin—have been collectible for some time, it is only recently that old tin items of all kinds have hit the fancy of the gatherers of treasures. This new interest of antique collectors has caused the prices of old tin to spiral upwards rapidly, and good pieces and unusual items are getting quite hard to find. So it is that the craftsmen of today are being called upon to repair, copy and reproduce the tinware of the years gone by and revive the art of tinsmithing.

The main job of the old tinsmiths was putting roofs and spouting on houses, porches and barns. In spare time or bad weather they did the "little work" of making household articles, buckets and cans.

Charles Messner, an accomplished tinsmith, was primarily a roofer. While recovering from an injury about a decade ago, he started experimenting with tinsmithing. Using old shop tools including a charcoal stove to heat his coppers, usually mistakenly called soldering irons, he produces a variety of wares including candle molds, teapots, lanterns, cookie cutters, cookie cutters, and more cookie cutters. He has produced about sixty shapes and sizes of these cutters and is still being asked for "that other kind."

Joseph Messersmith, who has worked in stained and leaded glass for more than half a century, made a tin chandelier for a friend. Another friend saw it and, of course, wanted one. Mr. Messersmith, having stated that he had no old tin, soon found an entire old tin roof dumped in his yard. And then the fun started. His specialty is reproduction of lighting devices. Quite a variety of sconces can be seen in his annual display.

Horman Foose is another tinsmith who reproduces antique items. Many of his designs, however, come out of his head. He also does some repairing but finds it is easier to make a new item than repair an old one.

These men can deftly manipulate a plain sheet of tinplate into a useful and decorative object. Of course, each tinsmith's work is quite distinctive and is readily distinguishable from the ware produced by another. ⑤

Tinsmith at work at the Kutztown Folk Festival.

Joseph Messersmith, a lamp maker and noted tinsmith, is one of the Kutztown Folk Festival's outstanding craftsmen.

Robert Bourdon,
Twentieth Century Blacksmith

William C. Davis

If Robert Bourdon had ever known that buying an old flintlock rifle for his collection would lead to his becoming one of the few traditional blacksmiths in the country today, he might have taken up butterflies instead. You see, the gunlock's spring was missing. A simple matter—any gunshop should have a lockspring. But people aren't using flintlocks anymore, and it turned out that springs are even harder to find than good flints. Failing this, Bourdon tried to find someone who would craft a spring for him, just as its predecessor had been handcrafted a century and a half before. Here, too, he was stopped. The only alternative seemed to be to make it himself.

Bourdon had always felt some interest in metalwork, but had neither training nor experience in the trade. On the Pennsylvania farm where he was living in 1947 was a simple blacksmith shop, the kind most people would have turned into a storage shed or playhouse for children. It represented a challenge to the intrepid Bourdon who, working with the tools

he found in it, began to experiment in the forming of his needed lockspring. It took five tries to produce a part for the rifle, but when his trial and error self-training resulted in success, he knew the thrill of working with metals.

Additional projects were suggested by the needs of his hobby and the unceasing demands of his farm equipment, which constantly needed repair. Slowly a variety of tools began to accumulate. Hours of intense study of blacksmithing methods and techniques followed, and soon Bourdon was delving into the specific workings of individual smiths of days gone by, the ways they put their hammer to the iron, and their trademarks. It was not long before the compulsion to have an authentic lockspring lay well submerged in the excitement of what became for Robert Bourdon a way of life.

He looks the part of the blacksmith. Tall, ruggedly handsome, openly friendly, Bourdon, in his leather apron and worn denim shirt, could easily

From the October 1972 issue of EARLY AMERICAN LIFE. Used with permission.

have stepped out of Longfellow, taking a pause from the forge to talk with a passerby. Born in Woodstock, Vermont, sixty years ago, he studied art under a scholarship for three years and then began a career as a graphic artist.

Vermont and his love for skiing called him home in 1949 when he moved to Stowe, Vermont, and bought an old farm in the shadow of Mount Mansfield. His main business was teaching the art of skiing, but his graphic art training eventually led him into photography and writing as the manager of the Mount Mansfield Company County News Bureau. He made several promotional films and wrote two books on ski techniques.

Smithing was still mostly a hobby for Bourdon until the early sixties when he decided to quit the ski business and devote his full time to the anvil. His first catalog was produced in 1964.

In 1968 he was invited to work with Professor Antonio Benetton in Treviso, Italy. Here, working with other European smiths, he gained valuable experience and technique which was not available in America.

Work with wrought iron in the traditional manner has nearly died out except for Robert Bourdon and a few others like him. For one thing, most of what passes on today's market for wrought iron —the beautiful black metalwork on countless thousands of stairs and railings, doorlatches, fireplaces and even sculpture—is actually mild steel. Much cheaper to produce and containing a higher carbon level than wrought iron, mild steel is harder, more prone to rust and more difficult to work. Genuine wrought iron is very scarce. Most of it today is processed in Sweden, and high importation costs make it prohibitively expensive.

Beyond the material itself, the methods of working it—have not changed drastically. The colonial blacksmith strove to turn out as smooth and graceful a product as possible, using his craftsmanship to work out or conceal evidences of hammering. Today, however, and especially in commercially produced wrought iron, the cruder the finish, the more desirable the product. Deep, rough, hammer marks are a part of the art form.

Robert Bourdon, modern blacksmith and artist, in a rare mood of relaxation.

His forge is traditional, but air is forced by an electric blower.

Thumb-press opening is punched on the anvil with a hand punch.

Above: Edges of latch handle are formed on the anvil.
Below: These tongs made by Bourdon are whitesmith work.

Robert Bourdon practices the best of both worlds. Many of his works are copies of traditional iron pieces, and in these he strives to duplicate not only the design but also the finish of the original. Bourdon, however, makes a variety of freehand pieces of his own design; and with these he gives full play to the variety of surface textures that can be achieved with the hammer. He sees in hammer marks a bit of the smith's personality, his attitude toward the iron and his creative instinct. But whatever mode Bourdon employs, traditional or contemporary, he makes sure that his wrought iron products have that touch of unevenness, the almost-but-not-quite-symmetric dimensions, that distinguish hand-wrought pieces from those stamped out by machine.

"Wrought" iron is aptly named. The name stems from an ancient Anglo-Saxon derivative which means, simply stated, "work." And work is the principal ingredient in any forged wrought iron piece. Robert Bourdon uses genuine antique tools collected from various places in Vermont augmented by a vast array of special purpose instruments made, as in any working blacksmith's shop, by the smith himself to answer specific needs. His shop is modern and efficient with the best of twentieth-century improvements added to traditional methods and equipment. He uses coal for forge heat, but blows it with an electric fan. His shop is heated and lighted electrically, a far cry from the dim and drafty workrooms of past ages.

Once the coals are hot, and his iron bar is heated to a light yellow—forging heat—he works fast. Before the iron cools, a single operation must be performed—punching a hole, hammering out a cusp or shaping an edge—and then the piece goes back to the forge to be reheated for the next step. Sometimes a single piece must go back in the fire a dozen times or more, and a relatively simple-looking creation like his "Lima Bean" swivel door latch will take one and one-half hours to make, including the forging of its nails.

Bourdon even makes his own nails in the old manner. They are called five-clout nails, a name that is as graphic as it is descriptive, for five clouts with a hammer are used to form the head—one on each of the four sides and a fifth to form the flat top. He points out that the rest of a two-and-a-half-inch nail takes forty or more blows.

Onion-tip handle with a common door hook.

Bourdon's own home fireplace. The andirons are of simple design with hand-turned spit.

This modern blacksmith designs and makes a wide variety of fine pieces. His chief influences are the traditional patterns of old English and early American smiths, but he is not bound by convention. He devotes a great deal of time to the design and forging of beautiful iron chandeliers, dividing the remainder of his work days among his several other specialties.

His catalog, "Early American Wrought Iron" is no longer in print. Bourdon says, "It was of great help when I was getting started, but I found that it put me in the 'Ye Olde Crafte Shoppe,' stamped-out-iron category. And this is the wrong impression, for everything I make is done by hand in the old manner and has my own particular touch. In other words, I try to make each piece a work of art. Though much of my business is making fine latches and hinges, there are few things that I haven't made at one time or another, including such difficult items as an iron chalice, sculptures, pipe tongs and other whitesmith work."

This is only the beginning, however. Robert Bourdon, like his colonial predecessors, turns out everything in iron that a home may need: weather-vanes, door bolts and knockers, trunk handles, belt buckles, floor lamps, candle holders, table legs, railings and bannisters, kitchen pot hangers, curtain rods and, appropriately enough, hammers and hatchets. Customers are always welcome to visit his shop, now located on Scribner Hill in Wolcott, Vermont. He moved there less than a year ago, built his new shop, and constructed his new antique house, copied in part from the stencil house at the Shelburne Museum in Shelburne, Vermont. Over its living room fireplace hangs the gun which started Bourdon on his smithing career, its lockspring still functional.

Robert Bourdon has been at his forge and anvil for nearly fifteen years now, and for the past six years it has been his sole livelihood. He approaches his work with enthusiasm and respect, combining all of his interests to make an avocation a vocation. He even puts his years as a championship skier to good use, and has turned out a number of widely acclaimed ski sculptures in iron. In his shop in Vermont there still flourishes a piece of early American life that is too good to let pass, and Robert Bourdon is keeping the trust well. ⑤

Coffee Cakes and Quick Breads

Darlene Kronschnabel

This is the time of the year when lots of freshly perked coffee and the aroma of fresh baking makes us feel warm inside. There are certain things that make homemade baking a special country treat. The wonderful fragrance of something baking in the oven and a houseful of family and friends always seem firmly joined in our memory.

No matter what kind of day, sunny and crisp or snowy with blustery winds, coffee cakes and quick breads are welcome. Warm and fragrant, fresh from the oven, they add a sweet touch to breakfast, the kaffeeklatsch, the afternoon coffee break or late night snack. Rich throughout, with fruits, preserves and nuts, they are hard to resist.

Quick and easy preparation and a delicious blend of flavors make the following recipes favorites in any kitchen. Wait till you get a whiff of these tasty homemade treats as they bake. They're made to share with a friend as soon as they pop from the oven.

Serve the streusel-type coffee cakes warm with lots of butter. Spread cream cheese on thin slices of the cherry and cranberry bread. Whatever the variation or whatever the occasion, these homemade coffee cakes and quick breads will always be good to the last crumb.

APPLE CINNAMON COFFEE RING

2 11-oz. cans refrigerated cinnamon Danish
    rolls with raisins
1½ c. (1 large) cooking apples, peeled and grated
½ c. brown sugar, firmly packed
½ c. raisins
¼ t. cinnamon

Generously grease bottom and sides of one 10-inch ring cake pan. Arrange 8 rolls (1 can) cut-side-down in bottom of prepared pan. Combine apples, brown sugar, raisins and cinnamon; spread mixture over rolls. Stagger remaining 8 rolls over apple mixture. Bake at 375° for 30 to 35 minutes until deep golden brown. Immediately loosen edges and invert pan to remove coffee cake; spread with icing. If desired, garnish with chopped nuts. Serve warm. Makes one coffee cake.

Apple Cinnamon Coffee Cake

COCONUT COFFEE CAKE

½ c. light brown sugar	¼ c. soft shortening
2 T. all-purpose flour	1 egg
2 t. cinnamon	½ c. milk
2 T. melted margarine	1½ c. flour
⅔ c. flaked coconut	2 t. baking powder
¾ c. sugar	½ t. salt

Sift dry ingredients. Combine brown sugar, flour, cinnamon, melted margarine and coconut. Set aside. Thoroughly mix together sugar, shortening and egg. Add milk. Add dry ingredients. Spread half of batter in greased and floured 8-inch square pan. Sprinkle with half of the coconut mixture. Add remaining batter, then rest of coconut mixture. Bake at 375° for about 30 minutes. Makes one coffee cake.

Coconut Coffee Cake

CRANBERRY BREAD

1½ c. wheat bran flakes	½ c. chopped nuts
2 c. all-purpose flour	1 egg
1½ t. baking powder	2 T. vegetable oil
½ t. baking soda	1 c. orange juice
½ t. salt	1 c. halved cranberries
1 c. sugar	

In large mixing bowl, stir together wheat bran flakes, flour, baking powder, soda, salt, sugar and nuts. Set aside. In small mixing bowl, beat egg until foamy. Add vegetable oil, orange juice and cranberries. Mix well. Add to dry ingredients, mixing thoroughly. Spread evenly in well greased 9 x 5 x 3-inch loaf pan. Bake in 325° oven about 70 minutes or until wooden toothpick inserted near center comes out clean. Cool 10 minutes. Remove from pan. Cool completely on wire rack. Makes one loaf.

Cranberry Bread

ALMOND REVEILLE CAKE

1½ c. all-purpose flour	2 eggs
2 t. baking powder	1 c. milk
½ t. baking soda	½ t. almond extract
1 t. salt	1 c. rolled oats (quick or
1½ c. sugar	old-fashioned, uncooked)
½ c. butter	Sliced blanched almonds

Sift together flour, baking powder, soda, salt and sugar into bowl. Cut in butter until mixture resembles coarse crumbs. Add eggs, milk and almond extract; mix well. Stir in oats.

Pour batter into 2 greased and floured 8-inch round cake pans. Sprinkle with almonds. Bake in preheated oven (350°) about 25 minutes or until golden brown. Cool on wire rack about 5 minutes; remove from pan. Serve warm. Makes two coffee cakes.

NOTE: To freeze coffee cake, remove from pan and allow to cool to room temperature on wire rack. Wrap in moistureproof material; freeze. To serve coffee cake, unwrap and thaw at room temperature. Reheat in slow oven (300°) 15 to 20 minutes.

HONEY GLAZED CINNAMON RING

2 11-oz. cans refrigerated cinnamon Danish rolls with raisins
⅓ c. sugar
⅓ c. honey
¼ c. nuts, chopped
2 T. butter
½ t. cinnamon
2 T. honey

Generously grease bottom and sides of 10-inch ring cake pan. Arrange 8 rolls (1 can) cut-side-down in bottom of prepared pan. Combine sugar, ⅓ cup honey, nuts, butter, cinnamon and the icing from one can of cinnamon Danish rolls; spread mixture over rolls. Stagger remaining 8 rolls over sugar-honey mixture. Bake at 375° for 30 to 35 minutes until deep golden brown. Immediately loosen edges and invert pan to remove coffee cake. Cool 5 minutes. Combine 2 tablespoons honey and remaining container of icing; drizzle over coffee cake. Serve warm. Makes one coffee cake.

PINEAPPLE CRISP COFFEE CAKE

1½ c. sugar-coated corn flakes	¾ c. sugar
1 T. butter, softened	1 egg
1½ c. sifted all-purpose flour	1 8¼-oz. can crushed
2 t. baking powder	pineapple, well-drained,
½ t. salt	reserving syrup
¼ c. butter	¼ c. flaked coconut

Crush sugar-coated corn flakes to measure ¾ cup. Melt the 1 tablespoon butter in small saucepan over low heat; add sugar-coated corn flakes, stirring until well coated. Set aside for topping.

Sift together flour, baking powder and salt. Set aside. Measure the ¼ cup butter and the sugar into large mixing bowl; beat until well-mixed. Add egg; mix well. Add water, if necessary, to reserved pineapple syrup to measure ½ cup; stir into egg mixture. Add sifted dry ingredients; mix thoroughly. Spread batter evenly in greased 9-inch round cake pan. Sprinkle coconut, pineapple and the cereal mixture evenly over batter, pressing gently into batter. Bake in 350° oven about 50 minutes or until wooden toothpick inserted near center comes out clean. Cool 5 minutes; cut into pie-shaped portions. Serve warm with butter. Makes one coffee cake.

LEMON SPICE COFFEE CAKE

⅓ c. butter	¼ t. nutmeg
¾ c. sugar	¼ t. cinnamon
1 egg	½ c. buttermilk
1½ c. all-purpose flour	½ c. seedless raisins
1½ t. baking powder	1 t. grated lemon rind
½ t. baking soda	¼ c. chopped walnuts
½ t. salt	

Beat butter and sugar together until creamy and fluffy. Beat in egg. Add sifted dry ingredients alternately with buttermilk, mixing well. Fold in raisins, lemon rind and nuts. Spread half the batter in a greased 9-inch square baking pan. Sprinkle with half the topping. Spread with remaining batter and sprinkle on remaining topping. Bake in 350° oven for 40 to 45 minutes. Serve warm. Makes one coffee cake.

CRUMB TOPPING

2 T. butter, melted	¼ t. cinnamon
⅓ c. brown sugar,	Dash salt
firmly packed	¼ c. chopped walnuts
2 T. all-purpose flour	1 t. grated lemon rind
¼ t. nutmeg	

Mix together.

Remember When...

Ann Kilborn Cole

*a glimpse of the age
that made the new antiques*

The thirty-odd years between 1890 and 1925 was a period of slow change. Life in this country at the turn of the century still retained some of the characteristics of the Victorian period, sentimentality, somberness, a sense of propriety and decorum, and even some of the Victorian bad taste. Nevertheless, there were omens of a trend to less formal living. As we passed the century mark, a restlessness began to be felt, and the United States, along with much of the world, no longer felt secure and isolated in a pool of well-being.

In England, the accession of Edward VII to the throne sparked a general loosening up in all fields. It was a happy time in which to be alive, no wars, no taxes, no disturbing ideologies. As the rebellion against Victorian conformity grew, more thought began to be given to convenience, comfort, space and freedom.

It was an anomalous time, in fact an anonymous time, with not enough character to give it a name if we do not adopt the English term, Edwardian, which accounts only for the first ten years of the century. But things in America were happening fast. In a very short span of years, scarcely a generation, we saw the opening of two big links with the rest of the world, the Atlantic Cable and the Panama Canal. The horsecar gave way to the mechanized trolley car and the subway, the automobile arrived, and the telephone came into use in many private homes. The first years of the century saw the home use of electricity, central heating, and indoor plumbing, at least in the cities.

Mother wore a linen duster,
Father used a straight-edged razor
and all the family
sang around the piano in the parlor.

The Bettmann Archive

By 1910, we were enjoying the phonograph, the nickelodeon, the carpet sweeper and silk stockings. In these years, except for the depression of 1907, there was money to spend and new things to spend it on. The rich grew richer and didn't care who knew it. They displayed their wealth in tremendous houses and lavish entertainment. A single ball could cost over $300,000. One social leader, Harry Lehr, gave a sumptuous dinner party for his dog, and Mrs. William K. Vanderbilt gave a dinner for a monkey.

Things accelerated after the depression of 1907. Until 1915 there was a turbulent period of industrialization, with a flood of new things to tempt the courageous buyer. World War I put a stop to much new manufacture, but during the war, and immediately afterward, America broke completely with tradition. Young girls drifted to the offices and manufacturing plants to take the places of men. Many women at home were forced to do more of their own work. Social barriers began to break down. College girls--what few there were-- began to talk about careers and began exploring fields beyond teaching and social work. Quantity rather than quality, unfortunately, was the prize concern of the manufacturer and builder in all lines. Houses were "jerry built" and goods were "ersatz."

Many items that attract today's antique collectors give us clues to the way of life in these transition years. We still valued some kind of formality and propriety. We had not learned to be truly casual in our homelife or in our clothes. Men still wore a variety of hats, and many--not just the politicians--possessed top hats, which were kept in leather hat boxes that you can find in antique shops today. For business, a man chose a derby. Tails were the proper dress for formal occasions; the tuxedo was tolerated only for stag affairs. A man carried as many gimcracks on his watch chain as a woman used to carry on a chatelaine hung from her belt. His beard went, but his mustache remained. He used a straight razor, which he sharpened on a strop--very handy when Junior had to be chastised. Perhaps he kept his personal shaving mug at his barber's, very likely one with his name on it in gold, or with a picture of his trade or profession transfer-printed on it in color.

By 1900 the silhouette of the woman of fashion had entirely changed. The bustle was gone. Balloon sleeves were in; the hourglass figure of the Gibson Girl was the vogue. Shirtwaists, one of the first concessions to the new informality, were adopted with perhaps a high-boned collar and jabot to keep the neck covered. The leg was still a limb, but ankles began to show. Petticoats began to dwindle in number until only one was left, and that likely a

> "By 1900 the silhouette of the woman
> of fashion had entirely changed."

silk one that rustled effectively. Bicycling was popular for women who often wore divided skirts "pour le sport." Schoolgirls wore bloomers and middy blouses for gym classes and that exciting new game of basketball. The flannel or mohair bathing dress of the 90's was out, but the female figure was still well-covered on the beach with stockings and beach shoes for good measure.

For the auto, a woman wore a linen duster and a veil tied down over her hat as protection against the wind and the dust of the road--there were only 144 miles of paved roads in the country in 1900. She never drove a car until the self-starter came in,

Cover of Motor Magazine, May 1919

but she could handle a fashionable electric brougham by moving a single handle. As my delighted mother exclaimed when we acquired an electric car, "Why, I can handle it with my white gloves on!" It was a ladies' car, with fancy glass cornucopia vases for fresh flowers, a luxury for deluxe cars. We kept ours in the old stable back of our city house where my father's faithful old horse, Dolly, and his buggy waited ready for sick calls night and day. The stable also housed a monster, a huge generator that supposedly charged the electric cells of the car. At such times the stable glowed in a blue light and the smell was freshened with ozone. But the generating machine broke down so often that finally the car, the flowers, and my mother's white driving gloves disappeared, as did so many of such innovations in those days.

The sheath gown arrived from Paris in 1908, a daring step forward in style. It was followed by the slit skirt and the hobble skirt that limited locomotion to shuffling, six-inch steps. Short skirts did not reach the knees until the Roaring Twenties. Formal dresses still had trains. Bonnets had given way to hats with brims that grew larger as pompadours grew higher. Girls wore their hair in "puffs" under their beaver hats, which were trimmed with ostrich plumes. There was always a veil caught under the chin and over the hat brim to keep the hair tidy and give a bit of glamour. Fans were still evident at evening affairs, usually of ostrich plumes, lace, or spangled chiffon. (Collectors never overlook these.) Pattern companies were encouraging women to make their own clothes, a threat to the family dressmaker and to the ready-mades that were beginning to fill the shops in regular women's sizes and even in stylish stouts.

Home entertainment in those days was mild in character, with guessing games, lotto, parchesi, and Old Maid to pass the evening hours. Most of these games can be found in antique shops today.

"... it is not going too far to say that there are no bargains in antiques today, early or late."

"Home entertainment in those days was mild in character . . ."

A party was dressed up with much crepe paper, place cards, and favors. Hostesses vied with each other in working out parties with unusual themes.

A few courageous card players forsook hearts and whist for bridge. There was a piano in every parlor and group singing around it. Music companies did a good business with sheet music of the popular songs that are collected avidly by buyers today. Remember "Mary Is a Grand Old Name," "Japanese Sandman," "I Love You Truly," and "Under the Bamboo Tree," and many more catchy enough to be revived today by modern combos?

Well-worn books on the library shelf were those of Edith Wharton, especially her tragic *Ethan Frome* (1911); Richard Harding Davis, the dashing Ian Fleming of his day, whose *Ransom's Folly* appeared in 1902; Finley Peter Dunne's Mr. Dooley stories, and, beloved of the ladies, Temple Bailey, whose books appeared as regularly as the seasons. On the silent screen (the full-length talkies did not come in until 1928) Mary Pickford, Douglas Fairbanks, and Charlie Chaplin delighted audiences in the new movie palaces in the second decade of the 1900's. Movie-goers roared at the antics of Mack Sennett's bathing beauties and

Family listening to phonograph, ca. 1920.

sighed over the daring sex symbol, Rudolf Valentino, in *The Sheik*. The *Castle Walk* introduced a new style of dancing, as well as the boyish figure and cropped hair displayed by Irene Castle.

This is the world from which our new antiques come. Many are still in use in homes, unrecognized as antiques and discarded ones that fill the shops are being gathered up by forward-looking dealers. Ten years ago they would have been found only in the junk or second-hand stores in which the white elephants and trash were dumped at housecleaning time. Today, you are lucky to find "sleepers" or bargains even in junk piles or at rummage sales. These sources have been well combed by antiques hunters. In fact, it is not going too far to say that there are no bargains in antiques today, early or late. Everyone is too well-informed, sellers and buyers alike. The junk shop, in many instances, has moved up in the social scale of merchandising and often announces "Antiques" on its sign.

One good thing about these new antiques is that they are fairly available; they have not been around long enough to have been entirely bought up. Moreover, they were mass produced and put out in quantity; a buyer does not have too much trouble finding what he wants. It is easier to pick up a piece of Limoges china than one of early spatter.

Sometimes buying is motivated by nostalgia. These new antiques are so young that many of us can remember them used in our own homes. "Why, my mother had a blue pitcher exactly like that when I was little. She used it for lemonade. I wonder what became of it," a buyer will murmur wistfully. ⑤

The Bettmann Archive

Such great pleasure in

THE SIMPLE THINGS

A nostalgic view of childhood toys

Bea Bourgeois

Courtesy, State Historical Society of Wisconsin

"But Mom, if you didn't have television, what did you *do*?" Questions like that not only encourage my resident gray hairs to increase and multiply; they also set me to pondering. What, indeed, *did* we do? What kept us amused, entertained and occupied in the thirties and forties? How did we ever manage to wander happily through childhood without "Captain Kangaroo," "Sesame Street" and "the Pink Panther?"

True, there were no Saturday morning cartoons. We did not have sophisticated equipment to record the family's breakfast conversations. We did not have a doll who repeated tinny recorded messages at the pull of a string in her back, nor did our dolls come complete

with boyfriend and luxury jetliner to whisk them to a Caribbean resort.

What most of us did have, though, was a fairly active imagination. Surrounded by adults who had just scratched their way through a crushing depression, we never questioned the slogan, "Use it up, wear it out, make it do, or do without." Our society had a tangible sense of permanence about it, and very few items were disposable. We learned to recycle just about

everything, long before that became the fashionable thing to do.

Our primitive walkie-talkies were not battery operated; instead, they were imaginary telephones made out of empty oatmeal or salt boxes held together with a long piece of string. Our rag dolls were born because Mother had enough material left over after sewing someone's Sunday best. After the mitten supply was completed, we used the excess yarn to make six-inch high dolls, hung lovingly on the Christmas tree. And what delight when the last of the thread slid off sturdy wooden spools so we could have them to make soldiers, or dolls, or whirring moon spinners. The wooden spool, alas, will soon be just another memory.

Apparently we took our pleasures in simple things. A bag of marbles provided an instant variety of games; a jackknife was all we needed to draw a circle in the dirt and challenge a chum to a round of mumbledy-peg. A piece of chalk—or a broken brick—drew a splendid hopscotch diagram; and everybody scooted around to find a smooth, flat stone to use for a "lagger." Indoor boredom was combatted by learning to wind string into a cat's cradle or other intricate patterns on your own two hands. Wooden tops were wound over and over until the color faded, and were spun regularly on the kitchen floor. And we spent hours advancing from ordinary up-and-down yo-yoing to such fancy show-off tricks as walk the dog, rock the baby, or around the world.

As the family finances improved, we were allowed a few more store-bought toys. Yes, it has become a dull cliché to remark "they don't make 'em like they used to," but there's a certain truth there nonetheless. Our dolls were soft and lovable, and they wore white peasant blouses and checked pinafores —made out of real material. How well I remember carefully dressing Shirley Temple in a black velvet coat with matching tam! And Sonja Henie—how I loved changing her elegant fur-trimmed skating costumes! (What fantasies she invoked: there I was, a world-famous figure skater, trapped in a mountain chalet during a blizzard —until dashing John Payne skied to the rescue!)

My special favorites, though, were Storybook Dolls®—little bisque people five or seven inches tall. My mother and sister added to my collection every Christmas or birthday, or as a reward for a successful piano recital. There were

Courtesy, State Historical Society of Wisconsin

Blocks, from the collection of Bob and Bea Bourgeois

Toys, from the collection of Justine Leonard

dolls for each month of the year, dolls fashioned after nursery rhyme folk, dolls who were dressed as Quaker maids or Western girls. Saturday's child, who must work for a living, even had her own straw broom and sensible cotton apron. I doubt that Barbie® in her satin lounging pajamas could ever have such charm.

It seems to me that our toys were made of sturdy stuff and that they had that elusive something called character. One of our delights was a tumbling acrobat, brightly painted, whose hands were joined to a piece of string stretched between two wooden sticks. Squeeze the sticks together, and he did a series of incredibly agile tricks. Today, the same fellow is made of plastic and so are his sticks. He not only lacks character, he breaks.

The automatic clothes dryer has all but eliminated a staple raw material from which many of our toys were made. The humble clothespin could be painted and dressed in fabric scraps; and an entire family, all different, was created. For the adventuresome child, a clothespin doll became a daredevil parachuter simply by tying string to the corners of a handkerchief and attaching it to an eye screw in Mr. Clothespin's head. Dropped from the ledge on the front porch, he blossomed magnificently on his gentle descent to the ground.

I remember spending countless happy hours with a toy named Dancing Dan, a loosely jointed wooden man about ten inches high. Dan had a hole in his back, into which was inserted a slim, metal rod. His only other piece of equipment was a smooth board about a foot long. To make him dance, I sat on a firm chair, slid one end of the board under one thigh, and

A STIFF BREEZE.

tapped the board with one hand while holding Dan's metal rod with the other. He did a fantastic soft-shoe while I sang "Way Down upon the Swanee River" or a clickety tap dance while someone played "Bye, Bye Blackbird" on the upright piano. A modern version of Dancing Dan is still available; but while ours wore a vivid checkered costume and a permanently happy smile, the current item is a faceless piece of plywood.

Mechanical windup toys were eternally fascinating; ours must have had mainsprings made out of some kind of indestructible steel. How many thousands of times did we wind up a favorite furry bunny and watch it hop madly all over the dining table? I seem to remember an entire circus of windup performers: the monkey who held a cymbal in each hand and clanged them noisily until he ran down; the daddy mouse who held his wee mouse child by both hands and, when wound, twirled in a crazy circle

swinging the little one up, down and around; and the clown who rode a unicycle in a dizzy circle without ever falling off.

It is a jarring experience to meander through antique shops and suddenly come upon the very toys my brothers and sister and I played with—surely not *that* many years ago! How I wish I still had our Knapp's electric questioner with its cheerful buzz that signaled a correct answer. And I have seen platoons of lead soldiers now classified as collectibles, if not antiques; I remember what fun it was to melt chunks of lead and pour the molten liquid (*very* carefully) into molds and, after the metal set, to remove a perfectly formed artilleryman or cavalryman.

The Lionel train set we so casually played with would, today, send a collector into raptures. Heavy metal engines—complete with cowcatcher—puffed out steam and cut through the darkness of shoe-box tunnels with their headlights. Behind them followed a grand assortment of metal cars: one with Curtiss Baby Ruth® painted on the side, another carrying real wooden logs to be rolled off onto a log loader, another filled with miniature wooden milk cans which plopped out onto the station platform. Our crossing signals were lighted, as were our Pullman cars, and unwary bystanders were warned by the deliciously mournful whistle as the train approached our town.

I watch my sons glide smoothly around our patio on $18 skateboards (the wheels of which have already been replaced once) and I think of my $2.00 pair of ball-bearing roller skates (which lasted forever). I am impressed at their understanding of that engineering

nightmare, the ten-speed bicycle; and I remember the bike I rode for eight years and passed on to a niece. It boasted wheels, handlebars, a seat, and pedals—nothing more. And I wonder just how much progress has cost us, and whatever happened to simplicity and imagination and outdoor games. How many summer nights did we spend trembling behind a dark tree, listening to a pal count to one hundred by fives, in a suspenseful game of hide-and-go-seek? How many muscles did we strain as the result of an exceptionally talented statuemaker? How often did scruffy kids of assorted sizes call out in excited voices, "Captain, may I?" How come we needed only an empty soup can on the way to school for a superbly noisy session

of kick the can? Is anyone still able to do their sixes in a game of jacks? Whatever happened to those games, anyway?

Praise be, some of the board games have survived. Our sons still enjoy building hotels on St. James Place, the better to ensnare their impoverished brothers as they travel the Monopoly® neighborhoods. The simple checkerboard still sparks the competitive spirit and shouts of "king me!" Maybe future generations will still play Sorry® and Scrabble® and Chinese checkers. Heaven knows they won't be able to pass on their super-duper road-race sets (whose plastic tracks never did fit together properly) because they will be long gone, sold "hardly used" at some forgotten rummage sale. ⑤

Courtesy, State Historical Society of Wisconsin

Fall Splendor

The myriad of autumn colors in the country, criss-crossing hills in golds and oranges is a pleasurable sight. Of all the seasons of the year, autumn is a favorite for many people because it offers cool breezes and a respite from work. It is the time of year when the earth readies itself for winter. It is a time of harvest; apples are ready for picking, some to be used for cider jelly or apple butter; others simply eaten for their crunchy sweetness. Autumn can be a time for a drive in the country to enjoy the landscape or explore the antiques of the area. Color abounds in the country, shouting "Come look at me!"

Golden October

Gladys Taber

Now the road to the village is blazing with color. Every leaf on every tree has a special glory—gold, vermilion, garnet, pale lemon. No two trees are alike, and a few still have green leaves, as if to say good-by to summer in a special way. I have never read any expert information on the variance in color, and no two autumns are quite the same.

As the leaves fall, some countryfolk begin to pile them against the house as a natural insulation against the long cold to come. This practice has come down from our forefathers and prefurnace days. The banked leaves are held in place by a low expanse of wire. Some leaves go on compost piles, some are burned—but not many for leaves are valuable in any season of the year.

In the village store we have an annual discussion as to whether the color is better than last year or not so good. For nobody can really remember just how October looks from year to year. It is never the same. I have watched the giant sugar maples around the house for many years, and the color varies— more gold than scarlet or more scarlet than gold. After the black frost the colors intensify until on rainy days the trees seem to be lighted with their own light.

October brings frosty nights and clear mellow days. The harvest is in, the soup kettle hangs over the open fire, and pumpkins decorate doorways in our valley.

In recent years rain is a constant preoccupation. There is never enough, and, after several days of hard, dark rain, at the market I will hear a farmer say, "Need more rain!"

I have the same well that was dug by the man who built Stillmeadow, in 1690. At least there is no sign of any other well, and this one has the old well house with the cable and cabin, now rusted, that were there in the beginning. The well is spring-fed, and the water is cold and sweet. Nothing drains into it, for it is surrounded by thirty-eight acres of woods and meadow. The water is pumped into the house as a concession to modern times, but it doesn't have far to go because the well is right by the back door. On a hot summer day you can lift the cover and breathe the cold damp air.

A fire burns on the hearth, now that the air has a tang in it. It is a small fire, for the long cold is still some time away. But the children like to pop corn in the old wire corn popper on cool evenings. Occasionally they decide to roast apples on sticks, but they have trouble keeping the apples from falling into the fire.

On cool evenings my dear friend Margaret Stanger drops in to do crossword puzzles with me, for we are both addicts. Her favorite memory is of my saying that I couldn't see what "Cart rouble" could be, and she said, "Well, try 'Car trouble'. " Ever since then she tells me when she's having "cart rouble." We got thoroughly stuck, both of us, on "Twenty-eighth President," which turned out to be "PRINCETON ALUMNUS." We felt this wasn't cricket.

The true song of autumn is the sound of the wild geese going over. Fortunate is the man who sees them—flying in a V as they do. Their cry is exciting and sad, for it is the signature of autumn. I have seen them only a few times, because they go over Stillmeadow very early or very late in the day. My neighbor Joe never misses them and comes to tell me that they have gone over. There is something free and wild in their flight; they belong to the wide skies.

It is time for a last turning out of cupboards while Erma is finishing the preholiday cleaning. Most of us save too many things. I always think of the old lady who had a huge suit box in the attic labeled PIECES OF STRING TOO SHORT TO USE. Sometimes, I think, we save equally useless memories, sad feelings, unhappy experiences. If we save only the shining memories, we are better off. Grievances are not for cherishing but for forgetting, yet I know one or two people who, like the old lady, store the absolutely useless.

I love the hunter's moon, for it is pure magic, riding high in a deep sky. I wish we would never try to land on the moon, for we all need mystery in our lives, and men have been dreaming under the moon since time began. Once we get there and establish stations, the moon will have no wonder for us.

I also feel we have a lot to do on our own small planet. I am glad I can still walk out under the glory of the moon at night and not bother about men landing there from a spaceship. I like the moon as she is, casting shadows on the leaf-strewn lawn. This is what I would wish to share—the beauty of an October night.

At one time, covered bridges
were commonplace in our country, but
in the last 100 years or so, they've all
but vanished. What's their story
and where have they gone?

ANTIQUE BRIDGES

Raymond Schuessler

There's hardly a kid in America who grows up not knowing what a covered bridge is—knowing but not really seeing. There are hundreds of renditions in books, but unless you've hiked or driven pretty extensively, the odds are against your actually seeing one. Thousands of them have either burned, rotted or simply been torn down.

Of the more than 5,574 bridges that once stood, only some 950 remain. Many of these are jealously guarded as monuments to "the growth of the American nation" by historical associations and covered bridge enthusiasts. Local groups, too, protect many. In the state of New Hampshire, the Covered Bridge Association has appointed vigilante committees to keep watch over the remaining fifty-five (of an original 200) bridges.

The Early Days

Though generally associated with an early period in American history, covered bridges did not originate in America. History notes the first such covered structure in 783 B.C. across the Euphrates River in Babylon.

Wooden bridges first became part of the American scene late in the 1700s and early 1800s, developing as pioneers—faced with a shortage of good fording places—constructed bridges by laying poles over fallen logs. As these unprotected structures soon weakened, they added supporting trusses and a roof to help protect them against the weather. Some were built by the community; others were privately built as toll bridges. Churchgoers crossed free on Sundays; a passenger on foot was charged 1 cent; a horse and rider, 4 cents; a cow, 1 cent; and sheep or swine, a half cent.

As time wore on, bridges creaked under the weight of ox-drawn carts when the country was largely wilderness. They clattered beneath the pounding hooves of saddle mounts and wagons. Without them, the West would have been won much more slowly and because of them, railroads penetrated the wilderness more rapidly.

From the January 1972 issue of PASSAGES, Inflight magazine of Northwest Orient Airlines.

Form Follows Function

But why were the bridges covered?

It was not, as one European visitor exclaimed, that "Americans have a quaint custom of building barns atop their bridges." But more as a farmer explained, "For the same reason women wear long skirts—to protect the underpinning." Quite simply, the roof protected the large supporting timbers from the rotting effects of sun and rain. After all, a covered bridge had a life expectancy of eighty years, while one left uncovered lasted only ten.

Covered bridges were practical as well as long-lived. Farmers driving their stock to market normally had trouble persuading cattle to cross open bridges.

When the same bridges were covered, the cattle entered happily, expecting to be fed inside. Allowing no reflection from the water below, the covered structures also cut down on the number of accidents caused from shying horses. It has been suggested too that they were responsible for drawing settlers to towns. There is an old story that claims a traveler didn't know what kind of town he was approaching until he crossed a bridge and then it was too late to turn back. But that is more legend than fact.

The basic principle for construction used with most covered bridges in the U.S. is credited by engineers to Theodore Burr, an American of Torringford, Connecticut, who used it in 1798 (patented in 1817). The same principle, developed in 1570 by

an Italian, Andrea Palladio, seems to have been forgotten and Burr is given credit for its redevelopment. Fundamentally, it is that of the king post truss. The longest timbers are used as diagonals, meeting in the center at the top of the vertical post. The base of the triangle thus formed is longer than available timber and made of two timbers each shorter than the diagonals.

Most of the New York State bridges now standing used the Town Lattice Truss which was patented in 1820 and 1835 by Ithiel Town, an architect of New Haven, Connecticut. It consists of planks joined together with wooden pins in a lattice pattern. Since it used lighter timbers than other styles—and was easier and cheaper to build—it soon became the most popular design.

As with most antiques, the hand-hewn timbers of these bridges are stamped with the personalities of their builders, and some have been standing longer than any nearby resident can remember. One old Pennsylvania Dutch farmer related:

"I can recall my father telling about the bridge builders. They were tradesmen, like wheelwrights. They built floors and sides of hand-chipped hemlock, oak and spruce; and roofs were of hand-rived pine shingles. No iron nails to rust out in those bridges, just wooden trunnels soaked in oil. They worked as long as three years to put up a bridge."

Veiled tales

Aside from being just about the best advertising media of their day, they were frequently the town meeting place as well. Here is an account of one of the last bridges near Cedarburg, Wisconsin.

"It was always a great gathering place. There was a good swimming hole right beneath it in the creek and many is the time we girls changed our clothes in the privacy of that bridge. Town meetings were held under it and ballots were cast there on Election Day. The grove along the creek banks was a popular picnic place. In case of rain, they simply moved the picnic onto the bridge, under the timbers. In wintertime, people used it for skating from and warming themselves. Originally, my mother once told me, people 'pitched in' to help erect the span from trees felled in the area and cut in the sawmills of Cedarburg."

There are numerous sinister tales as well: stories of hangings and highwaymen who lurked in the shadows of windowless darkness to prey on travelers. But there were laws to protect people, just as there were laws requiring towns to "snow" bridges—that is to shovel snow onto the floors of covered bridges for sleighs and sleds.

October

The hills are hazed with lavender;
  I wonder if they know
That soon their golden sides and crests
  Will lie beneath the snow;
And all the little trees will wear
  A crown of snowdrops in their hair.

The farmlands lie serene and still,
  Stripped of their summer spoil;
The golden sunlight of the fall
  Lies on the fallow soil
Like a rich blessing gently laid,
  As lovely as an old brocade.

The cattle browse among the trees,
  Sun-dappled and content,
The hills and trees and little fields
  In one great moment blend,
As if their elements were one,
  Welded together by the sun.

And all the children of the world
  Partake of this rich fare,
Like people at a wedding feast
  With flowers in their hair,
Weaving a song of love and pride
  Around the table of the bride.

Edna Jaques

Rural Living

I'm forever bound to the country scene,
  The rural way of living;
I love the smell of the fresh-turned earth
  And the joy all nature's giving.

I love to climb a snow-covered hill
  And gaze at the beauty below,
While a feeling of awe and tranquillity
  Floods my soul with a rapturous glow.

I love to walk in shaded woods
  And feel the cooling breeze
Softly saying an evening prayer
  As it weaves in and out among trees.

I cannot know what the future holds,
  But I hope that I can glean
From life my allotted time on earth
  As part of the rural scene.

Aileen Roberts Pozzobon

Trumpeter

An early morning trumpeter,
Without a sign of fear,
And stationed high upon a post,
Declares the dawn is near.
This very cocky chanticleer
Now has had his way,
Awakening the whole wide world,
Proclaiming a new day.

Marie Rogers Altpeter

What's Cooking

Darlene Kronschnabel

The fragrance of autumn's fully ripened fruit and their imperial tone can be captured "under glass" as luscious jams and jellies.

Time was, when making jams and jellies was one of the very few ways a homemaker could provide her family with any kind of variety in fruits during long winter months. Now that is all changed. However, the tradition of preserving jams and jellies is still popular. Preparing the fresh, plump juicy fruits is as much fun as eating the jams and jellies.

Nothing tastes quite like homemade jams and jellies. Their rich fruity flavor enhances thick slices of homemade bread and waffles. They are especially good served as a garnish for desserts, filling for jelly rolls, or as an ice cream or cake topping.

The harmony of grape and plum jelly, apricot and plum jam, pear and cranberry jam or ginger and peach jam are only a few homemade innovations. Even the most experienced jam and jelly maker in grandmother's day, might have had problems in improvising such recipes. Today, fruit pectin products take the guesswork out of jam and jelly making when recipes are followed to the letter.

Homemade jams and jellies are wonderful gifts, jelly-red and royal purple, jewels shimmering in crystal jars. Here are nature's fruits to be enjoyed and shared all year around.

CIDER JELLY

4½ c. sugar
4 c. apple cider
1 1¾-oz. box powdered fruit pectin

To make jelly, measure sugar and set aside. Measure cider into a *large* saucepan. Add fruit pectin; mix well. Place over high heat and stir until mixture comes to a hard boil. Immediately add all sugar. Bring to a *full rolling boil* and *boil hard 1 minute,* stirring constantly. Remove from heat, skim off foam with metal spoon, and pour quickly into glasses. Cover at once with ⅛ inch hot paraffin. Yields 5¼ cups or approximately 7 six fluid ounce glasses.

NECTARINE JAM

4½ c. prepared fruit (about 3½ pounds fully ripe nectarines)
2 T. lemon juice (1 lemon)
6 T. sugar
1 1¾-oz. box powdered fruit pectin

To prepare the fruit peel and pit about 3½ pounds nectarines. Grind or chop very fine. Measure 4½ cups into a *large* saucepan. Squeeze the juice from 1 lemon; add 2 table-spoons to fruit. Then make the jam. Measure sugar and set aside. Mix fruit pectin into fruit in saucepan. Place over high heat and stir until mixture comes to a hard boil. Add all sugar immediately and stir. Bring to a *full rolling boil* and *boil hard 1 minute,* stirring constantly. Remove from heat and skim off foam with metal spoon. Then stir and skim for 5 minutes to cool slightly and prevent floating fruit. Quickly ladle into glasses. Cover at once with ⅛ inch hot paraffin.

Yields about 6½ cups of 8 six-ounce glasses.

APRICOT AND PLUM JAM

5 c. prepared fruit (about 2 pounds fully ripe apricots and 1½ pounds fully ripe plums)
7 c. sugar
1 1¾-oz. box powdered fruit pectin
¼ c. water

Prepare the fruit pitting about 2 pounds apricots and 1½ pounds plums; do not peel. Cut into small pieces and grind or chop very fine. Measure 5 cups into a *very large* saucepan.

To make the jam, measure sugar and set aside. Mix fruit pectin and water into fruit in saucepan. Place over high heat and stir until mixture comes to a hard boil. Add all sugar. Bring to a *full rolling boil* and *boil hard 1 minute,* stirring constantly. Remove from heat and skim off foam with metal spoon. Then stir and skim for 5 minutes to cool slightly and to prevent floating fruit. Ladle quickly into glasses. Cover at once with ⅛ inch hot paraffin.

Yields about 8¾ cups or 11 six-ounce glasses.

PEAR AND CRANBERRY JAM

3 c. prepared fruit (about 2 pounds ripe Bartlett pears and 1 pound cranberries)
1 t. grated orange rind
5 c. sugar
¾ c. water
1 1¾-oz. box powdered fruit pectin

Peel, core and finely chop about 2 pounds ripe Bartlett pears. Measure 2 cups into large bowl. Grind about 1 pound cranberries. Measure 1 cup and add to pears. Stir in orange rind; add sugar. Mix well and let stand. Mix water and pectin in small saucepan; bring to boil and boil 1 minute, stirring constantly. Stir into fruit mixture. Continue stirring about 3 minutes. (There will be a few remaining sugar crystals.) Quickly ladle into glasses. Cover at once with tight lids. When jam is set (approximately 24 hours), store in freezer. Jam may be stored in refrigerator if used within 2 to 3 weeks.

Yields about 7 medium size glasses.

PLUM RELISH

3½ c. prepared fruit (about 2 pounds fully ripe plums)
¼ -1 t. *each* cinnamon, cloves, allspice
½ c. vinegar
6½ c. sugar
½ bottle liquid fruit pectin

To prepare the fruit pit about 2 pounds plums; do not peel. Chop very fine, and measure 3½ cups into a *very large* saucepan. Add spices and vinegar. Then make the relish. Thoroughly mix sugar into fruit in saucepan. Place over high heat, bring to a *full rolling boil* and *boil hard 1 minute,* stirring constantly. Remove from heat and stir in fruit pectin immediately. Then stir and skim for 5 minutes to cool slightly and prevent floating fruit. Quickly ladle into glasses. Cover at once with ⅛ inch hot paraffin.

Yields about 8 cups or about 10 six-ounce glasses.

APPLE BUTTER

R. J. McGinnis

There's a great deal more to making apple butter than the cookbooks will tell you. Theirs is a dry mathematical formula, and while butter of a sort can be made by following the recipes, the superior product takes a know-how which cannot be bound into the pages of a book.

Here's the way that Nora Weaver, of Belle Hollow, Tennessee, goes about making her famous apple butter. Mrs. Weaver, called Aunt Nora by all the children in the community, begins on her husband, Ben. On a fall morning, just before the first frost, Ben hitches the team to a bed wagon and with all the kids he can gather up in the neighborhood, drives to the orchard, stopping under each tree. The fallen apples are loaded into the wagon and the kids and Mr. Weaver ride over to the Belle Hollow cider press. The apples are crushed and pressed, and after Mr. Adams, the cider press man, has taken out his toll, the barrel of cider is hauled back to the farm where it is rolled up to the kitchen door and set up on a couple of sawhorses.

A spigot is driven into the barrel and Aunt Nora draws off a bucketful of the fragrant juice. She has already set up the copper kettle in the yard and has a brisk fire going under it.

The kettle is filled with cider and the boiling begins. The cider is boiled down to about half its volume, or until it is about the consistency of thin molasses. It is set aside in a cool place until the next day.

While the cider is boiling, being stirred constantly by Aunt Nora's youngest son, Andrew Jackson Weaver, Aunt Nora and some of the neighbor women are peeling and quartering the apples. Tart or sour apples, or what are known as "cooking" apples, are best because a sweet apple will not cook up. The cores are taken out cleanly. Fallen apples are just as good for butter as choice fruit, provided all the damaged parts are cut away.

After the required amount of apples are prepared (a bushel of apples will make about two gallons of butter) and the cider and spices are on hand, the cooking begins. This is usually started the next morning, early.

The apples are dumped into the kettle with just enough water to start the cooking. Soon after they start to bubble and steam, a small boy is set on a stool within range of the kettle, a long wooden paddle is placed in his hands, and stirring never stops until the butter is finished. A moment's hesitation may result in a scorched taste to the butter.

The quartered apples will cook down considerably. To keep the kettle full, Aunt Nora has a reserve of big pots (enamelware and copper, that is) of apples on the kitchen stove, cooking to the applesauce stage. These are added to keep the kettle full.

After the apples are cooked to the appearance and consistency of ordinary applesauce, the boiled-down cider is added, and then the sugar. A little less than half as much cider as apples is added. If you have four gallons of apples, you add two gallons of cider. The amount of sugar (granulated of course) depends on how sweet you want the butter. For ordinary tastes, four cups of sugar is added to every gallon of butter, but if you have a sweet tooth you add more.

At the same time the sugar is added, the spices go in. Here personal preference is the guide. Most people like cinnamon, so ground cinnamon is added to taste. Aunt Nora's family likes about a teaspoonful to the gallon. Cloves, nutmeg and ginger can be added also if you like those things. The best way to find out how much sugar and spices to add is to dip out a spoonful, spread it around on a saucer to cool, and then taste it.

After the desired flavor has been achieved, keep on boiling the mixture. It will by this time have reached the color of good strong coffee without cream. From here on, it is a matter of getting it to the preferred thickness. Some like it stiff, so that when it is dropped from the spoon, it remains in a little pointed mound; some like it "runny" so that it can be poured. This is how it's preferred for hot biscuits. It makes no difference, it's all apple butter.

After it has reached the point where everybody is satisfied, the kettle is set off the fire for canning.

Standing on a bench near the kettle is a platoon of boiled-out jars made ready to receive the butter. If you are a dyed-in-the-wool apple butter maker, you will be satisfied with nothing less than "crock" jars, each holding a quart, half-gallon, or even a gallon. These jars are hard to find nowadays, but are thought to be just the thing for apple butter, keeping the light from the contents and having some mysterious virtue of adding a supreme touch of flavor. The hot butter is ladled into the jars, a tin cap placed over the top and sealing wax poured around the edge. Don't let the butter cool in the kettle.

Some years, Aunt Nora has made as high as twenty-five gallons of apple butter, although the average yearly consumption of the Weaver family is about twelve gallons. The extra jars are just in case the apple crop fails the next year. ⑤

Country Winter

As the last shriveled leaves of fall drift to the ground on winter's first chilling winds, animals scurry about collecting food and seeking comfortable dens in which to hibernate during the long winter months. Amid nature's hurried preparation for winter's icy grip, country dwellers also prepare for their long stay indoors. Cords of wood must be cut to insure an ample fuel supply for wood stoves and fireplaces. Emphasis on the rigorous outdoor activities of past months shifts to the warm indoors where women calmly sew clothing and articles for additional warmth. The winter months quickly pass; and before the last snowdrifts have melted, sap rises in the maples. Thoughts quickly return to outside activities. Maple sugar is collected during this transitional period and refined into syrup to help provide the day's energy a man must have to cultivate the earth in preparation of spring.

They Warmed the Heart of America

Article and photos by Jacquelyn Peake

Toasting toes at an iron stove.

"Sara, it's here! Go get your brother and sister." Peeping through the snow-frosted panes of the living room windows, the mother's eyes danced with anticipation as she watched her husband and oldest son struggle to unload the 300-pound weight from the bed of their brand-new, green pickup truck. Within seconds she was joined at the window by two more rapt and curious youngsters. They watched the man and boy jockey the heavyweight onto a rented piano dolly, strap it down, and slowly, ever so carefully, roll the unwieldy cargo up the temporary ramp that spanned the front steps, across the porch, and into the living room.

The children stared, fascinated, as their father and brother gently lowered the treasure, a big, old-fashioned parlor stove, into its place of honor in the corner of the room. Like the staunch Victorian matron that it was, the stove immediately assumed command of the room and all therein. Five feet tall, clothed in impeccable black, wearing a glittering collar and an even more imposing crown, it was a dowager of unquestioned substance.

"It's beautiful!" one child whispered in awe. "Even prettier than in the store."

If you can remember Ty Cobb at bat, or Woodrow Wilson as president, or the sinking of the *Titanic*, you might have just such a nostalgic scene in your own memory. The arrival of a new parlor stove was, a few generations ago, a moment of exultant pride for any American family. The happy scene described above didn't occur, though, in a placid turn-of-the-century farmhouse. It happened just this past fall in a suburb of bustling space-age Denver, Colorado.

The new owners of this richly embellished antique stove have joined a growing trend back to the old-fashioned concept of using a wood- or coal-burning stove for home heating. While on a casual Sunday afternoon family outing just the week before, they had come upon this handsome old Round Oak, nickel-and-brass trimmed base burner, circa 1901, at an antique shop. Enchanted with its gleaming dignity and still cringing from a fuel bill of almost a hundred dollars the month before, they bought it on the spot.

With last winter's gas shortages still a painful memory and the cost of commercial fuel rising steadily, thousands of American families are rummaging through Grandma's attic and scouring secondhand stores looking for just such adjunct heating for their homes. One young family reported that they lowered the thermostat to sixty-four degrees after installing their "new" parlor stove. The result was a gas bill of exactly half that of the month before, with an expenditure for coal of only $3.50. In just three months the old stove paid for itself.

In addition, the new owners are discovering a delightful bonus. The gentle warmth of that old potbelly or base burner is decidedly more comfortable on a frigid day than gas or electric heat, and a lot more satisfying to cozy up to than the furnace register. As one retired minister said, "This stove seems to warm me, not just the air around me. I can't explain it but my bones have been warm ever since we got the old stove for the family room."

Of course, the whole thing could be psychological. Just seeing fire makes one feel warm, but as a college professor mused "even so, perusing the spring seed catalogs is a lot more fun when you're toasting your toes on the footrest of a friendly little potbellied stove."

Although their crude stoves couldn't compare with later models for efficiency, even the early Pilgrim settlers knew the pleasure of toasting toes at an iron stove. They brought the knowledge of rudimentary stove construction with them on their arduous journeys across the Atlantic. And some

Below: An Austrian range featuring opulent inserts of colorful porcelain. Right: A Victorian period base burner.

readily identifiable remains of a Dutch stove have been found at the site of a home built in Plymouth, Massachusetts, in 1638.

Those early stoves were crude, six-sided iron boxes usually set on legs beside a fireplace and used to supplement its heat. As time went on, they were improved by the addition of another iron box inside the outer one. This served colonial housewives as an oven for baking breads and cakes.

It took the ingenious brain of Benjamin Franklin, though, sparked by a firewood shortage around Philadelphia in the early 1740s, to come up with the first really original American contribution to home heating. His "Pennsylvania Fireplace," which he refused to patent so that it could be readily and inexpensively manu-

factured by any citizen, set the pace for home heating in this country for over a hundred and fifty years. His iron, open-hearth stove was engineered to be set into the existing opening of a fireplace and utilize the chimney's flue. Its opening was smaller than the original fireplace, so used less wood or coal. It was engineered so that more smoke went up the chimney than into the room and more heat into the room than up the chimney, a common problem with all conventional fireplaces, even today. Thrifty settlers then bricked up the remaining opening to close off any draft, and another of Mr. Franklin's inventions became a part of our heritage.

Few examples of these early stoves are still around. Heavy usage took its toll of most, and historians

know that hundreds of the bulky iron stoves were melted down for shot during the Revolutionary War. So, finding an authentic Pennsylvania Fireplace, or one of its many imitators, is pretty unlikely today.

But, the charming little pot-bellied stoves or the elegant base burners that followed? Ah, that's another story.

With the years of struggle for independence behind it, the new nation began its headlong rush to make up for lost time. Families packed up and headed to the beckoning West, ready to start living the good life that was promised by freedom and a burgeoning economy. Even though they scattered into far-flung communities hundreds and thousands of miles from the industrial East, those foundries and factories were soon able to ship them all the necessities, and many of the luxuries, of daily living through an ever-widening network of canals and railroads.

First on the list of "must haves" for many frontier housewives was a fancy parlor stove, efficient enough to keep her family warm during the harsh Western winters and pretty enough to cause satisfying waves of envy from other women in the neighborhood. She also wanted a good cookstove, one big and sturdy enough to produce three prodigious meals a day for her large family, and quite often for a hungry crew of hardworking cowhands or hired men. To fulfill these demands, foundries began producing stoves by the thousands; and in 1844 the U.S. Patent Office issued more patents for innovative iron stoves and improvements to old ones than for any other item.

Perhaps because they wanted their products to be thought as sturdy and lasting as the mighty oaks that shaded every Victorian village square, many manufacturers included the word "oak" when they christened each new model. There was Round Oak and Estate Oak, Live Oak and Dandy Oak, Artistic Oak and Rochester Oak. Other names reflected the personalities of their designers who almost universally had a taste for the dramatic: Great Majestic, Prominent St. Clair, Home Atlantic, Denver Queen, New Perfection No. 3. And, many carried fanciful slogans, the "commercials" of their day: "If I am good, please tell others about it" and "Kalamazoo, Direct to You!"

By the turn of the century, the 200 or so stove manufacturers in the United States were vying with

This blue porcelain charmer probably warmed some lucky lady's boudoir.

one another to see just whose designers could turn out the most elaborate parlor stoves, lavishing all their skill and whimsy on ever more grandiloquent creations. They embossed, carved, and embellished every conceivable square inch of iron; nickel-plated the broad upper collars and footrests; inserted up to eight doors and a dozen or more opalescent mica windows; then often topped the whole gingerbread concoction off with an elaborate brass finial. No royal wedding cake ever stood so grand!

They made stoves in the shape of Swiss chalets and full-maned lions, stoves with intricate grape arbors draped around the firebox, and stoves that resembled nothing in the world so much as Lilliputian Parthenons, complete with fluted columns and overhanging cornices. How those men must have loved their work!

By the turn of the century Sears, Roebuck and Company of Chicago was warehousing these beauties in some thirteen central shipping points and guaranteed delivery to any railroad station in the country

Even the kitchen range came in for its full share of chrome and ornamentation during the height of the Victorian era.

manufacturer at any price."

For its more thrift minded customers, Sears offered the potbellied stove, admittedly not as elegant as the celestial Sunburst, was, nevertheless, a real bargain at $4.95 for the forty-inch model or $11.25 for the big fifty-six-inch monster. It was guaranteed to "burn anything" and "25¢ to $2.00 will pay the freight to any point within 100 to 1,000 miles from our Newark, Ohio, foundry, according to distance and size of the stove selected." These bulky pig-iron stoves weighed in at a hefty 134 to 319 pounds, too. Even the postage was a bargain!

Even though the hardworking kitchen stove couldn't compete with its glamorous sister in the parlor for radiant splendor, it wasn't neglected by the pattern-makers. Many of those old Queen Atlantics or Home Comforts had every possible surface carved and embellished with fruit garlands, latticework and romantic borders. Some Austrian imports even boasted brilliant porcelain inserts.

Beauty is as beauty does, though, and the housewife of that early day was mostly interested in a cook-stove that was dependable and efficient. She wanted one with a roomy food warmer on top, a copper tank on the side for a constant supply of hot water, a firebox large enough to handle sizable lengths of wood, and an oven big enough to bake a week's supply of bread in a morning. The better models came with an intricate system of dampers so that after the fire was burning well, the cook could adjust one damper and the superheated air would circulate around the oven's walls, giving her even, predictable heat for her baking. Some even had a

"just three or four days from receipt of order." The mammoth 1908 Sears catalog listed one of their best sellers as "Our Acme Sunburst—Double Heating, Self Feeding Base Burner—just $23.95." This glittering creation was, their copywriter rhapsodized, "the very highest type of parlor heating stove . . . with very liberal use of mica (isinglass) and with the enormously large swell, light reflecting nickel plated dome, you get a light effect, an illumination from the fire not approached by any other base burner on the market. The attract-ive pattern and delicate tracery of the silver nickeled ornamented parts and dome, corner ornaments, name plate, draft register, foot rails and leg base are all beautifully nickel plated by our silver nickeling process, polished to the highest degree, and this beautiful finish, with only ordinary care, is practically indestructible. The reflectors above the fire-view doors double and treble the glow of the coals within and flood the room with light." Unblushingly, he concluded, "Such a heating stove has never been offered by any other

Junkyards will often provide a missing part for an old stove.

clever foot lever on the oven door so she could open it when her busy hands were full of pans.

The phrase "energy conservation" was three generations away, but the saving of fuel just came naturally in a time when all wood had to be chopped by hand and all coal hauled into the house by the bucketful.

To warm upper level bedrooms, often unheated in those days of down comforters and long woolen underwear, a pipe was usually attached to the hot-air flue of the big parlor stove and directed at a register in the floor above. Some of the heat that developed from the blazing fire below would then rise to these chilly rooms. When evening prayers were finished in the parlor and the coals burned low, dampers in the big base burner

were then judiciously positioned so heat would continue to rise throughout the night. How many tiny bare feet must have raced in nippy predawn hours to absorb the last vestiges of that warmth while flannel nightshirts were being exchanged for the day's tweed and serge!

If the memory of those days (or the thought of last month's heating bill) is making you long for a cute, little potbellied stove, handsome base burner or sturdy iron range to grace your home, then consider yourself in good company. More efficient than a fireplace and more ecomonical than turning up the thermostat, the old-fashioned wood- and coal-burning stoves of yesterday are right back in style.

Where to find one? Start by haunting the garage sales and auc-

tions in your town. Never pass an old farmhouse without stopping to see if, just possibly, there might not be an old Round Oak or New Perfection stored out back. Ask your neighbors. Who knows? One of them just may have Grandma's pride and joy stored in the attic. Scour every secondhand store within driving distance. These are the places you'll find your stove for very little outlay.

It may not always be in the best condition. There may be a crack or two in the firebox. A leg may be broken or missing. Very likely the grates will be long gone. But, if you find one you like, don't let a small amount of damage stop you from grabbing it up.

Small cracks can be filled with furnace cement. Rust will give way to repeated applications of kerosene, a stiff wire brush and much elbow grease. Missing bolts can be replaced. Rusted nickel can be re-plated, broken mica replaced. Even missing parts can sometimes be located.

One young couple came upon a handsome potbellied stove in a secondhand store, just the perfect touch for their "country kitchen." It was in fine condition except one back leg had been broken off and was missing. Young and full of enthusiasm, they decided to check out the nearby junkyard to see if they could find anything at all that might serve as a replacement. While she was sifting through a pile of scrap iron, offered by the dealer at 4¢ a pound, what did the young wife come upon but the very leg that was missing from their little stove.

Now, admittedly, this sort of luck doesn't happen every day; but junkyards often conceal at least a few old grates, iron doors and stove lids. They may be buried under a layer or two of dead washing machines and rusting bedsprings; but diligent searching will some-times ferret out just the part you need. No luck? See if you can find a local craftsman who works in iron. Many stove parts can be fabricated by someone with the right tools.

Don't want to go to all that trouble? Try the antique shops. You'll pay more for your stove there (anywhere from $100 up, mostly up, depending on its size and rarity) but it will be in working order and you'll be just hours away from a cheery fire in your own home.

If antique value isn't important but you want the comfort, pleasure and economy of a wood-burning stove, then you might consider one of the many excellent reproduc-tions on the market. Several found-ries have begun producing them at reasonable prices, from $150 for a simple Franklin stove up to $1000 for a big six-burner cookstove. A few, such as the Portland Franklin Stove Foundry in Portland, Maine, have even resurrected some of the intricate, old hand-carved castings and are making stoves virtually identical to those Grandma loved so well.

Once you get your stove home, no matter what its age, the only

things you'll need to consider are fuel and upkeep. Coal is available in many parts of the country at reasonable prices, listed in the Yel-low Pages of the telephone book under Coal and Coke Dealers. Wood can be bought already cut and split from dealers, or you can get it for little or nothing if you're willing to do some scrounging. Lumberyards will often let you clean up scraps around the cutting area. Sawmills sell "slabs" (the bark edge cut from logs before they're sawn into lumber) for a few dollars a truckload. Road construction crews often have to uproot trees. These are free for the taking, but get permission from the foreman, anyway.

Upkeep is simple and inexpen-sive. A coating of stove polish once or twice a winter will keep the iron body like new. Nickel and brass polish will do the same for those metals if you're lucky enough to find one of the real old beauties. Mica will eventually darken and break with constant use; so every three to five years you'll need to replace the little windows with new panes cut from sheets available at the hardware store. Just wipe porcelain with a damp cloth and polish cooking surfaces with a wad of newspaper.

We're very fortunate, those of us who live in America, this latter-day empire. We're a new country and our roots are close to the surface, within the memory of so many. Those old iron stoves are part of those roots; one symbol of a simpler day, a quieter time, an hour in our history that perhaps isn't gone at all, just temporarily forgotten in the rush to become great.

Lots of us are reaching back for those roots, too, trying to capture some of the independence and economy, and the strong family unity that once existed here in abun-dance. For many, an old iron stove in the parlor seems to be a good place to start.

Today the stove may arrive in a shiny 1977 green pickup truck in-stead of a horse-drawn wagon, but the lucky family that receives it into home and heart will soon know much of the same warmth and comfort and pride as did their grandparents.

It's kind of nice to think about, isn't it? $\boxed{S}$

THE WINTER WOODPILE

R. J. McGinnis

Elmer and I are a couple of diehards when it comes to sawing wood. Not that we have anything against the chain saw, which can mess up enough wood in a day to last you a year. We both admit the chain saw is a great invention, and a boon to loggers, but we like sawing wood by hand, the way people like to fish or hunt, and we have plenty of time, both of us. No one is pushing us, and we like to talk while we saw wood. With a chain saw you can't hear your own voice, let alone the other fellow's.

Shuttling rhythmically between us, our saw hums a drowsy, rocking lullaby. The clearers rake away the sawdust and winnow it out into neat little piles. The whole of nature murmurs with our saw. All about us the air teems with myriad insects, mesmerized by the warm, yellow sunlight. And the foliage is at its height, with the stands of dark-green spruces among the riotous maple colors, suggesting the presence within of dreamlike palaces.

"Best time o' year to saw your wood." Elmer's nasal twang blends with the thrumming of the saw. "Fell your trees and limb 'em while the sap's still in the leaves. Then the logs saw better and your wood dries faster." Little capsules of folk knowledge transmitted by Green Mountain kin survive in Elmer.

If it hadn't been for sawing wood by hand, I would never have come to know Elmer as well as I do. For years now Elmer has been helping me saw my winter wood. I say help, but it really is the other way around. Though I pay Elmer and board him (Elmer will not work for you unless you board and lodge him), he is the boss, the officiating high priest of these autumnal rites. Out of the maple, beech, yellow-birch and black-cherry logs snaked in the yard in front of the wood-shed, Elmer and I make music, with a crosscut saw as our only instrument, aided by a few saw-wedges, a couple of axes, a light sledge, and two flat files.

The yellow-birch log we're now bucking shivers

and causes the saw to shiver with it. For some reason the two smaller logs resting against it do not seem to hold it in place. We cannot maintain the needed coordination between muscle and metal which is the essence of enjoyable sawing.

"Restless, she is," Elmer mutters churlishly. Without straightening his body he reaches for the ax and slivers off a small wedge from a nearby log. This he "shims" in between the log and the skid nearest the thick end.

The saw takes up its happy song again. Yellow birch saws easier than maple and the unimpeded saw takes greedy bites out of the less resisting wood. There's an easy, effortless swing to the arm, but the sawing lacks the finer-grained, cleaner cut of maple. Still the sawyer's enjoyment is not diminished, for yellow birch is not gushy like balsam, which stifles the saw with pulpy, excelsior-like sawdust and waxes it with its gummy bark.

Sawing wood hasn't hurt Elmer any. On the shady side of seventy, he is ageless. Somewhere between fifty and sixty he got cast into a mold that still retains its form and hardness. He lives alone, raising potatoes, beans, pumpkins, sugaring a little, berrying in season, water-witching for summer folk, linin' bees in the fall, and sawing wood, not so much now as he used to, but still preferring that to any other chore.

With his country-wise counsel Elmer has saved me no end of trouble. But I always ask for his advice. Unless you ask, he will let you make a fool of yourself and say nothing. He will let you dig a springline up a rocky hillside to a spring he knows will run out the first dry spell. And when you ask him why he didn't warn you, he'll say, "You didn't ask me."

Even when you ask, Elmer presumes not to instruct you. "If it were mine, I'd do thus and so." Or he will direct your attention to the ways of nature, or to

Providence, or to the Lord Himself, as when I asked him whether I should seed my lawn in the fall or in the spring. Elmer thought a moment and then replied, "Well, now, when does the good Lord do His seedin'?"

"In the fall, isn't it?"
"Well, He ain't no fool."

Elmer is a living link of life as it was lived up here a hundred years ago. Tractors roar up and down the countryside; bulldozers uproot trees and level off mounds, changing the contour of the old familiar landscape; monstrous balers clatter over mowings and scoop up windrows with incredible speed, flicking the hay out in concentrated packages. Chain saws drone in the woods with the noise of airplane propellers; red oil trucks pull up into backyards and in a matter of minutes pump a month's heat into a drum buried in the earth.

In the midst of it all, with calm imperviousness, and enviable serenity, Elmer lives the old life, a life of absolute self-reliance and self-dependence. His chores, his heating and cooking arrangements, his water supply, the entire pattern of his life, or any part of it, cannot be disrupted by a dead spark plug, a dead battery, by blown-out fuses or transformers or condensers, by frozen pipes, by the tyranny of dripping faucets, or the whims of plumbers, mechanics, electricians. Elmer has never surrendered, even partially, reliance on his own ingenuity and ability to handle matters in his own individualistic way. He has never given up the humanly possible for the mechanically and electrodynamically uncertain.

Frugality is ingrained in Elmer. He wastes nothing, least of all the movements of his body. He is sparing with his gestures, sparing with the twitching of his face muscles. When he laughs only his throat laughs. His face and eyes never smile. The strokes of his ax are clean and precise, the bit striking where it's meant to. He draws the saw in his direction just so much and no more, and then releases it to me.

Each succeeding morning, as we near the end of our wood sawing, the air gets chillier. The frosty grass crackles underfoot, and the insect world is benumbed. But as the sun swims out from behind the spruce-crested ridge and throws its diaphanous mantle about us, we can hear the rustle of the earth as it stirs from its shallow lethargy. Bees and wasps begin to drone in the air, and to dart toward the house, where they hover and drum against the windowpanes, searching for cracks to crawl into winter quarters. The drumming sound of a partridge comes from the sugar lot; the sharp, reedy call of a blue jay flying abovehead has the sound of winter in it, as have the querulous, witch-like imprecations of a flock of crows chasing a hen hawk above the pasture.

Let it come. The huge pile of bucked-up hardwood drying in the sun is a comforting sight. There's reassurance in every block. I can feel the hardness and substance of the wood, the concentration of heat in it, the warmth against the stubbornness of a Vermont winter. When you saw wood year after year, the way Elmer and I do, and burn it to cook with and to warm your house, you become familiar with the temperaments, characteristics, and qualities of different woods. You come to know them by grain and bark, by their degree of hardness, by the way they burn and saw and split, and the scents they give forth as they burn. You come to feel about woods as you do about people, and you treat them accordingly. You do not have the respect for the hard-splitting, quick-burning yellow birch that you have for the clean-splitting, longer-lasting maple. Still you are indulgent with yellow birch because it is a generous, friendly wood; it will burn for you green when you are all out of dry wood. As for beech, it is good, clean wood, saws well, splits neatly, and burns brightly when dry. But there's something prosaic, plebeian about beech. It lacks the high nobility of maple and oak, or the impulsiveness of yellow birch.

"Well," says Elmer as the last block topples off, "you've got wood enough to burn." He takes a long, slow pull on his old pipe and blows a cloud of smoke into the brisk autumn air. The smoke smells more like sawdust than tobacco—that would be Elmer. ⑤

Corn drying racks secured to a tree allow climbing animals easy access to dried corn.

BACKYARD WILDLIFE HAVENS

Article and photos by George H. Harrison

The snow was falling heavily as I watched a cardinal crack a sunflower seed at our patio bird-feeding station. It was December, and I knew we were in for a good snowfall by the way the birds were behaving. Since about eleven that morning, a big flock of birds had been feeding like Christmas shoppers hurrying to get home before the storm.

We know a lot about what is happening in the outside world merely by watching our birds. We know, for example, when spring is coming by the changes in the male goldfinches' drab winter plumage to bright yellow and black. Another sure sign of spring is the tender way "Big Red" feeds Madame Cardinal in a gesture of courtship. We know that autumn is approaching when we see the first juncos at our feeders. We can even tell what week of the spring or fall it is by the arrival of certain migrating songbirds and waterfowl. The dates of their appearances vary only a few days from one year to the next.

My wife and I are bird watchers of the first order, but these days bird watching is "in." The sales of birdseed, feeders, books and binoculars have increased dramatically. I know state governors, telephone linemen, dentists and real estate salesmen who watch birds even while they are on the job.

The fastest growing form of bird watching is the backyard variety. More and more people are discovering how easy it is to attract birds and other wildlife to their patios, back porches or other places around their homes by setting out feeders and by planting natural food and cover.

We have been backyard bird watchers for a long time, but it didn't become a part of our everyday lives until we built an addition onto our home. The large thermopane windows look out onto a patio feeding station and a lake beyond. Now, the birds are with us or we are with them from the moment we awake until dark. Sometimes even after dark . . . like the New Year's Eve we had a screech owl peer in at us from the top of our birdbath.

Once the birds began coming to our feeders, we could watch them anytime we were near the patio. In fact, we find ourselves watching our 6- x 20-foot television screen to nature far more than our conventional table model.

The habits of our bird visitors are fascinating to observe. One snowy morning last December, as I was watching a chickadee eat a sunflower seed, it occurred to me that each species has its own way of

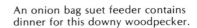
An onion bag suet feeder contains dinner for this downy woodpecker.

opening and eating the same kind of seed. The chickadee was the fastest. Darting in from the woods, he snatched a sunflower seed from the feeder, flipped up to a nearby tree branch and placed it between his tiny black feet to hold it. Then he hammered the shell with his sharp black bill until it opened. I counted fifteen strikes at the seed before the shell broke and surrendered the meat.

The neighborhood bully, the blue jay, came in next and swallowed a dozen or more unshelled sunflower seeds before leaving. I suspect that he coughed them up later for cracking and eating.

The nuthatch speared a sun-flower seed and then wedged it into the bark of a nearby tree. With the seed tightly locked in, the nuthatch struck the shell with his long bill until the treasure inside was his.

The cardinal attacked sunflower seeds in a totally different way. Standing in place at the feeders, "Big Red" rotated the seed in his heavy nutcracker-like bill until it was ready for the squeeze that crushed the shell and released the goodies.

The sunflower seed episode was just one of many fascinating and rewarding experiences we have had watching from the warm side of the glass.

A feeding station like ours is easy to set up almost anywhere, regard-less of where you live. Though the ideal situation is a patio or back porch surrounded by trees and shrubs, apartment dwellers with a window can also have a successful feeding station. Food is the essential item, and birds and other wildlife will come to an apartment window box as quickly as to an elaborate backyard display.

The four most popular kinds of wild bird foods are sunflower seeds, wild bird seed mixture, thistle seed and beef suet. (Thistle seed, a tiny and shiny black seed from Africa, is the newest food to become popular.) Though these four kinds are the ones most often used, I know people who put out peanuts, peanut butter, pecans, bacon, oranges, sweet rolls and donuts, dog and cat foods and much more.

Bird seed is available in most hardware, lawn and garden centers and grocery stores. Because it is the most expensive item in operating our feeding station, we shop around before buying. We have found that buying both sunflower seeds and wild bird seed mixture in fifty-pound bags saves considerable money. I buy thistle seed from a lawn and garden center in ten-pound quantities for sixty-nine cents a pound. Beef suet is available from your friendly butcher, and if he really is a friend, it will be free.

The questions most often asked are what kind of feeders to use and where to put them. There seem to be at least four levels where feeders can be placed in any backyard: on the ground, tabletop, on tree trunks and overhead.

The *ground feeders* in the North-eastern, Central Atlantic and Mid-western states attract cardinals, juncos, sparrows, blackbirds, jays, doves and, if you are lucky, phea-sants. Species will vary in other

Top Left: A feeder of wire mesh filled with suet is found by a hungry downy woodpecker.

Top right: Coat hangers, bent and secured at the top, form a feeder that can be easily filled with suet.

Opposite: Here is a feeder made from hubcaps. A black-capped chickadee cracks a seed on the feeder's edge.

A visiting squirrel snacking on sunflower seeds.

parts of the United States. These birds will eat from off the bare ground if you don't want to use a feeder. However, we use a log slab with a depression on the top for holding the seed. I found this natural feeder lying in the woods. We also use an old metal tray and a wicker basket as ground feeders.

The *tabletop feeders* are for finches, cardinals, chickadees, titmice, sparrows, evening grosbeaks, jays and juncos. In the winter, we convert our picnic table into a platform for holding trays, baskets and several wooden feeders with glass sides to show when the seed supply is getting low.

The *tree-trunk feeders* are primarily suet bags for woodpeckers, nuthatches, brown creepers and any other species which has a need for this insect substitute. A friend of ours built a simple suet basket using large-mesh hardware cloth for the sides and a plastic coffee can lid for the bottom. A small wooden dowel acts as a perch. The simplest suet holder, however, is a discarded mesh bag such as those in which onions are sold. Still another kind of tree-trunk feeder is a corn drying rack with cobs of corn skewered on the points. Chipmunks and squirrels love it.

Hanging feeders are primarily seed containers suspended from tree branches, the eaves of the house, or even the rain gutter over a window. More agile birds, such as titmice, chickadees, finches and siskins, use this type. Thistle seed feeders are the newest addition to the line of commercial hanging feeders. Some thistle seed feeders are hanging cylinders with tiny holes for access to the seed. A thistle seed sock is also available. It is made of fine nylon mesh which allows the birds to cling to the bag while they feed. Once the goldfinches discover thistle seed, they will stay with you forever.

Forever includes through the summer months. Most people who have bird feeding stations stop feeding in spring and resume in the fall. True, it is hardest for wildlife to find food during the winter, but much is missed if the feeding station is not maintained, at least on a small scale, throughout the warm months as well. We have had some of our best experiences in summer, when the adults bring in their youngsters. Last summer we had a family of seven chickadees at the staion.

On other days, we saw five nuthatches, four downy woodpeckers and five hairy woodpeckers. The cardinals, robins, goldfinches, song sparrows and red-headed woodpeckers all brought in their young last summer. What a delight!

Squirrels escort their youngsters to our feeders, too. In fact, I believe that every gray squirrel within a quarter mile of our house visits us daily throughout the year. During warmer months, we also have red squirrels and chipmunks. Some people try to keep squirrels away because squirrels often discourage birds from feeding. But we have enough feeders for every species and we get a great deal of pleasure from our squirrels, in spite of the gluttonous habits of the chipmunks. I know that one pair of chipmunks alone carried close to one hundred pounds of wild bird seed mixture to their underground home last fall. The gray squirrels, at least, eat the seeds at the feeders.

We also have night visitors. By the light of the full moon, we have seen cottontail rabbits and oppossums eating at the ground feeders.

Our success is not based solely on the food we put out, though food is the most important element. The best feeding station operation combines feeders with natural food and cover. Our patio is surrounded by trees and shrubs which provide cover and some fruits and berries. New research findings at Amherst University in Massachusetts have revealed simple and inexpensive steps for converting the most sterile of suburban backyards into an ideal wildlife habitat. A free pamphlet telling what to plant, where and when, is available from the National Wildlife Federation, 1412 Sixteenth Street N.W., Washington, D.C. 20036.

The Amherst study included the important role of water in the backyard wildlife habitat. When we built our patio, we included a small, recirculating, three-tiered pond which runs all year. During the

A dispute takes place
over the right to eat first.

coldest months, we use a cattle trough heater to keep the water from freezing. Even on the coldest days, we often have birds and squirrels drinking often. The open, running water is very attractive not only when all other water is frozen but also through spring and fall migration periods and on hot summer days. We attract nearly as much wildlife with our water as we do with the food we offer. Although any kind of birdbath or pond will work, the sound of water tumbling down over two spillways is a magnetic attraction to many passing birds.

Having wildlife around our home throughout the year has been very rewarding to us. On hectic days when our nerves are frayed, or on days when we have had disappointments of one kind or another, the feeding station always has a calming effect. To merely sit and watch the fascinating show of wildlings helps put our own lives back in proper perspective.

Now you can build a wildlife refuge in your backyard and have it certified by the National Wildlife Federation.

The Federation has created a program to promote the transformation of yards and gardens into sources of food, water and shelter for wildlife.

The new program is called the Backyard Habitat Program. Since it began in 1973, more than four hundred backyards throughout the country have been certified.

Information about the program and applications for certification can be obtained free of charge from the Federation's Dept. BY'76 1412 16th St. N.W., Washington, D.C. 20036

*"Just four walls so I can get in
out of the rain."*

Log Cabins...A Return to Rustic Living

Beth Huwiler

Let me tell you about my grandfather's log cabin. Although he built a log house, Grandpa was not an impoverished pioneer nor an Abe Lincoln. He was born in town and grew up to be a minister. He was never rich, but his family always had a sturdy city house to live in. He doesn't fit most people's image of a log-cabin dweller. But then, these rustic dwellings have come a long way since pioneers first built them.

The first log cabins were wilderness homes. In the years of the American frontier, as settlers moved west they built homes from whatever building materials were available. Because much of the land was forest, which had to be cleared before crops could be planted, the most convenient building material was wood. And since the settlers were usually in a hurry to finish their homes, they often built log cabins.

These makeshift dwellings were quickly erected. Trees of fairly uniform diameter were chopped and stripped of branches. The ends of the logs were chinked and then laid in crisscross fashion, the chinks meeting in the corners. Moss stuffed between the logs kept out drafts, and stones cleared from the land were often used to make fireplaces. With a hole for a door and others for windows, the cabin was complete.

As the years passed, log cabins fell out of favor. City dwellers found sawed lumber easy to acquire—and often cheaper than whole logs. As Americans became more sophisticated, they disdained their ancestors' cabins as primitive, old-fashioned symbols of poverty.

A few log cabins were built all along, though, primarily in wilderness areas. And in the past generation or so, as more people have built vacation homes and as respect for the homespun symbols of our American heritage has increased, log cabins have known a revival. And this revival is where my grandfather came in.

Besides being a preacher, Grandpa was a fisherman. There was nothing he loved better than getting away for a few days to sit on the banks of a lake and watch the Northern pike get away. During World War II, when Grandpa was in his fifties, he inherited some money from his parents' estate. And although Grandma tells me he protested, I don't think he really minded a bit when she suggested, "Why don't you take the money and buy some land near a lake, so you'll always have a place to fish?"

The land was a small lot on a lake about thirty miles from town. Grandpa found his midweek fishing expeditions delightful—so delightful, in fact, that after a few years he decided that he needed a shack on the land. "Nothing fancy," he insisted. "Just four walls so I can get in out of the rain."

"... nothing too fancy."

But Grandma again prevailed. The children were growing up and two daughters had already married. What they needed, she thought, was a cottage where the children and their families could spend vacations. Where they could all gather for reunions. "But," she agreed, "nothing too fancy."

Being a preacher meant that Grandpa never earned a great deal of money, but it also meant that members of the congregation frequently offered to help out—with goods or services. And when the word spread that Pastor Jeske was building a vacation home, an old German carpenter in the congregation came to visit. "I've just finished work on a hunting lodge," he said. "Come with me and take a look at it. If you like the style, I'll match it for your cottage."

The lodge was built of half-logs, inside and out, but they were vertical, while old-fashioned log cabins used horizontally placed logs. And on the interior, the logs were hand-chiseled to meet the floorboards. As soon as the family members saw the lodge, they fell in love with it.

Now came the time for compromises between Grandpa's fishing shanty and Grandma's vacation cottage. "We'll need a bedroom," Grandma said, and Grandpa grudgingly agreed. But two? "Well, all right." Adding a kitchen was "getting fancy," but then, they would want to stay at the cottage for more than a few hours, and certainly they couldn't go out to eat. As for a bathroom, Grandpa agreed that he didn't want to settle for outhouses. And yes, you needed a sink to wash your hands. But a shower? Preposterous! "After all," he said, "that's what the lake is for."

Then there was the matter of the fireplace. Central heating was out of the question. But when Gramps saw what a fireplace would cost, he almost put his foot down. Still, he might want to go ice fishing in winter, and if he did he'd certainly need to warm up ... and so Gramps agreed to a stone fireplace.

The building of the cabin was directed by the German carpenter, but it was a family affair. Grandpa bought whole cedar logs

with the inner bark still attached. The carpenter sawed them to the proper length and showed the family how to scrape off the bark. Then he chiseled the ends. When a number of logs were finished, a wall would be begun. Because the logs varied in size, it was impossible to determine how many would be needed. So the carpenter would saw and chisel some more, and the family would begin scraping again, doing their best to keep up with him.

When the walls were finished, an old-time log cabin was nearly done. But the family cabin was not. With his son John, Grandpa laid the floor from what flooring lumber he could get. (Wood was still scarce, although by this time the war had ended.) The ceiling was made of composition board, held together by thin wooden slats, as were the kitchen and bedroom walls—the living-dining room was finished with logs inside and out. And there were innumerable finishing touches, from windowsills to curtains.

During the thirty years since Grandpa's cabin was finished, more people have come to recognize the natural beauty and rustic charm of log cabins. If you would like to build one yourself, you can find information at your local library. It is possible to buy plans and even kits for log cabins.

Traditional horizontal log cabins are the easiest to build. But it is impossible to insulate this kind of cabin and keep the natural beauty of the logs inside and out. If you live in a climate that is temperate year-round, you may find this the best kind of vacation home to build.

Vertical log cabins are easily adapted to use with modern insulating techniques. They ordinarily use half-logs rather than whole ones. With one row of half-logs for the outside wall and another for the inside wall, it is easy to add insulation between them.

No matter what kind of log cabin you choose, it will provide years of enjoyment—even if you don't have an old German carpenter to help you build it. These cabins will make perfect homes for leisurely country living. For as Grandpa would say, they're "not too fancy." Ⓢ

Silent Sentries of the Skyline

Patricia Pingry

Drive through the countryside and observe the untold miles of fences and walls which snake across and march around the yards, the farms, the forbidden and, thus, foreboding land. They are of all materials and colors, they guard and defend all matter of wealth, and they provide and protect all sorts of privacy. Robert Frost declared "something there is that does not love a wall: but his neighbor replied "good fences make good neighbors." The truth is, fences, when designed to keep us in are loathsome, bothersome eyesores; but when they are constructed to keep what we fear out, they are quite all right.

The word fence is from the Latin *fendere*, to ward off, to protect. Traditionally fences or walls (functionally identical) were used for defense. The Great Wall of China was built to keep out invading hoards of Mongols. Hadrian's wall of northern England was the same type of wall, only it was for defense against the enemies from the Scandinavian area of Europe who once looked across the North Sea with malice and envy.

Walls have occasionally possessed a flair for dramatic beginnings, as when the Berlin Wall was erected during a long game of nerves between powerful countries. As for dramatic endings, none can compare with the miraculous demise of the walls of Jericho. It only took seven days of marching, the blowing of trumpets, and a mighty shout for those walls to "come tumblin' down."

In the early days of this country, fences and walls were erected as enclosures for protection. They guarded against Indian attacks, as in the case of the forts and stockades; they protected farmers' crops against hungry animals; and they prevented the domestic animals from wandering away or from attacks by predators.

The fence was often the first thing built by the settlers and pioneers, after the house, of course. Before the farmer had time to build a barn, he often had a crop of both grain and hay. He could harvest it, stacking the grain in the field, piling the hay where it was cut, then just build a fence around them both to keep the cattle out.

The type of fence built depended on the land itself. Farmers built fences from whatever material was surplus. In New England, stones had to be removed from the field before planting; so the farmer simply used these stones, piling them up as a barrier around his fields. These are now the famous and often photographed stone walls of New England.

Because these walls have stood since the first days of settlement in this region, they are of historical interest. They also, however, stood as concrete reminders to the farmer of his own history. John Burroughs, in *Signs and Seasons,* tells of a farmer whose stone wall stood for his family's past.

"An old farmer will walk with you through his fields and say 'This wall I built at such and such a time, or the first year I came on the farm, or when I owned such and such a span of horses,' indicating a period thirty, forty, or fifty years back. 'This other, we built the summer so and so worked for me' and he relates some incident, or mishap, or comical adventures that the memory calls up. Every line of fence has a history; the mark of his plow or his crowbar is upon the stones; the sweat of his early manhood

put them in place."

Farther down the Atlantic coast, however, there were no stones to be cleared. There, wood was plentiful, and forests stretched for miles and miles. These trees had to be cleared from the land before the farms could be planted. What logs were not used for cabins and barns formed zigzag boundaries along the farmers' land. As far west as the Colorado River of Texas these "worm" or "stake-and-rider," or more commonly known "split-rail" fences, snaked across the land. These fences, while useful, easy to build and attractive, required continual care.

Split-rail fences fell victim to the weather occasionally and to man constantly. Southern steamboat captains had a ready source of firewood for the boat's furnaces. They simply tied up at the dock and sent their workers out to gather split rails.

In addition to steamboat captains, soldiers also dismantled the fences. During the Civil War, dry rails which had stood for centuries provided an abundant and ready firewood for the Yankees. Eighty thousand of the rails were burned at only one plantation in Spotsylvania, Virginia. The Union army burned rail fences to such an extent that the lack of fences began to affect the Southern army's food supplies.

Soldiers of the South helped those of the North in burning so many rails that the Southern farms were left with no protection for their crops. Farmers either didn't bother planting crops which the animals would devour, or planted them only to constantly stand guard and ward off the hungry cows. These barren fields soon alarmed Confederate president Jefferson Davis and he ordered an immediate halt to the practice of burning rails by the Southern soldiers. Unfortunately, he could do nothing to prevent the Union soldiers from destroying fences. By the end of the war, few remained; and one of the first needs of Reconstruction was the mending of fences.

Pioneers continued to move west; and in the forested areas, they cleared the fields of timber and again erected wooden fences. The type of fence depended on what type of wood was left over after the house and barns were built. Many men later remembered their boyhood as endless days of splitting logs and building fences. One of these was John Muir who, as a boy, built fences in Wisconsin. He later recalled that task.

"As I was the eldest boy, the greater part of all the hard work of the farm quite naturally fell on me. I had to split rails for long lines of zigzag fences. The trees that were tall enough and straight enough to afford one or two logs ten feet long were used for rails, the others, too knotty or cross-grained, were disposed of in log and cordwood fences. Making rails was hard work and required no little skill. I used to cut and split a hundred a day from our short, knotty oak timber, swinging the axe and heavy mallet, often with sore hands from early morning to night."

Splitting rails may have been hard work, but since the days of Abraham Lincoln, it has been a romantic and honorable profession and pastime. And, it has been strictly American. Immigrants to America noted this peculiar fence, so different from those of Europe. One farmer's wife, Rebecca Burland, wrote back home to Yorkshire, England, of these amazing crooked fences wiggling over the land.

"The method of fencing is peculiar; they use no posts, but having prepared their rails, they lay one down on the ground, where they wish to make a fence; not precisely in the same direction as the line of their intended fence, but making a small angle with it. Another rail is then laid down with its end overreaching the first, with which it forms a cross like the letter X, only instead of the crossing being at the centre, it is near the end of each rail. A third is then made to cross the second as before, and so on to a definite length. On each side of these several crossings a stake is driven into the ground to prevent their being removed. Other rails are then placed upon these, crossing each other in a similar manner, till the fence is as high

Opposite: A log fence zigzags across a Rocky Mountain meadow. (Photo: Freelance Photographers Guild)

Excerpt by Rebecca Burlend from A TRUE PICTURE OF EMIGRATION. Reprinted with the permission of R. R. Donnelley & Sons Company.

"An old farmer will walk with you through his fields and say 'This wall I built at such and such a time, or the first year I came on the farm, or when I owned such and such a span of horses,' indicating a period thirty, forty, or fifty years back."

as it is required. Generally they are about nine rails high. From the description given here, the reader will perceive that the fences are not straight as in England, but in a continued zig-zag. The reason for this difference is timber and land are of comparatively little value in America while their method requires less labour than ours."

There was a time when timber and land were less valuable than labor in America; but not for long. As the pioneers and settlers pushed still farther west, they often found that trees became more and more scarce. In barren lands, "furrow fences" were constructed from the stubble left in the field. These fences, of course, didn't keep out any animals, but kept the land and soil from washing away. In Nebraska, however, the farmer built three-foot earthen ridges from the clay soil and kept the animals out and the soil in.

At first, in this western land of plentiful acreage and few settlers, cattle roamed free. All too soon, however, the fences went up. At first they were of smooth wire, but beginning with its invention in 1874, barbed wire became the scourge of the West. Today, barbed wire is enjoying an unusual popularity. It is collected by wire enthusiasts who search for various examples of the many types of wire patented and distinguished by different barbs. Western cattle today, however, are fenced in by the almost invisible, yet efficient single strand of wire charged with electricity.

Fences moved into town from the country; and today, a fence becomes man's way of staking out his territory whether it be a thousand acre ranch or a forty by forty foot city plot. Fences are no longer used only for defense. As suburbia becomes populated by redwood fencing to provide privacy, metal chain links for protection, and pointed pickets at silent attention in their prim rows, fences now stand for civilization. They provide borders and mark boundaries between both friend and foe; and modern society judges its inhabitants as did Emerson: "He was a first-rate neighbor and he always kept those fences up."

Creative Crochet

Mary Becker

Crochet was once limited to making doilies and bedspreads from fine thread, but it is once more coming into its own. In the hands of contemporary designers it has exploded with color, texture and pattern that appeal to all ages. The range of threads suitable for crochet isn't restricted to the fine doily threads or even heavier knitting worsted used for sweaters and shawls. When worked with the huge new bulky synthetic macrame cords, crochet can produce fast results that are even more exciting because the magnified stitches have a totally new look.

Of course, these cords will be worked with large hooks that are available in sizes, *N, P, Q* and *S*. To find one that is comfortable for you and gives the correct gauge, try several sizes. The hook should be large enough to catch the entire strand of cord or yarn without splitting it and small enough to give the fabric body.

Both basket and rug can be completed very quickly. The basket base is worked around a wire ring for stability. Another ring is enclosed in the final row to keep the upper rim firm. The basket is made entirely of single crochet, chain and slip stitches. The handles are made by slip stitching back and forth along a chain, and are then sewn into place. Because of the gauge of the cord and the hook, the basket can be completed in about three hours.

The rug is made from trebles, single crochet and slip stitches and is finished with a bold chain stitch fringe. It will take about eight hours to complete.

Jumbo Elephant Cord Basket

Size 20″ in diameter, 7″ deep not including handles

Materials 5 spools 144 ft. UniCraft Jumbo Elephant Cord; 15″ and 19″ wire rings. Size "P" (10 mm) Bernat crochet hook or size that gives you proper gauge.

Abbreviations Beg-beginning; ch-chain; inc-increase; lp(s)-loop(s); rep-repeat; rnd(s)-round(s); sc(s)-single crochet(s); sl-slip; st(s)-stitch(es); yo-yarn over; hk-hook; "Work even" indicates no increases or decreases.

Gauge: 3 sc = 2″; 5 rnds = 3″

Basket bottom:

Important: Number in parentheses is count of sts at completion of rnd. Finish each rnd of basket as follows: sl st into 2nd ch of ch 2 at beg. of rnd. This ch 2 topped by sl st is considered a joining st and is not included in count of sts for the rnd.

With sl knot on hk, ch 6, sl st into knot to join.

Rnd 1) Ch 2, 6 sc into ring. Sl st to join as indicated above. (6)

Rnd 2) Ch 2, 2 sc in each sc of previous rnd. Sl st to join. (12)

Rnd 3) Ch 2, * sc in next sc, 2 sc in next sc. Rep. from * (18)

Rnd 4) Ch 2 * sc in next 2 sc, 2 sc in next sc. Rep from * (24)

Rnd 5) Ch 2 * sc in next 3 sc, 2 sc in next sc. Rep from * (30)

Rnd 6) Ch 2 * sc in next 4 sc, 2 sc in next sc. Rep from * (36)

Rnd 7) Ch 2 * sc in next 5 sc, 2 sc in next sc. Rep from * (42)

Rnd 8) Ch 2 * sc in next 6 sc, 2 sc in next sc. Rep from * (48)

Rnd 9) Ch 2 * sc in next 7 sc, 2 sc in next sc. Rep from * (54)

Rnd 10) Ch 2 * sc in next 8 sc, 2 sc in next sc. Rep from * (60)

Rnd 11) Ch 2 * sc in next 9 sc, 2 sc in next sc. Rep from * (66)

Rnd 12) Work even over 15″ ring as follows: Lay ring on ch at upper edge of last row of sts. Work sc as usual: * hk through st, (See fig. A) yo, pull lp back (2 lps on hk) reach over ring, yo and pull through both lps on hk. Sc is completed. (See fig. B) Rep from * around. (66)

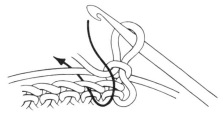

Fig. A

Fig. B

Basket sides

Continue to inc 3 sts each rnd by working 2 sc in following sts:
Rnd 13) 11, 33, 55 (69) Rnd 14) 1, 24, 47 (72)
Rnd 15) 12, 36, 60 (75) Rnd 16) 1, 26, 51 (78)
Rnd 17) 13, 39, 65 (81) Rnd 18) 6, 33, 60 (84)
Rnd 19) 10, 38, 66 (87) Rnd 20) work even (87) Rnd 21) Work even over 19" ring as in rnd 12. Weave end in at upper edge of basket and seal with bit of glue. Weave in end at center of basket bottom to close opening.

Handles

Ch 18. Row 1) sl st back along upper lps of ch.
Row 2) ch 1, turn. Sl st back through front lp.
Row 3) Sl st long edges of handle together. Sew one end of handle to basket. Sew other end to basket allowing 9 sts between ends. Repeat for handle on other side of basket.

Rectangular Rug

Size 28" x 42" including fringe

Materials 6 spools 80 yard UniCraft Acryjute. Size "P" crochet hook or size you require to reach gauge.

Abbreviations Ch-chain; hk-hook; lp-loop; sc-single crochet; sl-slip; st(s)-stitch(es); sc ch-single crochet chain; yd-yard; yo-yarn over.

Gauge 7 sts = 4"; 1 row of trebles and 1 row of sl st = 2".

Rug Work sc ch as follows: With sl knot on hk, ch 1. Sc into sl knot. Continue by working sc thkrough 2nd lp from hk (See Fig C) 45 times.

Row 1) Ch 4. Work treble in each of 45 remaining sts beginning in 2nd st as follows: * yo twice, hk through st, pull lp back (4 lps on hk) yo and pull through 2 lps (3 lps on hk) yo and pull through 2 lps (2 lps on hk) yo and pull through both lps on hk. (Treble completed) Repeat from * 44 times. Each row of trebles has 45 trebles plus ch 4.
Row 2) Ch 1, turn. Sl st back across row working through back lp.
Row 3) Ch 4, turn. Work trebles in each of 45 remaining sts, beginning in 2nd st.
Row 4) Same as Row 2.
Row 5) Sc in each sl st of previous row working through back lp.
Row 6) Same as Row 2
Row 7 - 30) Repeat Rows 1 - 6 four times more.
Rows 31 - 34) Repeat Rows 1 - 4.

Finishing: Sc along two long sides of rug.

Fringe: Cut 2-yard piece of yarn, fold in half. With rug lying vertically in front of you, insert hk in first lp at lower right corner of rug. Pull lp (center of 2-yard piece) back, ch 12 using ½ of 2-yard piece. Pull 12th ch lp until end slips through to lock. See (fig. D). Pull tight and trim end. Repeat with second half of yarn, inserting hk into 3rd lp from right edge of rug. Cut additional 2-yard pieces of yarn. Continue to work fringe from right to left in every other lp. ⑤

Fig. D

Fig. C

THE CRAZE FOR QUILTS

Wendy Murphy

Blazing Star

Baby Blocks

Quilting is a craft with a homely history that goes as far back as the Romans and probably even farther back to the ancient Chinese. But it took the Americans to find fun in the doing, thereby creating a folk art that is uniquely our own and uniquely vital today. Sociable busywork for some, creative art for others, sources of income for still others, quilting has been revived and its practitioners can once again be found at their needles from coast to coast.

To put quilting in its simplest terms, ancient craftsmen discovered that two layers of fabric could be made into a warm coverlet if separated by some sort of insulating filler and the whole held together by a few sturdy stitches, called counter points or quilt points. As the craft evolved, these stitches were worked into ever more elaborate linear patterns that became a decorative end in themselves. The first quilted bedcovers produced in America were as close to their English prototypes as memory and a limited supply of imported yard goods could make them. But the high cost and difficulty of obtaining materials led the hard-pressed colonial housewife to improvise, and therein lies the origin of the piecework quilt.

Two centuries before anyone gave a name to it, the thrifty woman of the New World recycled every usable scrap of retired clothing, bedding, and upholstery fabric, sewing them together until she had pieces large enough to cover a bed. On a surface already so busy with color and pattern, she was inclined to make her quilting stitches less showy than English taste demanded. The finished job was called, somewhat apologetically, a Hit-and-Miss or Crazy Quilt.

Eventually, mills began to produce fabrics that were cheap and plentiful on this side of the Atlantic. Presumably many women could go back to doing things the easier way. Just the opposite happened. It's apparent from the great burst of quilt making in the nineteenth century that it was the very difficulty of the task that satisfied, for the make-do crazy quilts of old were joined by still more complicated pieced and patched designs. The chief difference was that the creator was free to *plan* the arrangement of pieces, to cut the fabric to suit the quilt rather than the other way around. The bedcover now became a "canvas" on which a woman could paint with fabric, expressing all her innate sense of color and form.

Her budget and the pattern she chose determined how the quilt would be constructed: pieced quilts, which might consist of several thousand segments, were suited to geometrical designs; the patched or

A "friendship quilt" was made by a group of women as a gift to a neighbor or to an entire family. Often each woman embroidered her name on one of the squares she had sewn as a sign of friendship. Because these quilts were commonly reserved for special use, many that are found today in attic trunks remain in very fine condition.

appliqued quilt was somewhat more wasteful of material in that the ornamental parts were laid on a background fabric, but with a compensatory gain in design flexibility. Either way the quilt maker usually worked out her motif so that it could be repeated in uniformly sized squares, convenient for carrying about and working, one at a time, in idle moments.

A star, a flower, a wreath, a patriotic symbol and abstract arrangements of circles, triangles and squares were favorite motifs, recast again and again as women traded ideas with one another. Sometimes the name of the pattern stuck — Goose Tracks, Courthouse Steps and Log Cabin seem to have meant the same thing to the ladies of Maine and Colorado; but often pattern names were changed to suit the commonplaces of the region in which they were used. Typically, the eastern Ship's Wheel became Prairie Star when translated to the frontier; Le Moyne Star, which originally paid homage to an early governor of French Louisiana, was simplified in other parts to Lemon Star. Whimsy and a rugged sort of imagery named such patterns as Puss-in-the-Corner, Drunkard's Path, Hearts and Gizzards, Delectable Mountains, Old Maid's Ramble and Wild Goose Chase.

Once a woman completed all her squares she seamed them together. Then, laying the completed top on the floor, she traced with chalk or pencil the stitch lines the quilters were to follow. Lastly, she basted top, filler and bottom together.

Only then were the neighbors invited to join her in that happy institution known as the quilting bee, a most descriptive term for the buzzing conviviality that accompanied a session at the quilting frame. In a time when idleness was judged a sin, these cooperative sewing parties were a welcome excuse for getting together. As invitations went most often to those with nimble fingers, it was a wise young woman who made her quilter's reputation early in life and insured her social success.

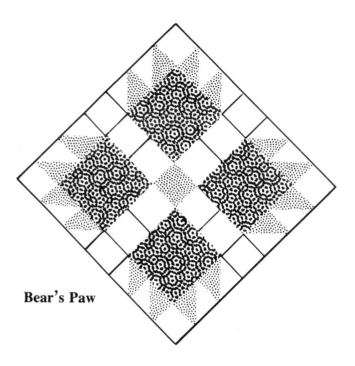

Bear's Paw

The party was an all-day affair, starting early in the morning when the ladies set up the frame and "put in" or stretched the basted coverlet over its four sides. Then, taking their places — usually two ladies to a side — they began to stitch their way toward the center. As the work progressed, conversation spilled forth. Harriet Beecher Stowe in her novel *The Minister's Wooing* describes a New England bee circa 1860. "One might have learned in that instructive assembly how best to keep moths out of blankets, how to make fritters of Indian corn undistinguishable from oysters; how to bring up babies by hand; how to reconcile absolute decrees with free will; how to make five yards of cloth answer the purpose of six; and how to put down the Democratic party."

At day's end, the men came to admire the finished work and to collect wives and sisters. Usually they stayed for a festive supper. When the quilt was intended for some special purpose, a bridal quilt for example, the frolicking was likely to be all the gayer, with singing, dancing and gallant toasts. Young girls traditionally made a number of everyday quilts — perhaps a dozen — in preparation for marriage, so when this, her "best" quilt, was put on the frame, it was tantamount to an engagement announcement. Quilts could also be group gifts, in which many hands produced both the patchwork and the quilting; a "freedom quilt" marked the coming of age of a young man; an "album quilt" was a sort of testimonial to some honored member of the community; a "friendship quilt" might be given to a family that had suffered some reverse. For the bereaved family, there even were "mourning quilts" (black and white only) and "memory quilts" that incorporated scraps of the departed's clothing.

Some time around the 1870's the craft suffered a marked decline. Mass-produced blankets and a greater freedom for women made both the quilt and the quilting bee obsolete in all but the most rural areas. Aunt Indy's Monkey Wrench and Miss Ida's Churn Dasher were banished to the attic trunk. Today these ladies would be astonished to see their work hanging on museum walls and studied in scholarly journals.

Despite all the recent excitement, it's still not too late for the amateur collector to find old treasures in out-of-the-way places, and new ones in little pockets of America where women supplement their income by making patchworks in the traditional way. But there's nothing mysterious about the technique of quilting and if you can't find the patchwork you want, why not make it. As one Yankee punster put it, quilt making is a great way "to keep the peace and get rid of the scraps."

A good idea any time 🅖

LOG CABIN QUILTS

Darlene Kronschnabel

**Materials for Log Cabin Quilt (Finished size 78″
x 102″)**
1 double-bed-size, plain-colored, flat sheet
1 twin-bed-size, plain-colored, flat sheet
½ yard 45″ fabric of 6 different prints identified
A, B, C, D, E, F,
1 yard 45″ fabric of 3 different prints identified
G, H, I
1 double-size polyester batt 90″ x 108″
Optional: Matching thread and knitting worsted
yarn for ties (if the quilt is to be tufted).

The Log Cabin Quilt was one of the first scrap quilts in America. Originally, plain, everyday scrap material was used to form the light and dark patterns. Later, Victorian quilters used bright silk and velvet to form their fashionable throws.

One of the best-loved of all the pieced quilt patterns is the Log Cabin Quilt. It is also one of the easiest and fastest quilts to make. Many different patterns can be achieved by manipulating the light and dark values.

The basic Log Cabin Quilt has numerous names, all depending upon its color and block arrangement after piecing. The more familiar names within the Log Cabin Quilt family are Barn Raising,

Straight Furrow, Courthouse Steps, Clocks, Zig-Zag, Windmill Blades and Pineapple. The name of the one shown here is Sunshine and Shadows.

Traditionally, Log Cabin Quilts are a contrasting blend of light and dark prints. However, this versatile pattern is equally attractive using plain-colored muslin or percale sheets with an assortment of multicolored prints. Early Log Cabin Quilts were often made with dark, somber-colored pieces, since this was the most readily available material. Today, there is a wide range of bright material to create happy, colorful Log Cabin Quilts suitable for many decorating themes.

Instructions

From the twin-size sheet, tear the following strips.
2 3″ x 103″ strips for border
2 3″ x 74″ strips for border
48 strips, 1¾″ x 2½″ (Plain 1)
96 strips, 1¾″ x 5″ (Plain 2 and 3)
96 strips, 1¾″ x 7½″ (Plain 4 and 5)
96 strips, 1¾″ x 10″ (Plain 6 and 7)
48 strips, 1¾″ x 12½″ (Plain 8)

Using Prints A-I cut or tear as follows:
Print A, cut 48 squares 2½″ x 2½″
Print B, tear 48 strips 1¾″ x 2½″
Print C, tear 48 strips 1¾″ x 5″
Print D, tear 48 strips 1¾″ x 5″
Print E, tear 48 strips 1¾″ x 7½″
Print F, tear 48 strips 1¾″ x 7½″
Print G, tear 48 strips 1¾″ x 10″
Print H, tear 48 strips 1¾″ x 10″
Print I, tear 48 strips 1¾″ x 12½″

Carefully stack the pieces in a flat box or put in separate envelopes to keep them all together and handy.

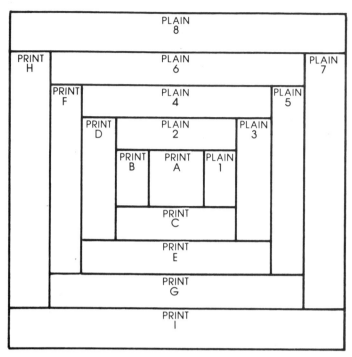

Diagram A

To Make Block

Follow the whole block chart for placement (Diagram A). Each block consists of 16 "logs" and a center square.

Starting with the center square, Print A, sew Print B to one side and sew Plain 1 to the other side using ¼" seam allowance. Press the seams outward. Continue to build by adding "logs," one print and one plain, to each side, pressing the seams, until the block measures 12½" and is square.

Construct 48 square blocks in this manner. Press all blocks.

Next, sew four blocks together, carefully matching the corners. Four blocks pieced together create a dark-colored diamond, bordered by four light corners (Diagram B). Complete 12 four-block units.

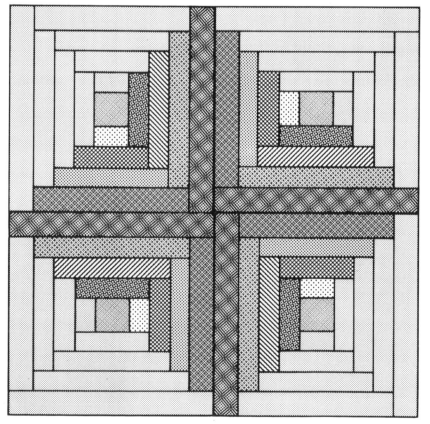

Diagram B

214

Diagram C

Finishing the Quilt

Prepare the flat, full-size sheet for the backing by opening and pressing out all seams.

Lay the backing on a large, flat surface. Place the polyester batt directly on top. Then place the Log Cabin top on the batt, face side up.

Make sure all layers are smooth and even. Pin all corners. Stretch and pin the three layers on a large quilting frame, as tightly and evenly as possible.

The quilt is now either tufted or hand quilted.

Tufting or tying is a fast and simple method of finishing the quilt. Use a large needle and knitting worsted. Using the yarn doubled, push the needle from the top through the three layers of material to the back, leaving about 2″ of yarn ends on top. Push the needle back up to the top side, about ¼″ away. Tie yarn in a firm double knot. Clip ends evenly, leaving about ¾″ to 1″ ends.

The quilting stitch is a short running stitch that goes through all three layers of material (Diagram D). These small, close stitches run along or right on the "log" seamline. The simple up-and-down, even stitches create an attractive design on the back of the quilt.

To finish the quilt, remove it from the frame and trim all sides evenly. Turn under ¼″ seam allowance. Pin sides together. Using tiny, invisible stitches, hand sew all four sides with matching thread. Ⓢ

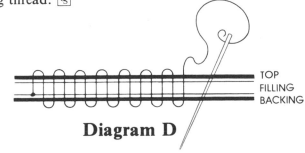

Diagram D

What's Cooking

Pancakes:
A Hearty Beginning

Marybeth Owens

What better way to ward off the chill of a winter's day than by starting out with a steaming stack of pancakes direct from the griddle? The aroma from the kitchen and the anticipation of your family and guests will almost surpass the delight that comes from savoring each forkful.

Originating in the old world, pancakes became an integral part of America's "farm-style" breakfast. Who wouldn't give a little more energy to the morning chores after eating a stack of buttermilk pancakes topped with freshly churned butter and drizzled with homemade maple syrup? Today, the taste for the treats of Grandma's day lingers on. Pancakes and the many variations that have evolved, are found in most restaurants and are the featured fare of some establishments.

Preparation time is quick and the methods simple which make pancakes a welcome addition to any busy cook's repertoire. You can further the versatility of pancakes by varying the sauces you use to accompany them. Fruits and nuts incorporated into your pancake planning will help in nutritionally balancing your meal.

Pancakes may be kept warm in the oven on "low." Cover the stack with a damp towel or put a small pan of water in the oven. This will keep the pancakes moist.

The recipes that are found here will add variety to your menus. Pancakes are a traditional breakfast item, but can also be a welcome change for lunch or dinner.

BASIC PANCAKE BATTER

*Anything goes from this point—
use your imagination.*

1 c. milk
1 c. whole wheat flour
¼ t. salt
4 eggs, separated

Beat together milk, flour, and salt. Beat egg whites until stiff and lightly stir in egg yolks. Fold eggs into the flour mixture. Cook on lightly greased griddle until brown.

BUTTERMILK PANCAKES

*Try adding bits of dried fruits,
nuts or berries to the batter.*

1½ c. all-purpose flour
½ T. baking powder
¼ t. salt
½ T. sugar
1 egg
1¼ c. buttermilk
2 T. melted butter

Sift together flour, baking powder, salt and sugar. Beat egg vigorously, then stir in buttermilk and butter. Combine with dry ingredients, using as few strokes as possible—overbeating toughens pancakes. Mixture will be lumpy. Drop batter by spoonfuls onto a hot, greased griddle. When large bubbles appear and begin to burst, turn pancakes, then brown on second side. Serve at once. For a variation, add 1 cup drained blueberries to the batter.

WAFFLES

A creamy delight of Dutch ancestry.

1 c. sifted all-purpose flour
4 t. baking powder
¼ t. salt
3 eggs, separated
1 c. heavy cream

Sift together flour, baking powder and salt. Set aside. Beat yolks vigorously, then add cream. Continue to beat until smooth. Stir in sifted dry ingredients and beat until smooth. Beat egg whites until stiff. Fold in beaten egg whites. Refrigerate batter for half an hour. Bake in a preheated waffle iron until crisp and delicately browned. Serve with butter and warm honey or maple syrup.

POTATO PANCAKES

A variation to accompany any main dish.

3 medium potatoes
¼ onion, grated
½ c. flour
2 eggs
   Salt and pepper
   Finely chopped parsley
   Vegetable oil

Grate raw potatoes. Add onion, flour and eggs. Add salt and pepper to taste and parsley. Mix well. Fry pancakes in ¼-inch hot oil. Turn when brown and fry other side. Pancakes should be thin. Serve with sour cream or applesauce.

Published by Ward Ritchie Press, Pasadena, California

BUCKWHEATS

A frontier favorite.

½ pkg. active dry yeast *or* ½ cake
   compressed yeast
¼ c. lukewarm water
2 c. milk
2 c. buckwheat flour
½ t. salt
1 T. molasses
1 t. baking soda
¼ c. warm water

Dissolve yeast in lukewarm water. Scald milk, then cool to lukewarm. Blend together yeast, milk, buckwheat flour and salt; beat for 2 minutes. Cover with a dish towel and let stand at room temperature overnight. Next day, mix in molasses, baking soda, and ¼ cup warm water. Pour onto a hot greased griddle (griddle is hot enough when several drops of water tested on it sizzle). Brown on both sides. Serve immediately with butter and warm maple syrup.

GERMAN APPLE PANCAKE

A deep-dish treat that guarantees success.

6 eggs, separated
¼ c. flour
¼ c. melted butter
¼ c. milk

½ t. salt
2 T. butter
3 apples, sliced
   Cinnamon-sugar mixture

Beat egg yolks. Stir in flour, butter, milk, and salt. Fold in slightly beaten egg whites. Heat the 2 tablespoons butter in a large skillet. Pour in the batter. Top with apple slices. Cook over medium heat for about 5 minutes. Remove from heat and place in a preheated 400° oven. Bake 15 minutes or until golden brown. Top with sugar and cinnamon mixture.

Gertrude Wright

PANCAKES SAN FRANCISCO

A luscious dessert—be prepared for compliments.

1 c. sifted all-purpose flour
3 t. baking powder
1 t. sugar
¼ t. salt
1 c. milk
¼ c. light cream
2 T. melted butter
1 egg, slightly beaten
   Melted butter
   Brown sugar
2 c. strawberries, halved and sweetened
   Marshmallow Mix

Sift together flour, baking powder, sugar and salt. Set aside. Add milk, cream and 2 tablespoons melted butter to the egg and beat well. Add dry ingredients to egg mixture and beat until smooth and creamy. Fry as pancakes in 6-inch size. Brush serving plate with melted butter. Sprinkle on a little brown sugar. Stack six or more pancakes, alternating sugar mixture and pancakes. Cover top with some of the Marshmallow Mix and broil until golden. Heat strawberries to a boiling point. Cut the pancake stack in wedges and top with hot strawberries. Serves 6 to 8.

MARSHMALLOW MIX

½ c. sugar
2 T. water
2 egg whites, stiffly beaten
1 T. butter, softened

Combine and beat until smooth.

Published by Ward Ritchie Press, Pasadena, California

GREAT-GRANDMOTHER LINDSTROM'S SWEDISH PANCAKES

This recipe is sure to stay in the family.

5 eggs
2 c. milk
1 c. sifted flour
¼ t. salt
3 T. melted butter

Beat eggs well. Add milk and beat thoroughly. Add flour in small amounts and blend until smooth. Stir in salt and melted butter. Fry on hot griddle. Top with pats of butter and sprinkle lightly with confectioners' sugar.

Jill C. Pelling

NATURAL SYRUPS

Natural syrups include honey, molasses, and maple syrup. Mix honey and butter together or add cinnamon to the mixture to taste.

FRUIT SAUCE

Sweeten favorite berries or peaches and let steep in their own juices. Fill each pancake with the fruit mixture, roll up, and sprinkle with confectioners' sugar or serve with whipped cream.

MAPLE PECAN SAUCE

Cook ¾ cup maple syrup over moderate heat for 6 to 8 minutes or until it thickens slightly. Remove from heat and stir in ½ cup coarsely chopped pecans or walnuts. Spoon over pancakes or waffles.

RAISIN SAUCE

1½ c. water
⅓ c. seeded raisins
¼ c. sugar
⅛ t. salt
2 T. butter
1 t. flour
¼ t. nutmeg or cinnamon

Boil water, raisins, sugar and salt for 15 minutes. Melt butter in a saucepan and stir in flour until blended. Slowly add hot raisin sauce. Stirring, bring to a boil. Add nutmeg or cinnamon and serve over plain pancakes or waffles.

Collecting sap for maple syrup

It's Honest to Goodness Maple Syrup! *Bea Bourgeois*

Mmmmmm—Sunday morning breakfast! Somehow, even the thought is warmly comforting. Weekday dawns are hectic, with hastily scrambled eggs and the dispensing of instant cereals. Ah, but Sunday—a yawn, a stretch, a slippered trip to the front door for the properly fat newspaper; then, after a decent interval, some golden French toast, or a stack of pancakes or golden waffles . . . any or all of these delights smothered in what you probably think of as maple syrup.

Guess again! If you're ever looking for a useless pastime, read the ingredients listed on the label of that syrup bottle standing in your refrigerator. No, don't get up—read mine: "Corn syrup (67%), sugar syrup (29%), maple sugar

syrup (2%), cellulose gum (for body), sodium benzoate and sorbic acid (preservatives), artificial flavor, caramel color." So, in this era of chemical additives, processed foods and synthetic flavorings, you could be breakfasting on soybean-base meat substitute, non-dairy coffee creamer, imitation powdered breakfast drink, and maple syrup with very little maple in it. Frequently (but regrettably) a typical American meal.

It wasn't always like that, and for some American families it still isn't. Obviously it's still possible to make pancake and waffle batter "from scratch"; you can still squeeze real juice from real oranges; honest-to-goodness pork sausage is still a tasty byproduct of honest-to-goodness pigs; and,

given the right set of circumstances, you can even produce real maple syrup. We are happily blessed with syrup-making relatives in northern Wisconsin; nothing commercial, mind you, just enough for their own table with a few pints left over as a generous treat for us city folk. Like every other homemade or home canned product, their maple syrup is "a spoiler"—it spoils forever your acceptance of the thick, gluey stream which comes gulping out of store-bought bottles.

My brother-in-law and his wife tap their fourteen or fifteen trees every year. Their system is basically the same as the one used by much larger syrup-making operations, but their equipment is far less sophisticated.

"I make my spigots out of pieces of metal pipe, drill a hole about a half inch into the tree and push the spigot in. Then we just sit back and let her drip." Ed and his wife set their buckets on the ground alongside the maple tree and only recently have decided to cover the buckets with plastic bags as a measure to keep out dirt, leaves and bugs—and also to thwart "them darn gray squirrels, they're just about the worst." The squirrels and their friends the rabbits like nothing better than to hop up to the bucket for a free sample of Ed's maple sap.

"About the only improvement I've made is that now I ride the snowmobile to gather up the buckets when they're full." It is difficult, if not impossible, to trudge over crusty snow and frozen ground carrying buckets of sap—unless you don't mind spilling half of what your buckets collected. Pioneers who gathered sap found that they needed a stone boat or a wooden sled to haul the buckets out of the woods to a central "boiling down" spot.

"Then we empty all the buckets into a great big kettle, usually Irene's canning kettle. I build a fire in the yard and let 'er boil away till she's done." A six-gallon kettle of sap will have to boil for four to five hours so that enough water evaporates to turn the sap into syrup. That much syrup will produce about a quart of real maple syrup; Ed figures that it takes anywhere from 30 to 35 gallons of sap to get a gallon of syrup. With that in mind, it's not difficult to see why the status of real maple syrup has escalated from a staple on the pioneer's table to a modern-day delicacy!

The weather is a major consideration in the tapping of maple trees. Ideally, there must be cold nights followed by warm days which will force the sap to run. And it must all be gathered before the leaves go into bud. Tapping, then, is generally done from mid-March to mid-April—always with one eye on the thermometer. I asked Ed if the sap ever froze in his buckets. "Yep," he replied, "but it didn't hurt it none."

After the sap is boiled down, the syrup is strained through flannel to remove any foreign substances, and poured boiling hot into clean jars.

I wondered if Ed and his wife ever made maple sugar. "Only accidentally," he chuckled. "If you don't watch that boiling sap real careful, you've got sugar whether you planned on it or not." Perhaps this is how maple sugar candy came into being. My husband remembers an ancient Indian woman who lived near their farm and the delicious maple candy she made in the shape of leaves. In their May baskets, all the children in his family would find a maple sugar "leaf" along with a few dried apples—the gift of their elderly neighbor.

Mapling, like so many other homely arts, was introduced to white settlers by various Indian tribes. American pioneers, of necessity, were jacks-of-all-trades. In order to carve a tolerable life out of the land, they had to be not only excellent farmers, but tinsmiths, hunters, butchers, tanners and carpenters as well. Anxious to be totally independent of England after the Revolutionary War, the pioneers strove for total self-reliance. Learning to tap the maple tree and boil down the sap for any number of sweet delights was one more step toward freedom.

In *The Maple Sugar Book*, Helen and Scott Nearing share an intriguing tale concerning the Indians' own discovery of maple syrup:

"There is an Iroquois legend about the sap of the maple and how Woksis, the Indian chief, first tasted it as a sweet syrup because he had an ingenious wife. Woksis was going hunting one day early in March. He yanked his tomahawk from the tree where he had hurled it the night before, and went off for the day. The weather had turned warm and the gash in the tree, a maple, dripped sap into a vessel

Left: Tapping a maple tree the old-fashioned way. Right: The modern method.

Horses are still put to work at maple syrup time.

that happened to stand close to the trunk. Woksis's squaw, toward evening, needed water in which to boil their dinner. She saw the trough full of sap and thought that would save her a trip to get water. Anyway, she was a careful woman and didn't like to waste anything. She tasted it and found it good—a little sweet, but not bad. So she used it for cooking water. Woksis, when he came home from hunting, scented the inimitable maple aroma, and from far off knew that something especially good was stewing. The water had boiled down to syrup, which sweetened their meal with maple. So, says the legend, was the happy practice inaugurated."

In commercial operations, tapping maples has become considerably more sophisticated than throwing a tomahawk into the bark of the tree, although the first step remains boring a hole—easily done today with a drill. Indians and early settlers inserted "spiles" or spouts carved from elder, sumac, birch or balsam wood. Today's spouts are made of heavy metal, and notched at one end so the sap bucket can be hung rather than simply set on the ground alongside the tree. My husband remembers that his father used to carve spouts out of poplar twigs, with a surprise ending for the children. When he had enough spouts, he'd roll the twig between his palms

to loosen the bark, slip the bark off, cut a notch in one end, then slip the bark back on and cut a matching notch—presto, a homemade whistle!

Professional maplers now use buckets made out of galvanized iron, a giant step from the birch bark buckets the Indians used. Pioneers improved somewhat on bucket production, making theirs out of ash or basswood or, finally, tin.

Large syrup producers have a separate building used as a boiling room; small family operations proceed with the fire in the yard, or even use their own kitchen stove. "We decided to quit doing that because of all the steam, and be-

Maple syrup is graded according to pre-set standards for color and density.

An evaporator reduces boiling time compared to the old kettle boiling method.

"About the only improvement I've made is that now I ride the snowmobile to gather up the buckets when they're full."

cause everything in the house got covered with sugar crystals—including our eyelashes," Ed recalls.

Boiling down must be done quickly and carefully, always with one eye on the pot. The fire can't be too hot, or else the pans will scorch and the sap will boil over. If the fire isn't hot enough, the syrup will stay in the pans too long, which darkens its color and gives it a heavy, murky flavor. Sap that is neglected can quickly turn to sugar, as Ed noted, and while maple sugar is delightful, it isn't exactly what you want when you set out to make syrup.

The venerable hard maple trees have blessed us with even more than their sap—which is truly their life's liquid—to enrich our lives. Maple wood is highly prized in making fine furniture and flooring, boxes and crates, bobbins and spools. Pioneers used bird's-eye or "curly" maple for cabinet making and for gunstocks. Hard maple is still a favorite wood of violin makers.

Four states—New York, Vermont, West Virginia and Wisconsin—have chosen the sugar maple as their official state tree. And even city dwellers can enjoy the natural sweetness which the maple so kindly distributes in late winter or early spring.

Several years ago, the city planted small maple saplings on our block to replace the majestic elms which were dying of Dutch Elm disease. We have all enjoyed watering our little maple, pulling weeds from around its base, and watching it grow sturdier year by year. Last March, our youngest son bounded excitedly into the kitchen waving one sticky finger, bubbling with questions about the identity of "the sticky icicle hanging on our tree!" It took a bit of explaining by his father to convince David that he was tasting a genuine frozen maple sap icicle—better by far than any imitation-flavored popsicle he had ever eaten. Even in small ways we can still be grateful to the maple for what our long-ago forebears called "the distilled essence of the tree." Ⓢ